All Roads
Lead to Rome

All Roads Lead to Rome

SABRINA FEDEL

Delacorte
Romance

Text copyright © 2024 by Sabrina Fedel
Cover art copyright © 2024 by Peter Braun

GetUnderlined.com

Educators and librarians, for a variety of teaching tools, visit us at RHTeachersLibrarians.com

Library of Congress Cataloging-in-Publication Data is available upon request.
ISBN 978-0-593-70521-6 (trade pbk.) — ISBN 978-0-593-70522-3 (ebook)

The text of this book is set in 11.75-point Adobe Garamond Pro.
Interior design by Michelle Crowe

Printed in the United States of America
1st Printing
First Edition

For Flossey, who will always be the
best part of Italy for me,
and for Mary O. for letting me be
her honorary dad

I am certain of nothing but the holiness
of the Heart's affections
and the truth of Imagination.

—John Keats, a letter to Benjamin Bailey,
November 22, 1817

One

Rome is sweltering as it waits patiently for the sun to set over the Spanish Steps. It's the kind of vapid heat that makes me wonder how the lions had the energy to leave their cages, let alone maul anyone.

I'm in John Keats's bedroom, the room he died in, overlooking the sprawling steps below. Horses sweat in the middle of Piazza di Spagna as they wait to give carriage rides, immovable in the small throng of late-May tourists. Most of the passersby don't even know this was Keats's house, despite the enormous crimson plaque on the side of it. They come here for selfies on the famous steps and never give John's shrine more than a careless glance. For me, the Keats-Shelley House is the best part of the neighborhood. I wonder if he stood exactly here, watching the people outside the way I do.

Anna Maria comes and stands beside me. "It's closing time, Story," she says in Italian. "No more people-watching today."

"Mmmm."

She follows my gaze to a cluster of kids my age, dressed like conspicuous American teenagers. They've stopped at the bottom of the steps. A group of tourists in matching red T-shirts flows around them like a school of minnows sliced apart.

"Wait," she says, "is that the infamous Dip Squad?"

I purse my lips and nod. They're all there: Kelsey, Guin, Alicia, and the twins, Patrick and Jack. We're the kids of the American diplomatic corps stationed in Rome, but I've called them the Dip Squad since last fall when they welcomed me with one prank after another to show me how things work here. They thought I was stuck-up because I keep to myself so much. The worst was when they convinced me a stray cat near the embassy belonged to a cute Marine assigned to guard duty. They told me the cat had been lost for days, so I brought it to him. He thinks I made the whole thing up to hit on him. He still smirks every time I visit my mom at work.

"Which one is the dark-haired boy?"

"That's Jack."

"But Patrick is the mean one, sì?"

"Sì."

"Jack is pretty cute." She elbows me.

I scrunch my nose, and she laughs.

"You should stand up to them. They don't seem worth being miserable over."

"They're not. But I'll be out of here soon. Jack is the only one I'll ever have to see again."

"He's the one going to Princeton with you?"

"Sì."

"Story, don't let other people keep you from living the life you want," she says, poking my arm. "Come on, I have to get home. I have an exam tomorrow." Anna Maria is in her second year at Università di Roma. She works two afternoons a week at the Keats-Shelley House, where I spend more time than is normal for a seventeen-year-old girl, even one as nerdy as me.

We say ciao as she locks the door, and she heads to the metro. The Dip Squad has, blessedly, disappeared. I've promised my mom I'd go to the Gucci store on Via Condotti to buy a ridiculously overpriced necklace the ambassador wants to give to a visiting dignitary. I don't understand why people flock to designer stores to buy ugly things for thousands of dollars when they could find vintage treasures on the Via del Governo Vecchio for a few euros, but I don't get most things about people.

When we moved here last August, I found my way around by using a copy of Fodor's *Italy in 1951* that I bought in a used bookstore. "Never out of date" it says on the cover, which makes me laugh, but the Eternal City is pretty eternal. There's something obscenely unromantic about a smartphone map.

As I reach the edge of the piazza, I spot Patrick's blond buzz cut leading the Dips back in my direction. I duck into a gelateria.

"Buonasera," says the middle-aged man behind the counter.

"Buonasera."

He looks at me expectantly, because most people come into an ice cream shop to actually get ice cream. My mom will have takeout waiting at home, but I might as well have dessert now, since I need to give the Dips time to go past. I look over my choices.

"Un gelato alla stracciatella vegana, per favore."

People burst through the door, and I turn my head, thinking it must be the Dips coming to harass me. But it's a guy and girl about my age, both of them looking like wealthy tourists. The girl looks a lot like the American singer Jasmine. But celebrities and celebrity look-alikes are as common as good pizza in this part of Rome. She has her dark hair in a ponytail like me, and we both have on yellow, though I'm wearing a vintage summer dress that Audrey Hepburn might have worn, and she's wearing a romper some stylist probably thought was retro chic.

The man behind the counter asks me in Italian what size gelato and whether I want a cone or cup, but he's watching her.

"Una piccola coppetta, per favore."

"Sì, signorina."

The girl's voice is almost hysterical. "Do you think they saw us?"

Maybe they're hiding out from the Dip Squad, too. The bad part about being a loner is there's no one to share your jokes with.

"I'm sure they didn't." The boy has a Scottish accent. He cranes his neck to look over her head without getting too close to the window.

"They can't see me with you."

"They won't, keep the heid," he replies, but then he changes course. "Ah no, I think they're coming."

I'm paying the man while they make this exchange, and he's listening intently.

"You are Jasmine, no?" he asks her in heavily accented English.

"Yes! Is there a back way I could go out?"

The man nods, and Jasmine slips behind the counter. He ushers her to the back as if he suddenly thinks he's working for the CIA. "I'll meet you back at the hotel," she calls to the boy while she slips the gelateria guy a fistful of euros.

I walk past the Scot and step outside. A quick scan for the Dips only shows me a group of people with cameras rushing toward the shop, ready to run me over. My gelato is already sweating, so I take a bite. The boy comes out of the gelateria, and they snap his photo.

"Where's Jasmine?" they all yell at him as if he isn't close enough to hear them. The flashes are so bright, I squint even though their lenses aren't pointed at me.

"Who?" the boy says.

"We all saw you go in with her!" one shouts as the rest clamor about where Jasmine is and click their cameras.

"Where is she, Luca? Where's Jasmine?"

"You're mistaken," this Luca kid says as the whir of cameras almost drowns him out. He steps toward me and grabs my elbow as if it's a beer mug. Melting gelato flies off my spoon. "This is the girl you saw."

And that's the moment I envision going down in history with the Dip Squad if they ever saw these photos: my mouth open, filled with stracciatella, surrounded by paparazzi blinding me with flashes as I'm held up like a prize marlin by some guy named Luca while he covers for the reigning Queen of Pop, whose music I don't even like.

The paparazzi seem to be thrown. Several of them lower their cameras to examine me.

"I could have sworn it was Jasmine!"

"She has a ponytail! And she's wearing yellow."

"You said it was Jasmine," one says in Italian. The rest are using English but with accents from all over Europe.

"Damn, I thought it was!"

"Who's this girl?"

"Nobody!"

While I'm perfectly aware of my nobody status, this seems pretty harsh, and the Scot hasn't even given me so much as a "please play along" look. It's like he just assumes I'd be thrilled to have these people insult me just so I could be in a photo with him.

"Well, this nobody is going to head out now." I say it in the language of Rome, because there's something about Italian that makes it sound a lot more serious than saying it in English.

"Who are you?"

"Who is she, Luca?"

"Is this your latest, Luca?"

"Where'd you find her? She doesn't seem like your type."

I stare at this Luca kid to let go of my arm, but he doesn't. He's looking between them and me, clearly calculating how much risk to benefit there is in throwing me to the lions. I shake my head at him.

"She's a tour guide," he says. "Obviously."

I just look at him. I don't think I look like a tour guide. I also don't think my Italian is fooling anyone that I'm a native, including him. Maybe it's the quickest way to get these people away from me, though. Luca is clearly somebody they consider worth taking pictures of. If I'm nothing more than a tour guide, then there's no chance those open-mouthed-bass pictures of me are getting published in any of the celebrity magazines Guin and Kelsey love.

"Sì, sì," I say, and stop speaking Italian before they realize I'm not actually a local. I do my best to impersonate Anna Maria's accent when she speaks English. "I was hired for the day, that is all." This is nothing like *Roman Holiday*.

"You lot need to back off," Luca says. "She isn't used to this kind of attention. She's just a local girl my butler hired to show me the sights."

His butler? Hoo boy, as my grandfather from Maine says. I nod at them, and I don't even need to pretend I'm annoyed. But it's still better than getting into any of these online magazines.

"See, nobody!" I say in my Italian-accented English. "Now, please let us alone, as I want to bring my client to Fontana di Trevi before the after-dinner crowds! Vieni!"

The paparazzi lower their cameras and mumble to each

other. I turn toward the street that will take us to the fountain and pull Luca along by the rolled-up sleeve of his expensive button-down. I'm practically on Gucci's doorstep, and now I need to take a thirty-minute detour, but it was the first monument I could think of that would be pretty close but still lead us out of their circle.

"That was pure dead brilliant," Luca says as we leave them behind, looking back at the paparazzi, who seem unsure of whether they should follow us. One or two do.

"You're welcome." I drop my wilted stracciatella in a trash bin along the bricked pedestrian street.

"Oh, right, of course, my manners. Thank you, Miss—?" He looks at me expectantly.

"Herriot. Astoria Herriot. But most people call me Story."

"Charming," he says, and I can't tell if he's being sarcastic.

"Look, I need to go to Gucci for my mom. So I'll take you to the Trevi, we'll pretend we're talking about it for a few minutes in case they're watching, and then we'll separate, okay? That should be enough to get rid of your entourage. And if they ask, you can tell them my clock ran out."

He pulls his head back as if he's a little shocked by my brusqueness, so I add, "No offense or anything." Sometimes I feel like introverts should wear T-shirts that warn people we don't know how to interact.

"None taken." He strides along beside me, a little more slowly than I'd like. "So, where did you learn to speak Italian like that? Do you live here?"

"Just for the past year. I'm a Dip kid."

He looks at me like maybe I'm a little unhinged.

"My mom's in the diplomatic corps," I add.

"Ah!" he says. "So that's why you knew exactly where to go for the Trevi."

I shrug. "Roma is classic."

He laughs. "Well, yes, the ancient Romans and all."

"No, like Audrey Hepburn classic. Rome is one of a kind."

He puts his lips together like he might whistle, I guess to keep from laughing at me. "I stand corrected," he says. "It must be right barry to live here for a wee bit."

"Barry?"

"You know, great, fantastic."

"Oh, yes. It is."

"Where else have you lived?"

"Well, home is technically Washington, DC, but we're hardly ever there. Let's see, Tokyo, Rio, Lisbon, Zagreb, and now here." We've reached the fountain. People scatter along the perimeter, trying to get selfies with it, but it's not so thick with tourists that you can't see well.

"So, tour guide, tell me about the Trevi."

My mouth twitches into an automatic frown, and he laughs. "Seriously, I bet you know all about it. Please?"

A paparazzo who followed us stands across the street casually keeping watch. "Well, you could spend hours talking about the Trevi, but I'll give you some highlights. The Trevi, named for the tre vie, or three streets here, is one of the oldest water sources in Rome, dating originally to about 19 BC. Then, in 1730, I think, Pope Clemens of some number, because I can never remember the numbers, held a contest to rebuild it."

Luca smiles at my loose grasp of the facts, and I sweep a strand of hair behind my ear.

"A relative of Galileo was awarded the commission, but he was from Firenze, and the locals pitched a fit, so they gave it to a Roman architect named Salvi. The fountain wasn't completed until after Salvi's death, about forty years later, but most of it's his vision."

"I knew you'd make an excellent guide," he says. His smile is dangerous, or maybe it's the way his grayish-blue eyes look at you.

"I'm not a tour guide."

I look around, afraid someone has heard how ridiculously defensive I sound of my nerd expertise.

"Of course. And who is around Neptune?" He points to the center statue.

"That's Oceanus, not Neptune. You can tell because he's supported by seahorses and tritons, who are half men and half mermen. Neptune would have a trifork and dolphins. Didn't you ever watch *The Little Mermaid*?" I point to the left of Oceanus, making a big show of it for the paparazzo. "See, the triton on the left is struggling with his horse, representing rough seas, while the one on the right represents calm seas." I glance behind us. The guy seems to believe I'm giving a tour. He's started to scan the crowd, probably for other celebrities. Rome is littered with them.

"I have seen *The Little Mermaid,* and wasn't the trifork called a triton in it?"

"No, Ariel's father is King Triton, that's what you're thinking of."

"Oh, I should have studied my Disney classics more," he says, so deadpan that I smile in spite of myself.

In front of us, a little boy throws a coin into the fountain, over his shoulder.

"And is that for love?" Luca asks. "He seems a bit young."

I laugh. "No, one coin over your shoulder ensures a return trip to Rome. Two will bring you love. Three and you're getting married."

"Got it, don't throw three."

"Definitely not. I should get going."

He drops his smile. "Aye, and I should get back to my hotel. Can you point me in the right direction? It's on the Via dei Condotti."

Of course it is. All the hotels there are for the uber wealthy. "So is the Gucci store. Come on." The paparazzo has disappeared. "I think we've lost your friends."

Luca looks around and seems to relax. I take him north toward Condotti by a different route in case there are still paparazzi waiting for him the way we came.

"So, why are you so popular?" I ask. "Are you a musician, like Jasmine?"

Luca looks at me with raised eyebrows and a bit of a smirk. "No, I'm not. I just hang around people like Jasmine."

"And why can't she be seen with you?"

He glances around as if making sure no one is listening. "Her EP with Rowdy Funkmaster is about to drop. The label has her under strict orders not to do anything that might give it bad publicity." He puts his finger to his lips and whispers, "Shhhh!" even though I haven't said anything. Rowdy is Jasmine's longtime boyfriend—everyone knows that, including me.

I want to tell him that maybe she shouldn't be cheating on the guy, then, but it's not my business.

"You won't say anything, right?"

I just look at him, because who would I have to tell and why would I brag about being this guy's cover?

"I'll pay you."

I shake my head. "I'd rather you didn't and we just forget this whole episode ever happened." Although, I'm still mad about my stracciatella.

He seems almost offended. But he's got the confidence of someone who is used to girls fawning all over him.

"So, what else should I see while I'm here?" he asks. "I mean besides the Colosseum?"

"So much. There's a street going up to the Villa Borghese if you walk to it from Piazza di Spagna that will give you a breathtaking view of the whole city, about halfway up. And the villa is a pretty cool place on a rainy day. No tourists, and it feels like you're in some golden-age-of-Hollywood movie. My absolute favorite places, though, are just little side streets and back stairways where you feel like you could be in any century you choose."

He's staring at me, and I feel the burn rush up my face. Honestly, I sound like a twelve-year-old who only leaves her house for cosplay. I need to not get carried away over talking history to strangers. As if I ever talk to strangers.

"How long are you here for? There are lots of day trips from the city that are pretty cool," I add to cover my awkwardness. I don't know why I bother, though. It's not like you can explain the essence of Rome to someone breezing through with a pop star.

"For the summer, I think. Although my plans aren't totally fixed. Friends, you know." He ticks his head to let me know he's really here for Jasmine.

I nod, like, yeah, of course, whose plans don't depend on friends? But I've never lived anyplace long enough to have real friends. A few pen pals and an occasional local friend like Anna Maria, but I'm not like the other Dips. They all clique together and become lifelong besties, splashing social accounts with photos of them looking amazing with comments like *omggg* and *ur unreal* and *stunning*.

We've reached the Condotti, and I point out the direction of his hotel.

"Well, thank you, Miss Astoria Herriot," he says in full Scottish gallantry. "Are you sure I can't do something for you? I could go with you to Gucci and buy you something. You could pick out whatever you like."

"That's okay," I tell him with a smile. "There's nothing at Gucci I want. But thanks, anyway." I almost wish my mom had said to buy something at Tiffany's. I've always wanted something in one of their robin's-egg-blue boxes. Not that I'd actually take a gift from him.

He hesitates, and I knit my face into a question mark. I'm pretty sure we've successfully covered up his clandestine shenanigans.

"Well, right. Thanks again. You were brilliant. Pure dead brilliant with that Italian accent." He smiles.

"Anytime," I say, and he steps back to let me cross in front of him in the opposite direction toward Gucci. I get an awkward feeling when he's behind me, as if he's watching me walk away. Suddenly all I can think about is how I'm walking, as if it matters, and I could swear I'm not walking normally. But at least I have enough self-respect not to look back. The bigger problem is that I almost want to.

Two

We don't have class the next morning. Instead, we're rehearsing for graduation at our private American school. It's all the Dips, along with some other American kids whose families are living here, a few Italian kids whose parents want them to learn in English, and a bunch of diplomatic kids from other countries. There's a six-foot-four Russian kid we think is a spy because he's constantly pumping us for information about what our parents do, and a weird kid called Ed, who won't tell us where he's from. Patrick insists he's a thirty-year-old cyber ninja on the lam from China.

A lot of kids have family coming in because it's Rome, and who doesn't want an excuse to come to Rome before the high summer tourist crush? We're sitting in the class that serves as our theater, music room, lunchroom, and parent-night refreshment stand while Dr. Stockton makes us go over the program so we don't disappoint our parents. I'm in the back, wedged between Jack and Ed, the weird kid from parts unknown whose real name is definitely not Ed, while Kelsey flirts with Patrick, and Alicia fixes her forever truffle-nude lipstick in her forever-at-her-fingertips compact. Guin's on her phone because it's the closest thing she has to a meaningful relationship.

The air-conditioning here isn't like in the States. The room is becoming moist, and we're all wishing Dr. Stockton would wrap it up and let us go, but he seems intent on keeping us as long as he can.

"Story," Jack says, "did you get your welcome package from Princeton?" He's sitting on his chair with it backward, and he leans to the side toward me. His straight dark hair falls just short of his green eyes.

I nod.

"I apply there," Ed says. "They tell me I need more documents. I tell them, 'No, thank you!'" He bobs his head up and down like this makes any sense.

Jack looks at him a moment and says, "Cool." Then he turns back to me. "I hope we get assigned to the same dorm. I'd like to know someone."

"Really?" I glance at him. "I thought you'd be perfectly fine going in there solo."

"Me? No. I'm used to having Patrick around. He usually does the meeting-new-people stuff. I'm six minutes younger, after all." His smile is effortlessly disarming. He'd probably be okay if he didn't have Patrick to follow.

"So how come he's not going to Princeton, too? Even your dad's connections couldn't get past his grades?"

Jack chuckles. "Probably not, but actually, that was my dad's idea. He thinks I need to learn to 'come into my own.'" He says this in the thick Boston accent his dad has. Jack has lived abroad long enough not to have it.

I nod and smile a little. "Well, I think you'll do fine without your brother. I guess I'm lucky I don't have a dad to worry about me like that."

Jack's smile vanishes. I don't really know how much the Dips know about my dad, or lack thereof, but my guess would be they know the gruesome parts. The diplomatic corps isn't that big, and people love gossip.

"I'm sorry Patrick messed with you so much. It's only because he needs a lot of attention and doesn't really know how to get it. It's nothing about you, honest."

I wonder if he means what he's saying or if he thinks it's better to strike a truce with me, since we'll be the only people we know going into Princeton. When I think back on it, I can't ever remember Jack being a jerk to me, but he never stood up for me, either.

"Well, I'm sure you'll make a lot of friends on the soccer team."

Jack's good enough that he plays with an Italian team here and got a partial athletic scholarship.

He smiles. "Yeah, but none of them will know what it's like to hide out in Rome's secret places, like the Keats house."

Did he see me yesterday in the window? "How do you—"

"Pay attention, please, people," Dr. Stockton barks out, and we all shut up and do a dry run of the procession once more. Then he has the Italian girl who is our valedictorian go through her whole speech. Again. She's about halfway through the part about how she'll never forget any of us, even though she doesn't know half our names, including Ed's, when Guin shouts out, "Oh my God!"

"Guin, please," Dr. Stockton says harshly enough that anyone with sense would be quiet. But that's not Guin.

"But, Dr. Stockton, this is huge!"

Dr. Stockton smooths his hair back into its comb-over. "Oh, for heaven's sake, what's wrong? Has the Pope died or something?"

Guin turns to me, her eyes as buggy as mine must have been in the paparazzi picture last night, and I know she's seen one of those photos. "How do *you* know Luca Kinnaird?"

"Who is Luca Kinnaird?" Dr. Stockton says as the room bursts into motion. Our valedictorian asks if she should finish her speech, the Russian kid grabs his phone, presumably to Google Luca, and Ed is saying with more incredulity than I think is necessary, "Story, with Luca Kinnaird, really?"

Even Ed knows who Luca is?

Guin is shoving her phone in my face. Yep, there I am, looking like a bug-eyed, tournament-winning mackerel, dripping stracciatella, while Luca is holding on to me as if he's some drop-dead-gorgeous movie star completely at ease with flashing cameras.

"We should be focusing on the procession," I say, hoping Dr. Stockton will put an end to this.

"Guys, check this out," Alicia says as she studies her phone, and a group of our classmates huddle around her.

"Can I see that?" I ask Guin. She hands me her phone with a glance that makes me feel like we're eight and she thinks I'll contaminate it.

"Story, how *do* you know Luca Kinnaird?" Jack asks, looking from his phone to my face.

I just shake my head and read about how Luca and his new "mystery girlfriend" were spotted in the Piazza di Spagna sharing a gelato and sweet nothings. The article says we tried to fool them by telling them I was Luca's tour guide. There's also a picture of me coming out of Gucci with a small shopping bag. At least my mouth isn't full of food in that one. *What tour guide shops at Gucci?* the article asks. *No, after seeing these two love birds at the Trevi, it's clear that heartbreaking Luca has another conquest to add to his collection. Nice try with the tour guide story, including some believable Italian by the young lady. In an exclusive, we've discovered she's an American exchange student, but the only thing she seems to be studying is our favorite Scottish heartthrob. Will Luca break this American girl's heart, too? We'll keep you posted, because nothing happens in Rome without us knowing!*

The screen goes dark, and I hand the phone back to Guin. For the first time since I've known her, she's right.

Oh my God.

Three

Dr. Stockton claps his hands. "People, people, can we try to get through this without a mistake, just once!"

Everyone turns and looks at him. "Will you let us go if we do?" Patrick asks. Even his smirk is blond.

"Yes, you may all leave when you have completed this correctly one time." I almost feel sorry for Dr. Stockton. He's terrified of Patrick because Jack and Patrick's dad is the US ambassador to Italy.

There's a soft mist across my forehead. Patrick looks around at us all. "Okay, guys, let's do this, one time, and get the hell out of here!"

"Patrick, language!" Dr. Stockton says, but his attempt to instill discipline flies past its target, who sits on top of a desk with the nonchalance of someone in charge.

Our parents are expecting a nice graduation, though, and we're all hot and irritated, so we try a little harder to get the day over with. Guin, Kelsey, and Alicia start to discuss how I could possibly know Luca Kinnaird, but Patrick is more interested in finishing, so he shuts them up. We finally get it right, and Dr. Stockton lets us go a little after lunchtime, but we haven't actually eaten because we worked straight through. I stay behind to help Dr. Stockton straighten the room, mostly to avoid any grilling my classmates must have in store for me. I stop by my locker to grab a couple of books, and the hallway is blissfully empty. The storm seems to have passed, until I step outside. A crowd has gathered at the student entrance.

Kelsey rushes over to me. "You should let me do the talking. I'm a natural!"

Before I can even react, cameras start clicking and whirring. I look around to get my bearings of the group that's staring at me. It's a mix of paparazzi and kids from school. There doesn't seem to be any open lane for me to walk, as everyone makes a semicircle around the entrance. I'm trapped between them and the building.

"You guys are making a big mistake," Patrick says. "There's no way Story Herriot is Luca Kinnaird's girlfriend. She doesn't even have any friends." A few photographers turn and snap his picture. Patrick smiles, completely pleased with himself.

"Thanks, Patrick," I say. *Way to look out for a fellow Dip.*

He just smiles bigger.

The paparazzi shout questions at me. Every one begins with my name.

"Astoria, where did you meet Luca?"

"Astoria, how long have you and Luca been dating?"

"Astoria, why don't you ever post on social media?"

"Astoria, is it true that Luca has a thing for Jasmine?"

I almost feel sorry for the me who's supposed to be his girlfriend having to listen to questions about him liking some super-hot music diva who used to be a Disney star. Jack moves in front to shield me. "Hey, whatever you all want to know, Story's relationship with Luca Kinnaird is no one's business."

My eyes widen. But maybe he just wants to be in the pictures the way Kelsey does. Guin has also somehow managed to get very close to me. It's almost worse to be surrounded by the Dip Squad pretending to be my friends than it is having those stracciatella pictures of me forever embedded on the internet.

I'm about to yell "I am not Luca Kinnaird's girlfriend!" when I hear my name called, and all the photographers turn. They clear a path. Luca comes striding through, cameras going off like fireworks. He walks right up to me, and I think Guin is going to hyperventilate.

"Sorry I'm late," he says, and kisses me on the cheek while wrapping his hand around mine. "Please play along," he whispers in my ear as he leans in.

Luca turns to the paparazzi. "Take your pictures, but we aren't answering any questions right now. Perhaps later, if you're all good boys and girls." He smiles his charming smile and slips his arm around my waist.

A few of them laugh. "You might see us tonight at the Jamie Talon concert," he adds, squeezing me close as a warning or plea to get me to go along. They fire a few questions anyway, but he ignores them. "Come on, I have the car just over here."

I hesitate, but I really want to get away from the cameras.

Luca smiles and pulls me along. My classmates' faces are price-less. Especially Patrick's. His smirk is completely wiped out, and his open mouth makes him look almost as idiotic as I did in the picture last night. Even Ed seems reverently awed. I'm going to have to spend the rest of the summer living down the humiliation when they find out this isn't real, but I'd rather it didn't start in front of paparazzi cameras. I let Luca tow me to a shiny red sports car that looks as if it could almost be out of an old movie. He opens the door for me. I climb in, and he jaunts around to the driver's side.

"I brought the Portofino because it's classic. And you like classics," he says with a smile. I'm presuming the Portofino is the car, which is fancier than anything I've ever been in. The Dips and paparazzi have followed us. Patrick lets out a low whistle. "Dude! Nice Ferrari!"

Luca starts the car, and it revs as if by its own free will. He flips his sunglasses down from his forehead and waves to the little crowd as he pulls out.

Patrick yells, "Bro, let's do coffee!" like they actually know each other. I look in the passenger-side mirror. They're stand-ing in a pack that gets smaller and smaller on the street behind us. As we drive off into the unknown, I'm not even sure what just happened.

Four

"Sorry about that," Luca says while he zips through the tiny streets of Rome as if it's not the least bit challenging. "Do you need to be anywhere right now?"

"I guess not," I say, because really, it's not like I ever need to be anywhere except for school. But I'd rather he didn't know that. My mom won't be home from work for hours. I start to wonder why he's carried me off. You read about rich people who do weird crimes sometimes. Maybe he's dangerous.

But his smile is sweet. "Brilliant." His phone is already plugged into the car, and he tells it to get directions to "La Contessa." I look at the screen on the dash. Whatever this place is, it's well outside of Rome, based on the kilometers and forty minutes it will take us to get there. Part of me wants to demand where we're going, and part of me just wants to get farther away from the Dip Squad and cameras. Whatever he wants from me, it's probably best to wait until I'm out of his car to ask. At least then I could run.

Luca tells me to play whatever kind of music I like and unlocks his phone with his thumbprint. I pull up his music app and search until I find something I like.

"Good taste," Luca says as the song begins to play. "Modern and yet classic, too."

I'm not sure if he's making fun of me, so I look at the scenery. After all, the guy likes Jasmine, so his taste can't be that good. Her songs are typical pop fueled by racy lyrics and confessional drama.

He can go pretty fast because the car hugs the road so tightly, but I don't have the faith in him that he has, and I grip the seat. He must notice, because he dials the speed back a few notches. The wind feels cool after how stifling school was, and I'm glad I put my hair in a bun this morning. I let myself bask in how good it is to escape the Dip Squad, even temporarily.

"There are some glecks in the glove box," he says.

"Glecks?"

"Sunglasses."

"Oh, thanks." I dig them out, relieved to stop squinting at the sun and the wind. I slip them on, noticing that they are not the cheap plastic kind from the newsstand.

"They look good on you."

I ignore this. "So, how did you find me?"

"I didn't. The paparazzi did. I just had someone find out what they knew. There was no way they weren't going to ambush you once they followed you to Gucci."

"How did they figure out who I am so quickly?"

"They probably went into Gucci after you and paid the

clerk to tell them your name from your credit card, or took a photo of it while you were paying. Someone followed you home, maybe to school this morning. Or they just found out once they had your name."

"I didn't even see anyone take my photo when I left Gucci."

"Well, you can tell from the picture they used a telephoto lens. They were probably in a car across the street, or partially hidden by a delivery truck or something." He frowns. "Half the time, you never know they're there. Especially in a crowded city. It's pretty easy for them to fit in, even with a really good lens on the camera."

"How do you know so much about how they work? And how do you stand it?"

He laughs. "It's part of the territory. I don't really remember life without them. You get to know their tricks after a while."

"What do you do that makes you so famous?"

"I told you, I hang around famous people. I don't actually do anything. I just . . . am."

He says this nonchalantly, but I feel like there's a current of bitterness running through his words. He doesn't elaborate, though, and I don't ask.

My favorite song comes on. I put my head back and enjoy the wind and the beautiful Italian countryside whirring by. I wonder if Grace Kelly felt like this when she was filming *To Catch a Thief* on the French Riviera, riding around in beautiful cars with Cary Grant. It's one of my mom's favorite old movies.

"I looked for you online," Luca says after a while. "You have accounts but no posts. How come?"

"I'm a professional troll," I say, and he chuckles. I don't really get why people look each other up online. No one is ever honest about who they are on the internet.

"Seriously, why no posts?"

We pass a cemetery with its tall sentinel trees. The Etruscans believed cypress trees have supernatural power and that their essential oil wards off demons. I think the best way to ward off demons is to keep your head down and stay away from them in the first place. The more people know about you, the more weapons they have to turn against you.

"I'm a private person."

Luca's face grows serious, and he gets quiet. Pretty soon, he pulls into the main piazza of a small town and parks. It's a typical village in Italy, old and pretty, without being special in any way. He hops out, and I start looking for the handle, which is practically hidden in the door. By the time I find it, he's come around and opened it for me.

"Thanks," I say. "So, why are we here?"

He smiles. "The food here is great, so lunch. And a business proposition."

I look around and nod. He's apparently not a serial killer, and I'm starving. And this should at least be interesting.

We cross the square to a restaurant that's housed in an ancient building overlooking a dry green valley. The heat of the day evaporates inside, which has been modernized in clean glass lines. Its beauty is in the contrast, with stone walls and exposed timber beams. It's late for lunch, even by Italian standards, and Luca gets us a table in front of a panoramic window. The perfume of fresh bread and rosemary lingers in the air.

"Is this good?" he asks before we sit down.

"Fine."

The waiter asks us in English what we'd like to drink. I ask for a limonata, and Luca says he'll have the same. We look over the menus, and nothing is inexpensive. Even the antipasti are at least twenty euros. When the waiter comes back with the drinks and bread, Luca orders a seafood pizza and I get a salad.

"Do you want the salmon with that?" Luca asks. "It's probably imported from Scotland."

"I'm vegan."

Luca nods. "Of course you are. Can't stand to hurt animals?"

"Yes. Although you can't really be completely vegan in Italy, so I eat some cheese and butter and eggs. But I try to make sure the animals are humanely treated whenever I can."

"Naturally. So, you like tofu?"

"God, no," I say, which makes him laugh.

"There's hope for you yet, Astoria Herriot."

"You can just call me Story."

The conversation lulls as we wait for our food. I look out on the beautiful valley below, while Luca studies me. I get the feeling he's used to getting the things he wants, almost like Patrick but without being mean about it. I don't think Luca has to be mean to get what he wants. The guy oozes charm. The real question is what he wants from me.

The waiter brings our food and retreats to the bar, where he and the bartender chat. The restaurant is empty.

"I see why you brought me here."

"No paparazzi, and no one to overhear." He smiles.

"So, what's this business proposal? And is it normal to make business proposals to your girlfriend?"

He chuckles. "I'm sorry we couldn't get you out of all this with that tour guide story."

"Me too."

Luca's smile disappears. "Well, the paparazzi seem determined to believe that you are my latest girlfriend."

"Your latest?" I stab a piece of lettuce with my fork. "How many have you had?"

This seems to throw him, and he vaguely says, "A few." He pauses before he offers me a slice of pizza.

"No, thank you."

"Anyway, it would really help Jasmine and me out if you could pretend to go along. You know, make public appearances with me so people don't realize—"

He hesitates, and I *almost* manage to not say "That you're helping her cheat on Rowdy Funkmaster?" But I say it.

Luca furrows his brow. "Are you a fan of his?"

"No, I've never heard of him except as Jasmine's boyfriend in the constant celebrity chatter none of us can escape. I mean, maybe I've heard his music, but I couldn't tell you what his songs are."

Luca sits back and relaxes. "Well, they've been struggling for a while, and they've basically broken up at this point."

"Basically?"

"I read that your mother's a lawyer. You must take after her." He says it simply, not meanly, but it makes me feel mean.

"I just think people should be honest. If she doesn't want to be with the guy, then she should tell him."

"She has," he says, and leans in closer before he whispers, "but she told him right before he went to rehab. He's there now."

I pull back and can't help it that my eyes grow wide. I guess I can understand not wanting to be with someone who has substance use disorder, but maybe she could have at least waited before she moved on to her next conquest. She's left a string of broken hearts in Hollywood.

"Look," Luca says, and he seems really annoyed with me. "I don't need you to approve, just to go along."

I take a big bite of my salad so that I don't say the first thing that comes to mind. But even after I've fully chewed and taken a large swallow of my lemonade, I'm still thinking the same thing.

"I'm sorry, why should I go along with you on this crazy idea exactly?"

Luca looks surprised, as if he can't imagine why anyone would not be willing to be his fake girlfriend.

"Well," he says, and then pauses awkwardly. "There are a lot of perks to running around in my circles."

"Like the Ferrari?"

He smiles as if he thinks he's scored a point. "Exactly. You'll get to go to all the best parties in Rome, see the best shows, meet, well, not the best people, but the people with all the access to the best things."

I just look at him. Then I take another bite of salad and turn my face to the window.

"You're not impressed by all that, are you?"

"Not really."

"So what are you impressed by? Do you want money?"

I drop my fork. "I'm sorry, do you think I'm an item for sale, like that Rolex you're wearing?"

The waiter jerks his head in our direction, and I really hope he only heard my tone and not my words.

"I'm sorry," Luca says, flustered. "That didn't come out right at all. Honestly."

"I hope not. This idea is ridiculous."

We sit in silence. Luca gazes out the window and taps his fingers on the table. I can't believe the nerve of this spoiled brat and his diva girlfriend, asking me to lie for them as if I have nothing better to do in life.

"Well, what would make it worth it to you?"

I stare at him, and he's actually serious. He's willing to make a deal, sure I must have a price. I think about this for a few moments, like maybe there is something I should ask for? But there's nothing he has that I need or want.

"There has to be something I can do for you? Do you want a trip? Front-row seats at Fashion Week?" He snaps his fingers.

"Or maybe there's someone you want to meet. The singer you played in the car? A five-star vacation on a private jet?" This kid could be a car salesman.

I think about maybe taking my mom to Hawaii. For just a moment, I see us hiking to see a volcano. It's something we've always talked about doing. But I'd never be able to explain how I got someone to give me a trip like that.

I shake my head.

He shakes his head back at me, clearly frustrated that he can't get what he wants.

"Look, I'm sorry I can't help you—"

"Won't—"

"Okay, won't. But I don't really want anything from you, and I don't want to be part of a scheme to help some girl cheat on her boyfriend. Or supposed boyfriend, or whatever he is. Especially while he's in rehab. Wow, that sounds even worse when I say it out loud."

"What if he knew?"

I stare at him. "Excuse me?"

"What if Rowdy"—he stops and presses his lips together for just a moment—"what if Jeremy—that's his real name—knew and said it was okay?"

"You're going to get him to do that?"

"Look, Jasmine has already told him it's over. He's going to rehab for him, not her. He agreed it had to be for himself."

"Are you sure he's not hoping to get back with her when he gets out?"

"Positive. She was calling it off no matter what, and he knows about me. I think that's what made him finally realize he needed help. Then the record label got involved and told them to keep it quiet until after the EP drops and makes its initial money splash."

I study him for a long moment. That would make it better. But I still don't want to be part of this. I didn't like having cameras all over me. And I really don't know how to be part of an in-crowd. But I feel sorry for this guy in rehab. "Would it help him?"

"You mean Jeremy?" Luca seems surprised I would ask.

"Yes. I mean, it would help him, too, since he's on the album, right?"

Luca nods. "He'd have some peace from all the questions while he's in recovery."

Late-afternoon sun comes through the window and makes me squint. I would like to help this guy out. But this is crazy. "No, I'm sorry. Even if this Jeremy were okay with it, I wouldn't fit into your world. No one would believe it."

"People will believe whatever the paparazzi spin for them. And the paparazzi will spin what they want the people to believe."

"So that means what?"

Luca shrugs. "My guess is that they'll paint you as an innocent darling and be waiting with bated breath for bad-boy Luca to break your heart. That's usually how it works. I'm one of their favorite villains. Jeremy will be out of rehab in July, he and Jasmine drop the album and, a few weeks later, announce a mutual breakup. She's not dumping a fellow in rehab, and he's not losing any face, either. And the album still sells."

"And is this what really matters? That the album sells?"

He shrugs. "What else should matter?"

That's the moment I know I'll do it. Because I know what matters, and he doesn't.

"What about Luca and Story? How do you save face for dumping me for her?"

"You dump me. For whatever reason you like. I'll wait a week or two, and Jasmine and I will be out in the open. No one will expect me to be without a girlfriend for long, and everyone already suspects I like her. It will blow over easily enough."

I gaze out the window. "I can dump you for any reason I want?"

"Yep. This can all be over by the end of July or early August at the latest. In the meantime, I'll treat you like a proverbial princess. And everyone walks away a winner."

I really don't like the whole idea. But Luca has hit on my one soft spot. There is one thing I've dreamed of doing one day and this entitled, self-absorbed ATM can make it happen now with a wave of his check wrist. I calculate in my head what I think the things he's offered me would cost, and it's enough to at least get me started.

"I'll do it," I say.

He smiles. "Brilliant!"

And now it's my turn to smile. "Yes. On one condition."

Five

"**T**hat's it?" Luca says when I've explained. "That's all? You want me to fund an annual memorial scholarship through a school? You don't want a diamond necklace or a Louis Vuitton bag?"

I scrunch my nose to tell him no. "I just want to get the scholarship started. And it has to be designated for someone coming from rehab. You can set it up through the university. I've already checked the legal aspects of it, and they'll do it if I can find the funding. This is something I've wanted to do for a really long time, but I didn't know how to raise enough money."

Luca leans back in his chair and crinkles his face as he looks out the window. I asked for an initial input of twenty thousand, but maybe he's going to try to bring it down to ten. I'm sticking to my guns, though. Scholarship or no deal. The interest on it isn't going to amount to very much each year, but it will at least pay for books or something. The waiter comes to bring us fresh limonatas and clear our dishes. He asks if we want dessert, but I shake my head and Luca sends him off to get the check.

Luca turns back, piercing me with the dark blue of his eyes. My request seems to frustrate him. "Why is this so important to you? Why is this the thing you'll agree to be my fake girlfriend over when you don't want any of the things normal girls would want?"

"It just is," I say. "And I *am* normal."

He leans forward and softens his look. "Sorry, you know what I mean. Average girls. And don't even try to tell me, Astoria Herriot, that you are average."

I smile because he seems sincere enough. But he's not charming me into a penny less. I'm about to tell him this when he leans back again, clearly calculating it all out.

"So, how exactly did you decide this scholarship is worth twenty K?" He has his phone on the table, and it lights up with a text in Jasmine's name. He looks at me instead of picking up his phone.

I can't believe he's such a jerk that he'll haggle with me over money for a scholarship because he expects me to want designer swag instead. I should have asked for thirty.

"Well, the things you've offered seem like they'd be at least that." But maybe I don't know, after all. It's not like I've ever chartered a private plane to Hawaii or bought a Dolce & Gabbana coat. "And, if I'm going to be spending my time to help you, I think you can spend some money to help other people."

I want to add "Especially since you seem to have more money than sense," but I manage to leave that unsaid.

He pinches his eyebrows and doesn't smile. "The thing is, that's not much seed money to run a scholarship fund with. You'd be lucky to pay for books with the interest on that each year."

"For some people, that could make a big difference. It's that or no deal." I hold his gaze, determined, but then I feel ridiculous and grab my drink.

"How about a quarter of a million?"

I sputter my limonata, choking.

Luca laughs.

"Dollars? Are you kidding me?"

Luca shrugs. "Look, I need to make a certain amount of charitable gifts every year for tax purposes, which my accountant has been on me about anyway. Why not this? Besides, the exchange rate is in my favor, and it will help my image. Especially once people find out about Rowdy."

I just stare at him, which he seems to find extremely amusing. This is way too good to be true.

"You know," he says, "seeing you speechless might be as much fun as I've ever gotten from having a tidy sum of cash to throw around. So does this mean we have a deal?"

I close my mouth and we shake hands.

"No one can ever know about any of this, though," he adds.

"Agreed." I push my glass away. The last thing I want anyone to know is that I'm helping this jerk's diva girlfriend move on from someone in rehab. I already feel like a total creep. But, if it helps his album with her do well, then it's helping him. Especially since he already knows the girl is gone. I just hope he's not fooling himself that she'll change her mind when he gets out.

"Nobody can find out," I say. "Ever."

He nods as the waiter approaches with the check. After the guy walks away with his cash, Luca catches my gaze. "So, tonight, Jamie Talon concert, aye?"

"Aye."

"Brilliant. I'll pick you up at six-thirty."

I can hardly wait.

Six

Luca lets me off around the corner from my apartment building, which is just a little south of the embassy. My mom might be getting home, and there could be paparazzi waiting.

"Can I borrow these?" I ask about the shades as he pulls to the curb.

"Keep them."

"Thanks." I step onto the sidewalk and close the door. Luca pulls into the street and flies away. I slip into a store and buy a baseball hat with the logo of a major soccer team, Juventus. I'd rather hide under an imitation Hermès scarf like a 1950s movie star, but that seems a bit too conspicuous for today's Rome.

Our apartment is in an updated, older building. It's where all the Dips not assigned to live at the embassy are housed. I scan the sidewalk for paparazzi. If they are here, then Luca is right, they're hard to spot. I keep my head down and go inside.

My mom is home. Bright, sunny windows overlook a court-yard in the back of the building. "I was thinking we could have pasta from that new place around the corner," she says. "What do you think?"

"I'm sorry, I had a late lunch." I drop my book bag by the door and kick off my Converses.

"That's fine. How was rehearsal?"

I rub my neck. "Hot and long and Patricky."

My mom laughs. "Well, you're almost free of him." She's reading, a teacup in her hand. Our lemon tree that stands sentry between the balcony doors is drooping.

"Have you watered Bert lately?" I ask.

"No, it's been a few days. He does look a bit sad, doesn't he?" I go into the kitchen and bring back a small pitcher of water. Bert has been with us since I was little, almost like a pet. I check his leaves for bugs and then take the empty pitcher back to the sink. I debated on the ride home how much to tell my mom about Luca. She's sure to hear about him if Guin and the rest of them mention it to their parents.

"Hey, Mom," I say as I start to put away the clean dishes sitting in the drying rack, "can I go to the Jamie Talon concert tonight?"

"Jamie Talon? That's a hot ticket. Whom are you going with?" She knows about all the events to see and be seen at because the diplomatic corps is like a giant concierge for the Luca Kinnairds of the States. Kelsey and company have been whining for months they couldn't get tickets, and even Patrick hasn't been able to hook them up.

"A guy I met this week." I try not to wince as I say it.

"A guy you met this week? How did you meet this guy? How old is he? What's his name? Is he from here?"

I laugh to make her relax. "His name is Luca Kinnaird, and he's only a year older than me. He's some rich kid from Scotland, and I met him by accident and somehow ended up giving him a little tour of the Trevi. He's just paying me back. That's all." I should have my fingers crossed behind my back.

"A rich kid from Scotland? And you barely know him?"

"It's fine, Mom. He's a little famous in the celebrity magazines, so he's not going to kidnap me or anything."

She raises her eyebrows and pushes a strand of brown hair back into its clip. "Well . . ."

"He doesn't have bodyguards, I won't accept any drinks from him, and I'm not hooking up with him. We'll be at a concert. I promise, I'll be completely safe."

"What's he famous for?"

I shrug. "Hanging around other rich people, from what I can gather."

"Take your pepper spray," she says, only half joking. "And keep your location sharing on and text me updates."

"Okay." I laugh and kiss her on the cheek.

"Story," she says, stopping me as I walk out of the room, "he doesn't sound like your type, but it's good to see you do something with a friend."

I just nod because Luca is not my type, and he's definitely not my friend.

After a shower, I stand in front of my closet. Nothing I own is even remotely similar to what I picture Luca's crowd will wear at the biggest concert of the season. The arena will probably be hot and crowded, though, so I settle on the nicest dress that I have, a pretty, sleeveless chiffon fit-and-flare in white with tiny blue dots.

Going to a concert with a rich guy isn't like anything I've experienced before. "When we're on for the paparazzi," Luca tells me in the car, "just follow my lead and smile. And, whatever you do, don't answer any questions."

"Right," I say, and watch Rome fly by.

We don't have to park blocks away from the venue or wait in line to get in. We drive up to valet service and are whisked across a roped-off area while paparazzi take our pictures. I ignore the multitude of questions flung at us about how we met and how far I've fallen for heartbreaking Luca. I just smile. This will be over in a couple of months.

Luca stops once to let them get a good picture, and then he moves us on. He must have done this hundreds of times, because it's completely effortless for him. My heart is pounding.

He takes my hand and leads me to the VIP section. Luca introduces me to more people than I can keep track of. Everyone is interested in me because they think I've captured the attention of Luca Kinnaird. Even I recognize some of these celebrities. I've apparently worn the wrong thing, though, because every girl I meet is wearing a body-con dress and comments on how "adorable" my outfit is.

As people are approaching or walking away from us, Luca gives me commentary on them. "He's handsy, stay close to me," or "She's going to ask you to lunch tomorrow. Don't say yes, trust me," or "He's a good chap, you should date him after you dump me." He says this last one with such a charming smile, it almost feels like an inside joke between people who actually care about each other. Thankfully, though, the music is too loud for much conversation beyond "Hello, brilliant to meet you!"

We go backstage for a meet and greet. People mill about and wait to get a picture with Jamie Talon. "You go ahead," I tell Luca when it's our turn, but he pulls me onto the backdrop with a look that says we have a deal.

Luca knows the opening act, a band from his hometown in Scotland that has started scoring hits in the past year. They come over and hug him. He introduces me, and then they talk to Luca about things at home. A guy named Craig asks me what I do.

"I'm headed to college in the fall. Back in the States."

He seems confused for a moment and side-eyes Luca.

"Should I be doing something else?" I ask.

"Naw, naw, A'm sorry," he says. "A'm being a total balloon. It's jest wae Luca at's usually models an' sangers and sooch."

Luca catches our conversation even though he's been talking to another band member. "A balloon's an idiot," he says to me. He looks at Craig and slips into a much stronger accent. "Goanie no dae tha? Stop bein' a chancer to th' lass."

"A'm sorry," Craig says to me, "we're comin' to tha end o' tha tour and A'm a bit gubbed."

"Tired," Luca says as he shakes his head at Craig. It's nice to see him irritated by someone other than me, although I'm a little surprised at him defending me.

"It's okay," I say as lightly as I can, and hope there's enough noise to mask the catch in my voice. Even though I don't care what Luca's type is, I get that not being his type is supposed to be an insult. I guess I should be glad the Dip Squad isn't around to hear it pointed out that I don't belong in this world any more than my own. My mom saying Luca didn't seem like my type earlier is almost funny now.

Luca puts his arm around my waist. "Don't mind him," he says, "all his eggs are double-yoakit."

"Aye, it's troo," Craig says.

I laugh it off, and they talk about other things. Luca's accent is so thick, I sometimes don't even know what they're talking about. He drops it as soon as we leave them and goes back to his usual standard English.

More people who know Luca come up to meet me, and he introduces us politely while cutting off their intrusive questions with amazing skill. I'm actually impressed. I let him do the talking as much as I can. Most of the conversation is empty gossip or material things like cars, Cartier, or "running up to Monte for the races," whatever that means. I really don't have anything to say.

When the meet and greet ends, we go back to our seats in the VIP section with a group Luca knows.

"We're all going out after," one soft Swedish girl says to me. "You and Luca need to come to the club with us."

"Not tonight, Saga, Story has an early morning tomorrow," Luca says. I almost laugh out loud when I hear our weird names together.

44

"How did you two meet, anyway?" she asks.

I have no idea what our cover story is supposed to be, so I just look at Luca.

"The way every fairy-tale couple meets, Saga," Luca says as he moves me to the other side of him. "Story was a damsel in distress, and I saved her."

I arch my eyebrows at him because I'm pretty sure it's the other way around, but Saga laughs at his vague but charming line, and then her attention is on the flickering lights as the show starts.

"So, what do you think?" Luca asks when Craig's band is on their last song.

"They're really good," I say, and he slips his arm around me as I lean toward him a little so he can hear me.

"You're hard to impress," he says, "so I'm glad you like them."

"Is that a compliment?" I ask as the stagehands change out the set.

Luca bobbles his head a little. "Sure." He says it with a smile, but I have no idea if he means it. And then the main event starts.

We're so close to the stage that I can see where Jamie Talon nicked himself shaving. But the music is good, even if my ears will pay for this later. Luca laughs when Saga gets me to sing along with her.

When the lights come up, Luca turns to me. "Shall we?"

I nod, happy to see this end before anyone asks me any more questions I can't answer about my boyfriend. Saga hugs me like we've been friends for years. "Another night, you'll come to the club, yes?"

I look at Luca, and he drapes his arm around my neck. "Sure, Saga," he says before turning us away.

"She's harmless," he tells me as we navigate the hall to the exit. "A little Swedish, but she has a good heart."

I laugh. "What does that mean?"

He gives me a sardonic smile. "You know, she's the tree-hugging, vegan type."

"Oh, right," I say. "One of those."

Luca laughs and takes my hand as a valet opens the door for us, and Luca hands him the ticket for the car.

The Portofino no longer seems unfamiliar as I sink into it. We zip across Rome, lit everywhere in its white marble and ancient travertine and tufa. The prettiness of it never loses any of its freshness to me, and the way home takes us past the Colosseum.

"I love it all lit up at night," I say. Luca slows the car over to a parking space and stops. We just look at it. A straggle of tourists walk around, enjoying the quiet cool of nighttime.

"It's pretty impressive," Luca says. "It's hard to believe their Rome and ours are the same."

"I don't know, I don't think they're that different."

Luca turns to me. "You do know about the gladiators, right?"

I smile. "Yes, but while their sports may have been extreme, it was still the elite power class doing one thing and everyone else doing another."

Luca just looks at me, his face contemplative.

"I'm sorry. I told you I wouldn't fit into your world."

He bobbles his head. "No, you don't. But I'm starting to think that might be a compliment to you."

I look down. "This is going to be harder than we thought."

"Yes. When are you finished with school for the summer?"

"Saturday is graduation. Why?"

"Well, I'll use that as an excuse for the next couple of days, that you're busy getting ready for it. And if anyone asks us why I'm not coming to your graduation, we'll say I didn't want paparazzi taking anything away from you or your classmates. Agreed?"

I nod. "People expect us to know more about each other than we do, though. I'm a little worried it's going to trip us up."

Luca purses his lips a moment. "Well, we're going to be spending a lot of time together over the next couple months. I know you don't fancy me much, but maybe we could at least become friends? That might make this all more believable."

"We could try."

He nods and pulls the car back into the traffic lanes. When he drops me off at my flat, we don't see any paparazzi. "Just in case," he says, "do you mind if I lean in and make it look like I'm kissing you?"

"Okay." He leans over and puts his hand against my cheek to hide our lips from any prying lenses, and then kisses my other cheek. He smells ridiculously good. Whatever cologne he wears isn't cheap. "You did a great job tonight," he whispers.

"A quarter-of-a-million job?" I whisper back.

Luca cracks up and pulls away, resting into his seat. "I'll

47

contact the university tomorrow and start the arrangements. Whose name should the scholarship be in?"

"Delaney John Herriot. The school will know. But, Luca, what if this doesn't work out? What if I can't deliver on my end of the deal?"

He shrugs. "It's not an engagement ring. You don't have to give it back. It's a donation for a good cause."

For the first time since I met him, I'm actually grateful. "Thanks. That means a lot."

He narrows his blue-gray eyes a bit. "So, who is Delaney John to Astoria?"

I hesitate, because as soon as I tell him, the light bulb will go off. But if he's willing to give me a quarter of a million dollars, then he has a right to know. "My dad."

Luca's face contracts into a big O.

The weight of all this suddenly feels like it might crush me, so I pivot awkwardly to my sarcastic side. "By the way, nice moves in and out of that accent tonight."

Luca smiles. "Well, I may have attended fancy schools, but I'm still a Scot at the end of the day. You don't have much room to comment, though, pretending to be an Italian tour guide."

I return his smile. "I guess not. Good night."

"Good night, Story."

I get out, and Luca waits until I unlock the lobby door and slip inside before he drives away. I watch through the glass as the Ferrari disappears, and I have no idea what I should think about this devil's pact I've made.

Seven

The next few days pass quietly. I face a barrage of questions from the Dip Squad, but I mostly shrug and say, "You'll have to check the tabloids." It's driving Kelsey and Guin out of their minds. Patrick just looks at me once and says, "Gotta admit, Herriot, I didn't think you had it in you. Even if it's not going to last."

"Leave her alone, Pat," Jack says.

I give him a smile of thanks. Whether his new friendliness is real or fake, it's better than the silence he gave me before. Especially since I'll have to see him around campus in the fall.

On Friday afternoon, I walk to the Keats-Shelley House to see Anna Maria. Occasionally I catch a glimpse of a camera, but no one surrounds me like before. I haven't gone anywhere except school since the concert, so I imagine they're busy chasing down Luca instead. His life seems to be one nonstop party.

"We need to celebrate your graduation," Anna Maria says as we sit in the tiny gift shop. A few customers come through, but the place is never crowded, even at the height of tourist season. "What are you doing Sunday afternoon? We could go to a nice restaurant, maybe after a shopping spree at Via del Governo Vecchio?"

"I'd love to, but I can't. I promised someone I'd go to an art exhibit at the Casino dell'Aurora Pallavicini." I cringe a little as I say this because I know it's going to make her eyebrows shoot up. I'm not wrong.

"Is this something to do with your mother's job?"

"No. I'm going with some kid from Scotland I met a few days ago. He goes to these kinds of things."

Anna Maria is not having my light take on it. She grabs my hand.

"Tell me everything."

So I tell her enough. I tell her that I met him at the gelateria up the street and we went on an impromptu tour of the Trevi. I tell her he took me to the Jamie Talon concert. I don't tell her about the paparazzi or that we went on VIP tickets or that I'm now his fake girlfriend.

"Is he handsome? Is he hotter than that Jack boy?"

"I don't know," I say, and shake my head. "They're both more gorgeous than they should be, but in different ways. Jack is boy-next-door handsome, but Luca is like *Dangerous Liaisons* beautiful. It's nothing serious. I just said I'd show him around while he's here."

She laughs but seems content. I'm pretty sure I don't have to worry about Anna Maria ever seeing me in a tabloid. They aren't something she'd read. I hang out with her until closing time, and then go meet my mom for dinner at one of our favorite restaurants.

"I'm sorry no one could come in for your graduation," she says.

I shrug. My granddad was supposed to come, but he tore his deltoid muscle, so he shouldn't be lifting a suitcase. My dad's parents were also on the guest list, but my cousin is about to have their first great-grandchild. I don't blame them for picking a baby over watching me walk through our lunchroom to get a piece of paper, surrounded by the Dip Squad. So it's just my mom and me, the way it's been most of my life. We go home and call all my grandparents.

"Okay, kiddo," she says when we hang up. "Big day tomorrow!"

"Good night, Mom."

She pulls me over to her and kisses my temple. "Your dad would be so proud of you."

I bite my lip.

"I love you. We love you. All of us." She slips some hair back from my face.

I squeeze her. "It's okay. I know." She's told me so many times that my dad's problems didn't have anything to do with me, I could recite the lecture verbatim. She means well, though, and that's what really matters, as my granddad says.

When I climb into bed and turn out the light, the glow-in-the-dark stars on my ceiling burn a faint green. I hope my dad would like this memorial scholarship. I wish I could tell my mom. And I will tell her. But not until after it's a done deal. She wouldn't approve of my methods. But she knows this is something I've wanted to do for a long time. The thing is, when someone's addicted, no one cares when they die except the people who really loved them. And even they're pretty tired of being afraid the life they want to save might be lost. It's kind of like watching someone die from cancer, I guess, except that they're helping their tumor grow. But my dad wasn't a loser, like the kids at my school in Rio said when he died. He had a disease that beat him. He was hurting, too. No one wants to be addicted. Maybe this scholarship will redeem him. No matter how wrong some of the things my dad did were, he was still a human being.

Tears slip from my eyes as my room lights up from a text. I pull my phone from the nightstand. It's Luca.

Hey, I just wanted to wish you Happy Graduation tomorrow.
Thanks.
Doing anything special afterward?
Not really. My mom and I are going to a restaurant we like down on Via Urbana. Then we'll probably walk around and get some ice cream. Definitely not as exciting as you're used to.
Excitement can get pretty boring after a while. I don't know that street. Where is it?
Near the Basilica di Santa Maria Maggiore, kind of between the train station and the historic district.
You need to show me more of Rome.
I smile in spite of myself. *Okay.*
What's your favorite color?
Blue. I like blues and pinks and purples. Why?

Just getting to know my fake girlfriend. See you on Sunday.
See you.

The next morning, eighteen long-stemmed pink roses are delivered, interspersed with bright blue delphiniums. The card says, "Happy graduation to my favorite Dip kid, Luca." He wasn't kidding when he said he'd treat me like a princess. I think about telling him it isn't necessary, but it's kind of fun. Besides, it's not like he's doing it. He's just telling his assistant to send me flowers.

It impresses my mom, though. "This boy must really like you, Story."

"I think it's just the kind of thing people do in his circle."

"Well, when do I get to meet him?"

"I'll make sure it's before the wedding."

She laughs, but my sarcasm lets her know I'm not losing my head, and she doesn't mention him again. The apartment, however, smells heavenly.

Graduation is as stupid as I expect it to be, except the room is a hundred and twelve times hotter than usual because of the number of guests crammed into it. My mom, of course, cries, and that's the one part that gets to me. I guess because I've only been here a year, I'm really not attached to anything I'm leaving behind except for her and Rome itself. But it does feel a little like the day after Christmas when I look around at all my classmates' big families gathered together while mine isn't.

When we get to the obligatory reception, the Dip Squad has suddenly become my besties. Even my mom notices as they flit around me over cannoli and fruit punch, but I tell her it's just because they're impressed by Luca's money. "He must be really rich," she says with arched eyebrows. I just shrug. I still have to see them around the apartment building all summer, and Jack for the next four years probably, but at least today is the last time I have to fake smile.

On Sunday, Luca picks me up for the art exhibit. I'm not sure how people dress for these things, but since it's in the middle of the afternoon, I wear a sundress and cover my shoulders with a white shrug, in case it's like going into church. I'm glad our apartment faces the back of the building, so my mom can't see the Ferrari from the windows as I slip into it. Kelsey and Alicia are coming down the sidewalk with iced coffees, and they whisper together and then wave to us as Luca pulls away.

"They seem—" Luca presses his lips together, at a loss, so I help him out.

"Typical. They are. It's like living in every teen movie you've ever seen. Kelsey is the queen, and Alicia and Guin are her worker bees. Although, Alicia's not as vocal about it. She just follows."

"And what are you?"

"Their favorite thing to sting. Unfortunately, they're more like wasps that can just keep stinging than like honeybees that are one and done."

"You should stand up to them."

"Say all the people who have never been picked on in their entire lives."

Luca shakes his head. "I'm just saying that you've got it all over those girls, from where I sit."

The compliment makes me uncomfortable, as all compliments do, even though it's just Luca being polite. But then I smile. "I guess from where I sit, too. I guarantee you they would kill to be in my place right now, fake and all, being whisked away in Luca Kinnaird's Ferrari."

He laughs. "While you would rather be somewhere else. Why are you shaking your head?"

"I was just thinking about what my granddad would say about your car."

"He'd like it, huh?"

"No, the opposite. He'd think it was . . . impractical."

"I see. So what would he say?"

"Probably something like 'You can't move a cow in that.'"

Luca laughs.

I already texted him yesterday, but I thank him again for the roses because he never replied. Maybe he didn't see it.

"You're welcome. I told Hodges pink roses and blue something. Is that what you got?"

"Yes. He's a good butler. Or assistant. Or whatever you call him."

"You think I'm pretty ridiculous, don't you?"

"Maybe a little. Mostly, I just think we're from very different worlds."

"That doesn't mean we can't have things in common."

"I guess so." Although it doesn't matter, since this will be over in a couple of months.

We reach the Casino, which isn't actually a casino but more of a convention center that's like a beautiful museum from olden days. There's valet parking, of course, but no red carpet to smile through.

Inside, Luca introduces me to our hosts, the UK ambassador and her husband. Champagne and hors d'oeuvres float by, and I meet people wearing clothes that look like they come straight from a runway. A photographer is walking around. I try to avoid him even though he's definitely not a paparazzo. I guess he's from *la Repubblica*'s society page, Rome's version of the *Washington Post,* because he's wearing a name badge on a lanyard. Most of the guests are older than us, which is probably good because it keeps me from standing out more for how underdressed I am. No one appears to be interested in the art we're actually here to see. People ask me what I do a lot, so I drop the name Princeton like it's a calling card, which seems to work well. When Luca becomes engaged in conversation with a Danish prince, I slip away to see the exhibit. The art is amazing, and I wish I could have brought my mom. I mean if I could even explain why we were here in the first place.

I'm standing in front of a marble sculpture called *Psyche Revived by Cupid's Kiss* by Antonio Canova when Luca finds me. Cupid is cradling Psyche's head as he raises her from the ground, his wings outstretched, and they're gazing at each other as if it's the last moment of the world.

"I've put in my appearance," Luca whispers, bending his head to mine and slipping his hands around my waist.

"This is so beautiful," I say, and take a step away from him. It's stupid to be nervous, but I look around anyway as if I'm doing something I shouldn't be. But this whole ruse is something I shouldn't be doing.

He stops and looks at the sculpture and then gazes at me just as closely. "It really is. You're a funny girl, Astoria Herriot. Do you know the myth?"

I shake my head.

"Well, there's a lot of 'don't do that,' and then she does it anyway kind of stuff, but, essentially, Psyche and Cupid are lovers, until she breaks a vow to not look at his face, and he abandons her."

"Just for looking at him?"

Luca nods. "Distraught, she asks Venus to help her win him back and is sent on a series of quests, the last of which is to go to the underworld and retrieve a dose of Persephone's beauty. But, on the way back, Psyche looks in the box she's been told not to look in, because she obviously hasn't learned her lesson about not looking at things you've been told not to look at, and she falls into a lifeless sleep."

He stops and looks at me until I look away. It's like he's determined to ferret out who I really am. Which was never part of our deal. I'm about to tell him that when he adds, "This is the moment when Cupid finds her and, wrecked with despair, revives her with his kiss."

There's something about the way the words fall from his lips that stops me. As if maybe he almost wishes it were true. "Wow, it's even prettier now that I know the story, despite your obvious disdain for Psyche's lack of self-discipline."

Luca laughs. "Well, all's well that ends well, because Cupid grants her immortality, and they get married and live happily yada yada."

"Don't you believe in true love?"

"Love, maybe. True, well, let's just say I haven't encountered it. I take it you do believe?"

I'd like to say yes. My parents really loved each other. But it wasn't enough to help my dad. "I don't know."

Beyond him, Patrick and Jack's parents are walking toward us. I turn my head quickly.

"What's wrong?"

"Two of the Dips I go to school with, Patrick and Jack, are the US ambassador's kids, and he and his wife are headed this way. I should have realized they'd be here. Remember the big blond kid who loved your Ferrari?"

"That roaster? Holy crivvens."

I smile and peek back. Someone has stopped them to chat. "Maybe they'll forget they saw us. It's not me they want to talk to, anyway."

Luca shakes his head. "Come on, I want you to show me something in Rome I'd never find without you."

He takes my hand and leads me to the exit, deftly getting us out of a couple of conversations on the way, one of them in French. I think my introverted self could learn a lot from him about how to handle people better, instead of using my snarky tongue or silently complying.

When we get in the car, he unlocks his phone and hands it to me. "Where to?"

"I don't know the street name, but it's near the Piazzo Vittorio." I type that into the maps app. He waits for it to load and makes the first turn. "There's no valet parking, though."

"You may have to carry me, then," he quips.

"I thought I already was," I say, and we laugh as the Ferrari roars its way across Rome.

Eight

"I hope you like this," I tell him when we've found a parking space. "It's a bit quirky."

"Quirky? From you? This should be interesting!"

"Very funny, come on."

The Piazza Vittorio is on the largest of Rome's seven hills, the Esquiline, but it's not a very good neighborhood. Graffiti covers buildings, especially on the metal doors that slide down over closed storefronts.

"Are you sure about this? It seems a little sketchy here," Luca says.

"Trust me." We sidestep some trash and a man sleeping on the sidewalk.

"Rome is a lot dirtier than Paris."

"Yes, but in Paris, no one will help you unless you speak perfect French. Here, anyone will help. Although, it's safest to ask middle-aged or old women."

"Noted," Luca says dryly. Maybe it was a mistake to take him anywhere but Via Condotti, with its plastic designer stores.

We enter a small park with the brick ruins of what once was a towering villa surrounded by a high iron rod fence. In a forlorn corner of the lawn, under the shade of a giant tree, is a fragment of brown stone wall with greenery around it. Attached to the wall is a rectangular marble doorway, with a circle of travertine above it and two weird-looking, naked marble men guarding it. The doorframe and the circle are etched with symbols and lettering, some of it nearly worn away. Afternoon sun brushes the top of the wall, and the grass around it is ragged and uncut.

Luca looks at me as if he's not sure whether I'm pranking him.

"You asked for off the beaten path."

He ticks his head in admission. "Seriously, this is the weirdest monument I've ever seen. And I'm from Scotland. Why is it famous, oh trusty tour guide?"

"It's the Porta Alchemica, or the magic door. It's the only surviving door of five, built in the late 1600s by the Marquie Massimiliano Palombara for his villa, which was here."

"A marquess, huh?"

"Yes. The Marquess of Pietraforte, who was known for his occult interests and his friendship with the very weird Queen Christina of Sweden. They were Rosicrucians, an occult order whose symbol was the Rose Cross." I make sure I say this with all the drama it deserves.

"I'm familiar with the very weird Queen Christina. So, what's so special about this doorway?"

"Well, legend has it that a mysterious stranger, Giuseppe Borri, who'd been expelled from the Jesuit College because of his occult interests, visited the marquess, promising he had the secret for using herbs to turn lead into gold. He even wrote the recipe down to prove he was a true alchemist. In the dark of night, Borri searched everywhere in Palombara's gardens for the powerful herb he needed. As fate would have it, the alchemist found the herb, and by dawn, he'd transformed it into gold, just before he disappeared through a magic door, never to be seen again."

"Please tell me there's more," he says when I pause. "This is so much better than my rendition of Psyche and Cupid."

I look around as if to make sure we aren't being spied on by spirits. "All the marquess ever found were a few flakes of gold and the secret formula, which he didn't know how to translate."

"That's unfortunate."

"Truly. The marquis was so distraught, he had the formula carved into his villa's doorways, in the hope that someone would chance upon them who could decipher the code."

"I guess that's a plan?"

I go back to my normal voice. "Well, a marquess can never have too much gold, after all."

"So I've heard."

"Palombara died shortly after the doors were inscribed. Some believe he was poisoned by Borri for revealing his alchemy secrets."

"Which were so well revealed that, four centuries later, no one can decipher them?"

"Exactly. But, royals, you know? Pazzo." I make a circular motion with my index finger at my temple.

Luca scrunches his face up.

"Or it could just be that you can't chemically change lead into gold with herbs, but there's no point in being technical over a little poisoning," I add.

Luca's face relaxes. "Okay, any more gems like this?"

"Nothing as occult, but there are tons of special places."

"Lead on," he says.

We drive fifteen minutes to Aventine Hill and park near the Piazza del Calvieri di Malta. This area is more like what Luca expects from his world, a quiet residential neighborhood. When we get to an elaborately carved stone wall with a huge door in it, I stop. Luca looks at me expectantly.

"So, this is the Priory of the Knights of Malta, who were brothers in arms to the Knights—"

"Templar," Luca supplies, obviously pleased he's beaten me to the punch.

I laugh, a little impressed. "Bonus points. Anyway, it was originally built by a nobleman who ruled Rome in the 900s, Alberic II. The Priory is now considered a sovereign state. The keyhole is known as the Aventine Keyhole. No one knows, though, if it was planned to be so special, or if it's just a happy coincidence. I like to believe it's a happy coincidence. I doubt, though, if anyone would've ever realized it's secret if it were."

"And what exactly is this secret?"

"Look for yourself." I gesture to the door.

He bends down on one knee and looks up at me. "It's not going to squirt me with black ink or something, is it?"

"No, just look. You really have no faith in me. It's hurtful."

He smiles and puts his eye to the keyhole. "Oh, wow. That's brilliant. That's the dome of St. Peter's."

"Incredible, isn't it? This is the only place in Rome where you can stand in one sovereign nation and see two other sovereign states at the same time."

"It's stunning. It's absolutely perfectly aligned." He stands up. "I'm hiring you for all my tours. Forget Princeton."

"Deal. It's one of my favorite things in all of Rome."

"I can see why. I also see why you wish it were a happy coincidence."

I shake my head. "You're unraveling all my secrets. Pretty soon, you're going to figure me out if I'm not careful." I say it jokingly, but something whispers to me that it isn't a good idea to let Luca see too far into my heart.

Luca smiles. "Can we go into the garden?"

"Only by appointment. You have to give me more notice next time I'm to take you on a tour."

"Duly noted. I'm hungry. Do you want to get some dinner?"

"Sure."

Luca checks his phone. There aren't many places in this neighborhood, but we settle on one in walking distance. Over an alfresco dinner, I ask Luca what he does besides jet-set.

"I'm nawt a total bampot," he says in his best brogue.

"Convince me."

He switches back to his usual accent. "I'll be in my second year at Oxford, studying business, as you're jetting off to Princeton to study, what exactly?"

I shrug. "I don't really know. The goal has always been to get there. I don't know what comes next. Something with animals or the stars, maybe the neuroscience of addiction."

"Animals or stars, of course. Why Princeton?"

"It's where my dad went to school. Well, both my parents. They met there."

"Ah, the pieces are starting to fall into place." He looks hard at me, but not in a judgmental way.

"My dad was a hockey player. In his senior year, he got a pretty bad concussion. At first, he seemed to get better, but now my mom thinks he had CTE."

"What's CTE?"

"That traumatic brain injury athletes in contact sports can get. Even after he recovered, he had depression that never really went away. By the time they were out of law school, he was having short-term memory loss. And he had pain from an old hip injury. The doctors prescribed opioids. I guess they worked a little too well."

"I'm so sorry," Luca says.

I look away. "He's just a number in some statistics chart at the FDA, and a bankruptcy ruling somewhere. One of an infinite number."

Luca reaches across the table and puts his hand on mine, but it's not like when he's just pretending, and I pull away.

"You aren't sorry?" I ask. "About the donation?"

"No, not at all."

I nod and press my lips together. I wonder if I should ask him about Jasmine, since that's what all this is for anyway, but it's also not my business, so I don't. I ask him what Oxford is like instead, and he tells me about his classes and professors. He doesn't talk much about his business courses, but he lights up over the science ones.

"Did you know," he asks, "that orcas are the largest member of the dolphin family, and even though they are known for killing whales, they're actually afraid of pilot whales?"

His eyes shine as he says this, leaning in toward me, and he seems really happy to have someone be interested in what he's interested in.

"Sorry, I didn't mean to bore you," he says after telling me some more about his marine biology class.

"You're not."

We look around the restaurant.

"So, what are your parents like?" He hasn't mentioned them, and I'm a little afraid I shouldn't ask. Maybe he has secrets to keep like me.

"Typical Scots upper class. Don't get me wrong, I love them, but we're a pretty stereotypical family."

"That sounds really nice. Do you have brothers or sisters?"

"Aye, four. I have two older sisters and two younger brothers."

"So you're smack in the middle?"

Luca thinks about this. "I am, but I'm the oldest boy, so in some ways, it doesn't seem like it."

"I always wanted siblings."

He smiles his charming smile. "They can be horrible, but it's good in the end."

"I'm lucky, though. I have a lot of cousins back home."

"So," he says when there's a piece of chocolate cake sitting between us, "now that you're officially free for the summer— wait, what was your script for the summer?"

"You mean before you grabbed me outside of a gelateria? I'm volunteering at a farm sanctuary on the outskirts of Rome."

"Are you pranking me?"

"No!" I laugh a little that he would actually think so. "I always spend my summers on my granddad's farm in Maine, after a couple weeks with my dad's family. I love my granddad's place. But since this is the last summer my mom and I will be like it's always been, you know, just the two of us, I decided to stay here."

"That's so sweet, I don't think I can eat my share of the dessert."

"You're not Braveheart, you know. It's okay to pet a kitten or kiss your mom."

Luca laughs. "Touché. Do you fence?"

"No."

"I think maybe you should. Seriously, though, people are going to expect you to be with me at the events I have to go to."

"Have to? Is it your job to party?"

"You know what I mean. It is kind of my job. People expect me to do certain things. Like the exhibit today. The ambassador asked me to come, so I needed to make an appearance."

"Okay, well, I'll still play along. I owe you that much for a quarter mil."

Luca relaxes.

"But I'm not giving up my volunteer work. Your parties aren't in the mornings, and I'll be back in the city by two or three. It's just Mondays, Tuesdays, and Fridays, anyway."

"We should be able to live with that. I'll check with Jasmine."

I don't say anything. If Her Majesty doesn't approve, we're going to have a problem.

"But listen, this Friday, we have a big charity gala. Black tie."

"Got it."

When we leave the restaurant, I tell him there's still one thing nearby I want him to see.

We stroll to the Santa Maria in Cosmedin church in the Piazza della Bocca della Verità, and I show him the giant marble mask that sits in the portico.

"I thought you said nothing as creepy as the Porta Alchemica?"

I tilt my head and look at it. "I think it looks more sad than creepy."

He narrows his eyes and contemplates it. "What is it?"

"It's the Bocca della Verità, the Mouth of Truth. They think it's Oceanus. It was probably used as a drain cover originally. It may also have been used as a drain for the blood of cattle sacrificed to Hercules. In that case, it's definitely creepy. But, more importantly, it was made famous by a scene in *Roman Holiday*. In the movie, the mask represents the fact that Audrey

Hepburn and Gregory Peck are not being truthful with each other about who they are."

Luca darts a glance at me before he looks back at the giant disk.

"Legend says only the truthful can place their hand inside the gaping mouth without it being lopped off. You can test it if you like."

Luca smiles. "Maybe you should try first."

"Oh, no, fake girlfriend would definitely get me"—I pause—"whatever the equivalent to decapitation for hands is."

"I guess we're both out, then. Does anyone in the movie get their hand bitten off?"

"Haven't you ever seen *Roman Holiday*?"

Luca shakes his head. "Let me guess, old movies are classic?"

"That one is. It's about a princess who spends a couple of days running away from her official duties in Rome, where she falls—"

Just then, someone shouts from across the street. We turn, and a paparazzo clicks his camera.

I look at Luca. "I think our tour is over."

"Come on, I'll take you home."

He catches my hand, and we retrace our steps to the Portofino. The paparazzo jumps on a nearby Vespa.

In the side-view mirror, I watch him follow us back to Via Veneto, and all I can hope is that this story has a happier ending than *Roman Holiday*.

Nine

On Tuesday, my mom uses her lunch hour to go with me to the Via del Governo Vecchio to look for a dress for Luca's charity gala.

"Story," she says to me as we poke through my favorite shops, "these women are going to be wearing gowns that cost thousands of dollars. Our budget is, um, a bit less."

"Luca knows we don't have that kind of money," I say, scanning some racks. "I just need to fit in enough so that people don't talk about me. But I still want to look classic."

"Well, I've got to get back to work. If you don't find anything, then take Anna Maria to Monti tomorrow. They have some trickle-down shops that are sure to have something."

"Thanks," I say as she hands me ten euros for lunch.

I don't begin my volunteer work until next week, but I'm starting to worry that being Luca's rent-a-girlfriend may be like having a full-time job. Hodges emailed our schedule for the next two weeks, and there's at least one thing every day. This Scot is definitely popular.

I don't find a dress, so I head home. Luca calls me as I slip in the door.

"Story, you're in."

"In what?"

"In with the tabloids. They think you are, and I'm quoting here, 'adorable.'"

"Oh, that's awesome. Now, I can forget about college and live my dream of being professional arm candy."

"Look, I get that you have higher aspirations than being Luca Kinnaird's latest, which, honestly, is refreshing, but the point is that if the tabs love you, then you're a lot safer in all this."

"You're right, I get it. But you do know how full of yourself you sounded just now, right?"

"You shouldn't take it that way. It's not me they're after. I could be anyone with my name and bank account, and they'd still want to date me. Most women are drawn to money and power. Look at all the weird-looking rock stars and dumb athletes who still marry bonnie wives, or at least women who are way out of their league."

"You have a point."

"Believe me, I'm not naive enough to think that Jasmine would want to be with me if I weren't Luca Kinnaird."

I want to tell him that maybe he should look for someone who would still want to be with him, but it's not my business.

"All right, I've got to go," he says. "Jasmine is just finishing rehearsal for the Berlin leg of shows, which start on Sunday. She leaves Saturday afternoon. I'll pick you up at six-thirty to-morrow."

"Ciao."

I open my computer and search for the tabloids. I don't even know what any of them are called. But when I click through, I'm in them. Leaving school with Luca, on the Jamie Talon red carpet, daring the Bocca della Verità, and leaving a baroque ensemble concert we went to yesterday afternoon. They've fig-ured out my mom works for the embassy as an attorney. They say I hail from Maine, although my mom and I would say DC. They say I'm Princeton-bound, and that makes me worry they might dig up dirt on my dad. That's something I hadn't con-sidered. I really don't need my dad's memory getting dragged because of tabloids linking me to a fake boyfriend.

Ever since this started, I haven't really processed it. Some-how, there's been a disconnect between the paparazzi following Luca around and all this information about me being splashed across the internet. I guess I thought it would mostly be about Luca, and I'd just be some obscure accessory he carried about, like a Pomeranian in a backpack. Instead, who I am and how I dress has become a topic of interest as everyone tries to figure out what Luca could possibly see in an "ordinary girl." The reality is, Luca Kinnaird would never have glanced at me if I hadn't been a convenient cover in the wrong gelateria at the right time. But now that I'm supposedly with him, I'm some-how different and newsworthy to them. It's all so fake.

I don't want some tabloid catching me without makeup and

speculating if I'm sick or need rehab. Or telling the world who they think I am. Especially when I'm pretending to be something I'm not. My breath gets tight just thinking about it. I retreat to my room and pick at chords on my guitar to refocus. My fingers hover over my keyboard to Google Luca, but I stop myself. Whatever these tabloids say is probably lies anyway, and I don't want to know anything that would make me feel worse about helping him and Jasmine pull this off. If I need to be friendly with the guy for the next two months, I should at least judge him on how he acts and not what some gossip column says about him. And, honestly, he's been nicer than I expected him to be. I can't get sucked into this nonsense of what's real and what's not online.

This will be over in a couple of months. The tabloids will forget all about me. Everything will go back to normal, except there'll be a scholarship in my dad's name. Maybe the reason we should break up is that I don't enjoy the attention. It wouldn't be a lie, and it shouldn't make either one of us look like a bad guy.

My phone dings with a text from Jack.

Kelsey and Guin are going nuts. You're on all those stupid sites they follow.

I know. It's so weird.

Doesn't seem like your scene.

It's not. I hate it.

Then you must really like this guy.

I have no idea how to respond. My fingers hover over the keyboard before I type, *He's nice. It's just summer fun.*

That's good. He's a player, Story. Don't get hurt.

I won't.

Are you doing anything now?

Just waiting for my mom to get home.

Wanna go to the bookstore on Urbana with me?

Jack and I don't usually hang out, but we have texted sometimes about school assignments or to complain about our AP Physics teacher, and once we grabbed pizza after working on a project we had to do together. But I wouldn't call us friends. If he had asked me to go to the bookstore with him before all this started, I probably would have said no. But maybe Jack's finally getting out from under Patrick's shadow before college. And maybe it's not a bad idea to have a friend going into school.

Sure.

Jack lives at the embassy, so he walks down to my apartment, which is on the way to Via Urbana. I meet him outside. He's wearing his khaki school shorts and a plain gray T-shirt. He's wearing a ball cap backward, and his dark hair is just long enough to be a little dangerous.

"Hey," he says when he gets close.

"Hey," I say, and fall into step with him. We both smile enough to be polite. "So, what are we buying?"

"My mom's birthday is tomorrow, and I want to get her a cookbook. She doesn't really cook much, but she collects them anyway." He shrugs as if he doesn't get it, but it doesn't matter because it's for her, not him.

I laugh. "I can see your mom doing that." She's the trophy-wife type, though she's always super nice to everyone. I don't know how she birthed Patrick. He could be Medusa's child.

"I figured you were probably the type of person who couldn't say no to a bookstore."

"Possibly," I say, and he smiles. It's only about fifteen minutes away, in an area that's not very touristy even though it's in walking distance to the Colosseum. There are a lot of restaurants along the way, and the smell of tomato sauce and roasted meat is everywhere. We pass a small groceria with stands on the sidewalk brimming with bright purple plums and strawberries still sparkling from being misted with water. A motorcycle roars past us. The long afternoon sun stretches to reach the other side of the street.

The shop is tiny, but there are all the sections needed for a proper bookstore. My mom and I come here more than we probably should. I help Jack pick his present, and we browse a bit. He makes jokes about some of the more serious or boring titles, holding up *The Living Dante* and making an excited face, or commenting, "Story, you *need* this book," when he comes across an illustrated guide to bonsai balcony gardening. He's funnier than I ever realized, but he also surprises me when he remembers something I said about poetry in English class way back in winter term. I never thought he paid attention to anything I said. I see a poetry book I wouldn't mind getting, but I need to save my money for the wardrobe budget for the Luca Kinnaird blockbuster I'm suddenly starring in.

Jack and I leave the bookstore and cross the street to get cold drinks from a shop that's just a little stall in the wall. I pick a strawberry drink while Jack gets iced lemonade. "It's on me," he says as he pulls out his wallet, "as a thank-you for helping me."

"Thanks. So how come Patrick didn't go shopping with you?" I take a sip, and we head back up the hill.

"His present is that he's going to the opera tomorrow because my mom wants us to go. He thinks that's enough of a present."

"Sounds very Patricky," I say, and we laugh. "Luca and I are going, too."

"Oh, cool, I'll probably see you, then."

We reach my apartment. Jack stops while I get my keys out. "Thanks for coming with me. I had fun."

"Yeah, me too," I reply, and we clink our plastic glasses together.

"I'll be sure to look for you tomorrow night."

"Okay, see you."

I slip inside and take the stairs to the fourth floor to avoid anyone at the elevators. I'm glad I've made peace with Jack. It's definitely going to be better, for the first time, to already have a friend at the start of school. My whole life has been one giant new-girl syndrome. I just have to survive these next two months, and then I can start fresh at Princeton, and no one but Jack will have the faintest memory that I supposedly dated Luca. But first, I have to sail past the paparazzi tomorrow night, and that now means worrying about Patrick being Patrick and trying to ingratiate himself with Luca while he embarrasses me.

Ten

'm eating breakfast the next morning when Luca calls. I answer the phone the way people do in Italy. "Pronto?"

"Story, what the hell?"

I put down my glass. "What's wrong? What the hell what?"

"You haven't looked at the tabs?"

"No, why would I? Do you look at those things every day?"

"You're splashed all over them. 'Is Astoria Herriot already cheating on Luca Kinnaird? Maybe Luca has met his match!'"

"I have no idea what you're talking about. Let me put you on speaker while I look."

Luca's angry sigh pulses from the phone. I'm trying to like him, but his obsession with influencer gossip is a bit much. Still, when I pull up a tabloid, I'm there with Jack. Laughing as we come out of the bookstore, buying icy drinks, and clinking our plastic cups together. Hoo boy.

"That's just my classmate. You know, the brother of the stupid blond kid. It was nothing."

"Well, it looks like something. It doesn't matter what it really is, it only matters how it looks. That's the whole point of us, remember?"

I shouldn't care that he says this, but his tone is so angry, it stings. "So what am I supposed to do? Hide in my house unless I'm with you? We went to a bookstore to get a birthday present for his mom. We're barely even friends. But we're both going to Princeton, so we're trying to get along better. It was nothing."

"Please don't let it happen again." It sounds more like a command than a plea.

"I'm sorry. No one has ever been interested in my little life before."

Luca pauses before he replies. "I guess it wouldn't have occurred to you."

"I'll be more careful. Believe me, I don't need anyone learning the truth. I can't wait to go back to being invisible."

This time when he pauses, I swear I can hear him angrily tapping on something. "You're not invisible just because you aren't in a tab."

I practically snort. "Really? You and everyone you associate with seem to believe it's the only thing that matters in life."

He doesn't answer. The silence is so long, I begin to wonder if he's hung up.

"Listen," he says at last, "I've got to go. Jasmine's calling. She's probably seen it."

"Okay, bye."

"Bye."

I set the phone down. My luscious piece of toast with vegan butter and quince jam suddenly tastes dry. How am I ever going to pull this off for two whole months?

Maybe Jack wanted to get into the tabloids and figured asking me to the bookshop was the way to do it. But that doesn't really seem like him. He's never been someone who seeks attention. Patrick is the one who sucks all the air out of a room. I was worried about what Patrick might do tonight, but now I have to worry about seeming to be too friendly to Jack, too. I don't know what to think about anyone anymore. I miss being a loner. You don't have to scrutinize people's motives.

I wonder if I should text Jack to tell him about the tabloids, but then he texts me.

Guin just told me our photos are in the tabloids. They made it seem like we were on a date. I'm really sorry. I hope I haven't messed anything up for you.

He seems genuine. And if I didn't notice we were being followed, why would he? *It's okay, Luca's seen them. He understands.* I feel like a jerk because we aren't even talking about the same understanding.

Okay, good, because I could tell him it was nothing if you need me to.

No, thanks, we're good. At least in our way.

Okay, cool.

I set the phone down and go shower. A little before twelve-thirty, I meet Anna Maria in Monti. We have a quick lunch and spend a couple of hours dress shopping through secondhand stores while she not-so-subtly pumps me for information about

Luca. I only say things that are true, which mostly amounts to me saying, "I don't know."

I've almost given up hope of finding a dress when I see a Christian Dior gown that looks as if it were made for a medieval princess. It's black taffeta with spaghetti straps. Copper embroidered flowers fall across it in delicate swirls. The skirt has a touch of black crinoline underneath. I hold it up.

"Che bella," Anna Maria says, pushing back her auburn curls. "Try it on!"

When I come out, she nods and smiles. "That's it."

"Apparently, though, all rich people are five foot seven or taller. I'm going to be dragging it across the floor all night."

She kneels down. "Well, you could give it a little flounce, like this, at intervals, and trim the crinoline, which is easy to do. I think it would seem like the dress was designed that way."

"You're brilliant!"

"Yes, but now I get to meet this beautiful boy sometime."

I nod but don't make any promises.

I pay for the dress, which is less than two hundred euros, since it's considered yesterday's trash, but Anna Maria has to babysit her nephew, so I'm on my own to find a dress for the opera. In a vintage store I've never been to before, I find a black slip dress for twenty euros. It's more "look at me" than I'd normally wear, but I'm supposed to seem like I belong with Luca, so I push myself out of my comfort zone. The less conspicuous I am, the better, and, in this case, that means being more conspicuous. I tell myself I'm like an actress playing a part, which almost makes it okay. Plus, there's a sliver of me that feels like

I have something to prove, on behalf of all the ordinary, over-looked girls everywhere. Because, really, the only difference between his world and mine is money.

I head home and get ready. It's almost six-thirty when Luca texts to say he's found a parking space and wants to come up and meet my mom.

Did she put you up to that?

No, just thought it would be the correct thing to do.

When I walk out to tell my mom Luca's coming up, her eyes pop at my dress. "Wow, my little girl is pretty grown-up suddenly!" I'm glad Luca isn't here yet, because I blush. "I have a perfect necklace," she says, and runs to her room.

She's just fastening a garnet-laced choker on me when Luca knocks. I open the door, and he raises his eyebrows at my appearance. "Okay?" I ask.

He nods but doesn't smile. "Definitely."

He steps past me, and I introduce him to my mom. He's over-the-top charming, complete with a sudden smile. It's the Luca he puts on display whenever we're in public, but he also manages to survey our apartment, without ever seeming like that's what he's doing. His gaze travels slowly over the novelty of a middle-class flat, and I get the feeling he's surprised by the smallness of it.

"Your home is lovely. So cozy!"

"Thank you, Luca. It's so nice to meet you. Story hasn't told me much about you."

"Well, I'm happy to answer your questions, Mrs. Herriot. But at the moment, Story and I should go, or we might miss the first act. Perhaps we could all have dinner together one night soon?"

"I'd like that very much."

I fake a British accent. "Yes, let's all dine together soon, shall we?" I deadpan between them, and they smile. I push Luca toward the door.

I don't ask Luca why he went out of his way to meet my mom. I'm sure it's because he wanted to vet me more after my screwup about Jack yesterday. Now he knows I really am the awkward, regular girl I seem to be, with the single mom and an ordinary apartment stuffed with books and watercolor paintings.

When we reach the car valet, I'm whisked out of the Ferrari to cameras whirring and flashing until we enter the theater. As we climb the grand marble staircase from the lobby, Luca whispers, "The best part about the opera is that they can't take our photo in here." I look up, and he smiles. We meet our hostess, a princess from Belgium. I didn't even know Belgium had a monarchy. The princess is an older woman, with dyed-blond hair, and you wouldn't suspect she was different from any of the other rich women here except for the two men in dark suits who hover in our box. Luca has already shown me how to greet her, so I know to dip down in a short curtsy.

"It's lovely to meet you, Astoria. Luca hasn't told us much about you."

"There's not much to tell," I say.

Luca glides his arm around my back and presses his thumb against me in warning. His hand is warm through the thin silk of the dress. "What Astoria means, Your Royal Highness, is that she's not very interested in celebrity. She's much more focused on her academic pursuits."

"Oh, I see," the princess says. "You must tell me about that."

So, I explain that I'm going to Princeton in the fall, this time dropping "Your Royal Highness" into the conversation where it seems appropriate. Luca relaxes his hand. The princess asks what my parents do. I tell her my dad died when I was eleven and go straight to my mom. Being the daughter of a diplomatic attorney seems to be an appropriate connection for a girl Luca might date, as she nods approvingly. I guess he's lucky the girl in the gelateria wearing yellow that day wasn't the daughter of someone Luca's world wouldn't find acceptable, although if they knew about my dad, they'd probably look at me like they would the daughter of a sanitation worker. But the princess is gracious as she introduces me to her other guests.

The lights flicker, and we take our seats. I catch a glimpse of Jack in the box next to us, and we smile and nod hello. Luca whispers, "Ah, the ripped guy from the tabs."

"Yes."

"We should say hello at the intermission so no one suspects I'm concerned about a rivalry."

I flip to my British accent. "As you wish, my lord. Anything to avoid pistols at dawn."

"Funny."

I've never been to an opera, but I like taking it all in. Luca asks me to translate, though there are English descriptions printed in the program. We sit with our heads close together as I whisper lyrics to him. At the first intermission, we go to the hallway for refreshments. I introduce Luca to Jack and his family. Luca is usually so relaxed, but with Jack it feels like he's sizing him up. I wish Mrs. Rooney happy birthday, and she thanks me for helping pick out her new cookbook. Patrick tells Luca they should hang out sometime but Luca is expertly evasive. I guess because his mom is there, Patrick doesn't say anything mean, like how surprising it is that Luca would date the most unpopular girl from our school. The lights flicker, and I'm glad to escape back to our dark box.

The performance is three one-act operas, and the last one is a comedy by Puccini about two young lovers. The girl is too poor to have a dowry, but the boy is expecting to inherit a fortune from an old relative, and then they'll be able to marry. The relative dies, and they find out he's left everything to a monastery. The lovers, now too poor to marry, beg the girl's father to help them. In a beautiful aria, she tells her dad she can't live without the boy, and her father loves her so much that he schemes to save them by pretending to be the dead man long enough to write a new will, even though he'll be arrested if he's caught.

When the song begins, I forget to translate for Luca. Instead, I'm just listening, leaning forward and transfixed, and when I see the dad's reaction to his daughter's desperate pleas, I have to wipe tears from my cheeks.

"Story, what's wrong? Why are you crying?" Luca whispers. He looks around as if he's afraid someone will notice me.

I shake my head and explain what the dad's doing even though he thinks the boy isn't worthy of his darling Lauretta.

"You're a sucker for a love story, aren't you?"

It's on my tongue to just say yes. "I think I'm a sucker for a father-daughter story," I say. My eyes burn. I turn back to the stage, away from Luca's penetrating gaze. For the rest of the performance, I focus on translating so I'm not overly emotional. Luca slips his arm around me as I murmur the lyrics into his ear, and I hope it's for show and not because he feels sorry for me. It feels sweet, but he's just an actor. Or as Jack says, a player.

When the opera ends, we're invited to dinner at a nearby restaurant with the princess and her entourage. She takes me by the arm as we leave the theater. "My dear, I hope you won't mind me saying, but I saw you entranced by Lauretta's aria, and how it brought you to tears. It's my absolute favorite piece in all of opera!"

"It's so beautiful!" Around me, cameras flash like heat lightning. "I've never been to the opera before. I wasn't expecting anything so lovely. Thank you for including me, Your Royal Highness."

The princess squeezes my arm and tells me that she sang opera when she was younger but, of course, couldn't do it professionally. She explains the history of Puccini's comedy, which is based on a canto in Dante's *Inferno,* which is based on a true story, as we make our way to the restaurant, and the history buff in me loves this. Luca trails behind with the others in the group.

"Oh, Luca, I'm so glad you brought Astoria with you tonight," the princess says, turning to him as we reach our destination. Candles glitter through the windows of a posh new restaurant, and the maître d' rushes to open the door. The place smells of rosemary and fresh bread and balsamic vinegar, and it makes my stomach growl.

Luca smiles and takes my arm from the princess. "Thank you, Your Royal Highness. So am I." We follow the princess into the restaurant, and I chalk up a small win for all us ordinary girls.

Eleven

t's after midnight when Luca drops me off. "You were pure dead brilliant tonight. The princess was really taken with you." He leans in and pretends to kiss me in case we're being watched. It's weird how familiar his touch is getting. He hesitates as he pulls back and gazes into my eyes a moment too long for me.

"She's very nice. How long have you known a princess?"

Luca relaxes into his seat. "My parents are old friends of hers. When she was speaking French, she told me what an improvement you are from my usual girlfriends." He looks over and smiles like he can't disagree with her. He really does know how to be charming.

I laugh. "It's nice to think someone from your world values something other than musical talent or model height."

Luca tilts his head noncommittally. "The princess is a rarity. Most people in my world, as you call it, judge people on their position on Forbes."

"So why do you care what the tabs say? They're a different measure than what you're talking about."

"Because connections make the world go around, Story. And what a tab says about you can impact your ability to connect. Plus, I don't want Jasmine to get hurt just because she wanted to leave a relationship with someone who is a very messed-up drug addict."

He turns to me. "I'm sorry, that was insensitive of me."

"People who are messed up on drugs are still people." I feel like I've been slapped in the face, but I shouldn't. "My dad was messed up and dependent on drugs. Just like Jeremy." My voice is quiet, and I feel a little like I'm betraying my dad by admitting this out loud.

Luca pushes back a strand of hair that's fallen in my face. "I know. I'm sorry. It was a stupid way to put it." His fingers linger on my face.

"So, luncheon tomorrow at the fundraiser for . . . ?" I ask to change the subject. He pulls his hand from my face and pauses to think about what cause we'll be supporting.

"Too busy juggling your secret-real and fake-open girlfriends to know what charity you're helping?"

Luca shrugs. "When you go to as many of these as I do, it gets hard to keep track. It's like musicians saying all the towns look the same. Something to do with Mozambique, I just don't remember if it's animals or people."

I nod and put my hand on the door.

"You hope it's animals, don't you?"

I look back. "I prefer animals to people, but I think there's enough inequality in the world to make either a worthy cause. Good night."

His "Good night, Astoria Herriot" comes from behind me like a soft breeze as I step up on the sidewalk. I don't turn around, but he stays to make sure I've gotten safely inside the lobby before I hear the Portofino take flight.

My mom is waiting up, and I give her the details while we sip tea on the sofa. I leave out that our hostess is a princess. I suppose I don't tell her because I don't really belong in this world and I'm only here by chance, temporarily. There is no way to explain the deal Luca and I made. I don't know how to even get close to it, like the flaming ovens the glassblowers in Murano use. I really hate lying to her. When this is all over, I'll tell her that Luca wanted to make the contribution, even though we're splitting up, because we're still friends, and besides, he has to make charitable donations to help his taxes. That sounds plausible. At least until you get to how much. But maybe she won't ask. Maybe my mother, the attorney, won't ask how much money Luca donated to my dad's memorial fund. I think my stats teacher would say I have a better chance of marrying royalty. But it's not like I extorted Luca. I only asked for twenty thousand. It was his idea to give me so much. I just wish it didn't make me feel so dirty. He's literally paying me to lie for him, even to the people I care about. Every time that thought crosses my mind, I feel like I need a shower.

When I'm finally in bed, my phone lights up, and I reach for it expecting Luca to give me some additional command for tomorrow. But it's Jack.

Just wanted to make sure you were okay.

Great, so he saw me crying, too. *Fine thanks, it was just a beautiful song and I was being sentimental.*

I get it, the whole father-daughter thing.

My fingers freeze over the keypad. I didn't expect Jack, or anyone, to get it. But it's nice not to have to explain.

Thanks.

It doesn't feel like enough, but what am I supposed to say? Sometimes there aren't really words for that kind of gratitude, and trying to find the words just makes it pathetic. There are no dots telling me he's going to answer, and maybe he feels like I'm being curt. I'm not used to these shifting dynamics. This is why I keep to myself so much. And then the dots come.

You're welcome. You're a good person, Story. Your dad would be really proud of you.

I close my eyes, and tears I didn't even know were right there fall to my pillow. I send Jack a purple heart emoji and put my phone on the nightstand. And for the very first time in my whole life, I feel like it's kind of nice to be seen.

Luca calls me early the next morning. "Story, have you seen the tabs?"

"What have I done wrong now?"

"Nothing. In fact, you're everyone's darling. Glamorous shots of you on the princess's arm are lighting up every tab. You're officially vintage stylish, whatever that is, and beauty and brains combined. And, most importantly, you are the perfect fit for a roguish Scot."

I can't really share his enthusiasm. "That's great."

"Story! It is great! Everyone's totally buying this."

I am happy no one seems to suspect the truth, but there's also something insulting about the fact that people need to be convinced. The only difference between us is that he has even more money and privilege than I have. It's ridiculous how people are valued just for being famous. Like he said, he doesn't even do anything.

"I'm worried they're going to keep poking around and find out things."

"Like about your dad? Or is there something else I should know?"

"About my dad. Luca, I don't want strangers digging apart his life. It's sad, and it's no one's business. People are really mean about addiction. I'm not sure I could take seeing that all over the internet."

"Well, the best defense is to go on offense."

"I don't know what that means here."

"They're asking why you aren't posting on your social media about us."

"I don't post on social media." I did once, last fall, put up a picture of Anna Maria and me at the overlook of Rome. Guin made a comment about how only noobs post tourist pictures of themselves, not Dip kids. Even though everyone posts pictures like that, I deleted it. There's no win from that situation. You're either taking it or retaliating.

"Aye," Luca says, "but you *could* post on social media. And, by doing that, you give them a little fodder so they don't go rooting around in your barn looking for snacks."

I'm a little thrown by Luca giving me farm metaphors. "I don't think it's a good idea. Besides, fodder is for cows, not people."

"You know what I mean, stop calling me out for mixed metaphors. And why isn't it a good idea? I think it's barry."

I sit up and let out a heavy breath. Morning sun lights up the oriental rug by my bed. The only really terrible thing about being a Dip kid is that we've never had a cat or dog because it's too cruel to make them go through quarantine with every move, so Bert, the lemon tree, is as close as we've come. But I think of the cats on my granddad's farm and how they'd be stretching out on this rug right now if they were here, and it makes me wish my life were simpler. I should never have agreed to this deal.

"Story? What's the problem?"

"If I post, then the Dips are going to make negative comments. Things like how there's no way Story Herriot is really dating Luca Kinnaird, or how Luca Kinnaird is way out of my league."

Luca laughs. "I think it might be the other way around, actually."

That stops me. But it's just Luca being polite. "Luca, I'm serious."

"Story, you can't refuse to live your life because some irrelevant person might be unkind to you."

"Maybe, but I also don't need to make myself a giant bull's-eye, especially with people who already hate me. Patrick told Kelsey you must have suffered a head injury to pick me over all the models you know. It's not safe for either of us. If they don't believe it, why should anyone else?"

"Patrick is off his nutter. But people will believe it a lot more if you post about us."

Compliments come so easy for him, I'm not sure he even knows he's making them.

"Plus, I've been thinking about why I would break up with you. It needs to be something that doesn't make either of us look like a jerk, and if I say it's because I don't like the attention, that's believable without hurting either of our reputations."

"All the more reason to post a few things. Then, when you do get reactions, you have a reason to say you need your privacy."

"Right, because being followed around twenty-four seven by cameras isn't weird enough."

"I don't get you, Story. You have no problem standing up to me."

I lose my edge. "That's different."

"Why?"

"Because you and I are fake. It doesn't matter. These people are my reality. I've had to face them, every day."

"So you're saying you can only be real with me because we're fake?"

"Okay, when you put it like that, it sounds ridiculous. It's complicated, though."

"You should just tell them off."

"It wouldn't change anything. And antagonizing them isn't worth it. I'll be gone soon, and things will be different."

Luca is quiet for a moment. I think I've won.

"Will it? Or will there just be new people you need to hide from?"

I don't answer him. Somewhere inside me, the little watchman who holds up the mirror is dinging his bell, trying to tell me that Luca might be right. But I've always hated that little watchman.

I pick at my nails. "I need to go. We can take a picture at the luncheon, and I'll post it."

"Thanks, Story. See you in a bit."

I hang up and drop my phone on the bed. There's only one thing I'm sure about. This is a much more dangerous game than I thought it was.

Twelve

The luncheon to raise money for a pediatric hospital in Mozambique is being held in the courtyard of a fancy restaurant not far from the embassy, so I've told Luca I'll just meet him there.

When I check with the valet, he tells me Luca hasn't arrived yet. I really don't want to go in by myself, so I wait outside. It's a mistake. I'm immediately swarmed by paparazzi. I'm starting to recognize them. There's the middle-aged guy who wears a fedora like he's in a 1950s cop show, and a young guy with brown hair with red highlights who has a mun and beard, and two women in their thirties who always elbow each other out of the way. The rest still blend together, though.

"Astoria, where is Luca?"

"Astoria, what was it like to meet a princess?"

"Astoria, why haven't you made it official on Instagram? Are you going to break his heart?"

They throw their questions so quickly, I wouldn't be able to answer even if I wanted to. I turn to the man in the fedora. "I'd like to go in now. Can you let me pass?"

"If you give me an exclusive," he says.

"I don't give interviews," I tell him.

They keep at me, taking pictures and blocking my way as they hurl questions. They can only hurt me if I overreact, though. "You should ask Luca," I say. "I believe he has a spokesman or something."

A man comes out of the restaurant and yells at them in accented English to leave before he calls the polizia. He pushes them back and escorts me inside.

"I am so sorry, Miss Herriot," he says. "Please, let me take you to your hostess?"

"I'd rather wait for my date, please." How does even the maître d' know who I am?

"As you wish, signorina."

I stand near the door and wish I had let Luca pick me up after all. It's not like him to be late. But then a group of people comes over to me.

"Miss Herriot," a lady says in English as she extends her hand, "I'm Giovanna Sardi. I'm so pleased you could come." She's slim and elegantly dressed, her blond hair upswept.

"Grazie. Piacere. How do you know who I am?" I could really use Luca's people skills right now.

"I recognize you from the photos, certamente."

I nod stupidly. She introduces me to the others, a man and a woman on her committee to raise funds, and a doctor from the

Mozambique hospital. We make small talk, and then our hostess ushers us into the courtyard. Signora Sardi introduces me to more people. I struggle through a conversation or two and then check my phone, but Luca hasn't sent a reason for why he's so late. He finally shows up a few minutes later, in a dark suit with a blue shirt and emerald tie.

"So sorry I'm late," he says as he kisses my temple. "I take it you've met Signora Sardi?"

They exchange hellos, and then she takes Luca and me around a bit before she moves on to other important guests who will drop wads of cash on her good cause.

We sit with a group of people who are mostly middle-aged. There's a businessman from the UK who knows Luca, I guess through his dad because he asks after him, and his wife. Then there are some Italian doctors and professors from the local medical school.

"Do you want some oysters?" the guy from the UK asks as he offers me the plate going around.

"Story loves oysters," Luca says out of nowhere.

I almost drop my glass as I turn to stare at him. From the look on his face, he's realized his mistake, but it's too late now. I turn back to the businessman and take an oyster and say thanks, but not before I kick Luca under the table. He coughs to cover his sudden jolt forward.

I set the shell with its slimy oyster on my plate. Even if I ate meat, it sure wouldn't be raw seafood.

"Oh, but I forgot about your allergy," Luca says.

It takes me a moment to catch up. "Oh, right, my allergy!"

I turn to the business guy. "I just got diagnosed. Nothing serious, but I probably shouldn't."

"Oh, my dear, I'm so sorry," he says.

"Should you wash your hands?" his wife asks, concerned for me.

"I'll be fine, really, I just shouldn't eat shellfish anymore," I say.

Several of the doctors chime in, apparently ready to give me a tracheotomy if I need one, but I promise everyone it's just a mild allergy.

That's when a waiter puts a dish of chicken in front of me. Luca pulls him over and whispers to him, and he immediately takes the plate away again.

I look at the businessman and his wife and say "allergies," at the same time I hear Luca say it. A few moments later, the waiter reappears with a vegan pasta dish, and I smile sheepishly at everyone. Thankfully, though, Luca is already maneuvering the conversation to the charity.

"Story, I'm so sorry," Luca says when we have a quiet moment as the luncheon ends, "I totally forgot to tell them you were vegan."

"I did the math on that when you almost made me eat oysters. What was that about?"

He grimaces. "Most people pretend to like them because they think it's the cool thing to do. Models are always chasing cool."

I give him a flat look. "Why were you so late?"

"Oh, sorry about that, too. I was with Jasmine and didn't realize the time. She was making me help her choose her final outfits for the tour performances, although I'm really not qualified for that kind of thing. You didn't have any trouble, did you?"

I'd say yes if it wouldn't sound petulant. "Not much. A minor paparazzi overload, but the maître d' rescued me. They were asking about my lack of posting."

Luca raises his eyebrows to say *I told you so*. We ask a waitress to take our photo beside an elaborate fountain in the courtyard, Luca's arm circling me. We decide we should both post it. That's when we realize we haven't even followed each other yet.

When I open my first app, I'm shocked.

"What's wrong?"

I show him my screen. I've gone from having less than a few hundred followers, mostly my family in the States, to several thousand people requesting to follow me.

Luca smiles. "Astoria Herriot, you're famous. But you need to set that to public now."

"Great," I say, with all the enthusiasm of someone getting off a carnival ride ready to throw up.

Luca laughs. "Use it."

I just look at him.

"Become a brand," he says. "An influencer. Sell your posts to advertisers. It can help you pay for that expensive school of yours back in America."

"Oh, I don't think so." I get a sick feeling even thinking about it. "I just, that's just not me, even if it would help me avoid student loans."

"It's easy money. You should take it."

I tick my head.

He shrugs. "Well, what do you even have?"

I show him the few platforms I use, and we follow each other.

"Now, what are we going to say about this lovely photo?" he asks.

"Do we have to say something?"

"Argh, Story, you're impossible."

"I don't want to say anything too sappy. First of all, it would make it less believable when we break up, and second, my cousins back home are going to have more questions about this than the paparazzi."

Luca zeros his blue gaze in on me. "Because I'm me, or because you're such a loner?"

I almost say "Both" because, while I doubt any of them have heard of him, his looks and fancy clothes are going to send them into a frenzy, let alone the shock of me posting. I shrug.

He laughs. "Okay, you just say something about having a lovely luncheon to raise funds for the charity, and make sure to hashtag the foundation, with me. And I'll say the same and add something stupid like 'with this bonnie girl.' That should do it. We don't need to make them think we're madly in love, just public enough that I wouldn't be interested in J."

I nod and post the picture. "Okay, well, am I off duty as Luca's latest?"

His smile drops. "I was kind of hoping you'd show me more of Astoria Herriot's weird Roma. But if you have things to do, we don't have to." He's ridiculously charming when he's not so sure of himself. I have nothing to do, of course. But I don't like telling him that. I try to think of something that wouldn't be a lie, but there isn't anything.

"Dai," I say, which means *come on* in Italian.

When we've escaped to the Portofino, I ask Luca what he wants to see.

"What are my options?"

I shake my head at him. "This is Roma. Your options are whatever you want them to be. Creepy, sweet, frightening, silly, historic. There's the Vespa Museum under a bike shop, or you might like the wax-enhanced skeleton of St. Victoria, or maybe you're homesick and would like to see Little London?"

"London is not my home. Never say that again," Luca says with mock offense. "Well, what are some of your favorite places?"

"I don't think you'd like any of them." Being a loner gives you a lot of time to explore.

"I loved your Porta Alchemica and the Aventine Keyhole."

I bite my lip because my favorite places are all hopelessly romantic.

"What?" Luca says, laughing at me. "I know you have favorite places."

"Well, there is the Pons Fabricus, which is the oldest Roman bridge in the city still in its original state. And the Ponte Nomentano is another beautiful bridge. And I like the Casina delle Civette, which is this weird kind of ode to German fairy tales. Or, just outside of the city is the abbey of Santa Maria del Piano, which they say Charlemagne built. But it's in ruins now."

"You would love where I grew up, you know that? I'll have

to take you." He says this as if our friendship doesn't have a shorter lifespan than a tube of Guin's petroleum-based lip gloss. But I don't say this. Something makes me believe that handing Luca a challenge is never a good idea.

Our first stop is Luca's hotel so he can change, and I meet the elusive Hodges, who emails me regularly about Luca's schedule. He's tall and slender with a shock of blond hair that is starting to gray. His black suit is perfectly tailored against a crisp white shirt and maroon tie.

"It's a pleasure to meet you, Miss Astoria."

"Likewise. You can just call me Story, though, Mr. Hodges."

"I cannot, Miss Story. Although, it's just Hodges." He says it sweetly, while letting me know that I'm threatening to disrupt a thousand years of British composure.

"Hodges," I say, "but not just."

He smiles. Luca emerges from his bedroom, ready to take on Rome in a blue T-shirt and cargo shorts.

It's ridiculous how good he looks whether he's dressed up or down.

The day is beautiful, not as oppressively hot as Rome usually is in June. I take Luca to the river walk below the Pons Fabricus, which connects the eastern shore of Tiber Island, a tiny strip of earth in the middle of the Tiber River, to the mainland. As we stroll around, Luca suddenly takes my hand.

I look up, and he laughs. "In case any paparazzi or fans are watching. Don't look so shocked, or they won't believe us."

"Of course," I say, but the idea of some random fan taking our photo is even weirder than the paparazzi.

We spend the rest of the afternoon sightseeing, and it's kind of fun to have a companion. After a while, I almost forget we could be on display as I get used to Luca's hand in mine or his arm around my waist or shoulder. It's dinnertime when we reach the village where the abbey is. You have to walk up a trail to get to the ruins, and Luca suggests we grab a picnic from the local groceria.

"Are you sure you can manage in those shoes?" he asks. "We've walked a ton."

"I'm okay," I say, although my feet have been hurting since we passed the Irish pub near the Pantheon, which was pretty raucous over some soccer game being telecast.

"Look, there's a shoe store," he says as we leave the groceria. "Let's get you some proper hiking shoes."

"It's okay, honestly."

"Story, it's the least I can do. Besides, if you can't dance tomorrow night, people will think something is wrong with our relationship. Come on." Luca pulls me across the street. It's a small store, but he still manages to find an expensive pair of trail runners for me.

"They cost too much."

"She'll take a size . . . ," he says to the lady waiting on us, as he looks at me expectantly.

"Thirty-six," I say. The lady goes to fetch them.

"You really don't have to."

"It's nothing." He pulls a package of socks from a display and hands them to me. My mom makes a good living, but buying an expensive pair of shoes for convenience's sake would still be something to us. Our worlds really are different.

"Thank you," I tell him as the lady rings it up.

Luca smiles. "You're welcome, Astoria Herriot."

We drop my espadrilles in the Portofino and find the trail to the abbey. The walk is steep, and we pass only a few people, all heading down the hill. Evening shadows make it feel as if Charlemagne might come charging by on his horse. The ruins have arches throughout the remaining stone walls, and there's a huge square tower with arched windows at every level. I pull up facts on my phone because I don't remember enough of the history. "You're not going to report me to the tour guide union, are you?"

"Not this time," Luca says, draping his arm across my shoulders even though there's no one else here.

We explore the ruins and then set out our picnic under a tree on the west-facing hillside as the sun sets.

"I wonder if Charlemagne really did build the abbey," I say.

"Imagine the history of these hills! Home is bonnie, but different, too. You've never been to Scotland, have you?"

I shake my head. "I haven't been to the UK at all."

"You'd love Scotland." He hands me a small carton of cantaloupe, and we have little roasted eggplant sandwiches. We drink aranciata from glass bottles, and Luca teaches me more Scottish slang, although most of their sayings "are not very polite," as he puts it, his eyebrows creased together as he vets them, and we laugh. Crickets come out to sing, and the stars are just starting to show. A three-quarters moon crests the horizon. For dessert, we have cookies and chocolates as the dark deepens.

"This is the best thing I've done since I got here," Luca says. "Thank you." He reaches over and puts his hand on mine, but his eyes are on the stars. I should pull away.

His phone vibrates in his pocket. He's been ignoring it, but the calls are coming closer together, and he finally answers.

"No," he says, "I heard it. I figured it was Andy or Adaira."

Luca looks over at me and covers the phone. "My best friend or my sister," he whispers.

I nod, trying not to be nosy. There's still a lot I don't know about him. Not that it matters, since this will be over before the days start to cool back in Maine.

There's a pause as he listens.

"Aye, fine, I'm outside of Rome, but I'll head back now. Story was just showing me some sights."

I start to pack up our trash.

"Don't be like that. I'll be back in an hour. I didn't know you'd end early."

I stand and shake the crumbs from my dress, and Luca stands, too. He mumbles something I don't hear and hangs up.

"Jasmine's upset that I'm not back yet." He says it more to the air than to me.

"Well," I say, "I'd be unhappy, too, if you were my boyfriend and you spent more time with your cover than with me."

He catches my gaze a moment before he nods. I don't think either one of them are used to not getting their way. "Well, it was a lovely day, anyway. Thank you."

It's my turn to nod. "Just doing my job," I say, and we silently follow the trail back to the car.

Thirteen

"Story," Luca says when he calls the next morning, "you continue to delight and amaze our paparazzi friends. They took some very cute pictures of you waiting patiently outside the restaurant looking like a lost duckling." The hint of sarcasm in his voice isn't lost on me.

"I'm sorry. I'm trying to fit in, honestly. I should have come with you."

Luca laughs. "Why are you such a shy loner?"

"I have certificates of achievement in both from Signora del Giudizio's School for Misfit Children."

"Ha! You must have been Madam Judgment's star pupil, wandering around Rome sightseeing instead of making friends. You can't hide forever, you know. Life will catch you up. I have to run. I'll pick you up at six, okay? Traffic to that part of the city will be tight."

"As you wish, my lord."

"Hilarious, as you say. Ciao."

"Ciao."

When Luca hangs up, I think about the tabloids. I really want to pretend they aren't there, but maybe Luca is right and it's better to keep your enemies close. Or maybe not. I set my phone down and start doing laundry. I can't get sucked into his lifestyle, worried about what people are saying about me. All I can do is be me and hope it's enough. It's not enough in my world, though, so I don't know how it could be in Luca's. At least in my world, I only have to take some jabs at school. My beatdown isn't a public spectacle. I vacuum and wash some dishes and then I water Bert and the rest of the plants. It's almost lunchtime, and I haven't looked at the tabloids.

But then I do. There I am, my whole day spread before my eyes. Pictures of me in front of the restaurant, Luca and I standing on the Pons Fabricus with his arms wrapped around me, the two of us laughing at the Ponte Nomentano and holding hands leaving the Casina delle Civette. It's almost enough to convince me we're the real deal. There's even a picture of us under the tree at the abbey. It might be nice to have these photos, if they weren't stalked and shared with the world without our permission, but they are, and that ruins even sightseeing with a friend.

There is also a lovely article quoting my "best friend," Guin Behringer, full of facts about my life, such as how we love to shop together on the "Via dei Condotti," and how she and I met Luca at an embassy party, and she had to tell him that I had a huge crush on him to get him to ask me out, and how I used to "have a thing" for our classmate, Patrick Rooney, son of the US ambassador. I almost throw my phone through the balcony door.

A few minutes later, Luca texts me.

So hey, Jasmine said she's sending you something for tonight, from her stylist.

You mean a dress? I already have one.

Idk. She just said she'd hook you up. Maybe jewelry. Let me know if you want some diamonds.

Hilarious.

I'm serious.

You are not normal.

Lol, I can rent you some, or at least Hodges can. Or hairstylist, makeup person, whatever.

I'm good, thanks. Like every ordinary teen girl, I learned my makeup tips from gay guys on YouTube.

Pro level. Okay then, see you at six.

After lunch, I walk up to the Keats-Shelley House and visit Anna Maria. She doesn't follow celebrity news, and it's really nice to forget the craziness for a while. She asks me about Luca, though.

"I guess I've seen him a lot."

"How much is a lot? Every day?" She keeps her dark-roast eyes fixed on me.

"Yes. I mean, he has a very busy social life, and he likes having a plus-one. That's all it is for him."

I help her set out some new notebooks with "Bright Star" in gold lettering on the blue cover.

"And what is it for you?"

I can't look at her. "It's something to do. He's funny and nice, but we come from very different worlds."

"How do you mean?"

Her gaze is like being hooked up to a polygraph test, but I'm not exactly sure what I mean. This whole thing with Jeremy doesn't feel right, but aren't I as guilty as Luca and Jasmine? Is it really even wrong? What right does the public have to know about Jasmine's dating life? But keeping the secret will make her money. I would never have started all this in motion, but I'm going along with it. I'm even getting paid for it, sort of.

"Rich people see everything as sitting there just for them, whether it's valet parking or tickets to some sold-out event. Maybe I've seen too much of it, being the daughter of someone who works at an embassy, but everyone accommodates them."

Anna Maria nods slowly. " 'I quattrini mandan l'acqua all'insù.' "

She's been teaching me idioms. "I don't know that one."

"Money sends water upwards. It means it can do the impossible."

"Most things, anyway. 'L'ultimo vestito ce lo fanno senza tasche.' " She laughs because that means the last suit is made without pockets, or as we'd say, you can't take it with you when you die. "I'd better go."

I walk home through a soft rain. Jack texts me, and raindrops splatter my screen in little iridescent pinpricks.

I didn't know you had a thing for Patrick.

Hilarious.

Does Kelsey know you're Guin's BFF now?

I will happily relinquish the title.

No wonder you've never liked our group.

I laugh. At least he can see them for what they are. *It'll all be forgotten soon. New town, new people to avoid.*

Jack marks my text with a like. *I promise to be a better friend at Princeton than I was here.*

I don't know how to respond. I settle on one word. *Same.*

As I open the door to my building, I knock over a huge box with my name across the top. It must be from Jasmine, and, from the size of the box, it's definitely a dress. It's probably gorgeous, but there's no way for me to explain it to my mom. I might be holding a five-thousand-dollar gown in my hands, and all I can wish is that she'd never sent it. My trickle-down dress was only $189 euros, but I love it.

I take the box up to my room and open it. There's a note from Jasmine on top of perfectly laid out tissue paper, sealed with a gold sticker. "All eyes will be on you, and I know you want to fit in for Luca's sake. My stylist picked this especially for you. It'll be perfect. Love, J."

"No pressure," I say out loud. I feel like a traitor to my Christian Dior for even looking at it. I can't imagine what this dress that costs thousands of dollars, picked by a professional stylist, is going to look like. I guess that's a good thing because when I pull the tissue paper away, I can hardly believe my eyes.

There's a famous designer's name on the label, but even Kelsey and Guin couldn't have picked anything this hideous for me. This cannot be a mistake.

The gown is a sickly color of chartreuse with layer after

layer of accordion ruffles, and they all seem to stick out at different angles. The neckline comes up to the throat and then does this weird Peter Pan collar thing, except it's cream-colored and huge like something a Puritan preacher would have worn. The sleeves pouf out, and the dress hangs slack. A minute ago, I was worried about my mom seeing me with a superexpensive designer dress. Now I'm worried that my fake boyfriend's secret girlfriend is a sociopath who wants to kill me on the altar of celebrity magazines. Maybe I deserve this for getting myself into this mess.

I try on the olive abomination just in case I'm missing something major about couture. Does it somehow become beautiful when you slip it on as if Cinderella's Fairy Godmother has transformed it? But no, an actual giant pumpkin would look better on me, plus it's way too long. I pack it up and shove it under my bed so my mom doesn't see it. I'll give it to Luca to return to his thoughtful diva.

I take a shower and try to wash away the memory of how I looked in that Puritan palooza, wondering why anyone would send someone a dress that ugly. Then I wonder how anyone could make a dress that ugly. Then I wonder how anyone who made a dress that ugly could still be a famous designer. Rich people make no sense to me.

When I'm all dressed, I check myself in the mirror. The Dior gown is beautiful. The way my mom and I tacked it up at intervals makes the crinoline show, and it really does look like something a fairy-tale princess might have worn. I'm wearing a rose gold necklace that picks up the copper coloring of the embroidery and a pair of satin black heels borrowed from my mom. I spritz some perfume on my wrists, and my mom slips a sparkling hairpin into my French twist.

Luca comes a few minutes early because my mom wants to take pictures of us as if we're going to prom, something I wouldn't have gone to even if my school had had one.

"Jings, Story, you look completely bonnie."

"Thank you, you look nice, too. My mom fixed my hair." I say all of it awkwardly because I'm not really experienced with handing out compliments or taking them, either. He has on a tux, and it doesn't look like a rental.

Luca has brought my mom flowers and me chocolates. She's so happy that I worry she's getting attached to this idea of Luca and me. I need to tell Luca to turn down the charm a notch. They have a mini gabfest while we take the pictures, and it's kind of fun to be in this beautiful designer gown and going to some fancy ball with a friend. Or almost friend. Or at least, someone whose company I don't find nearly as grating as I had expected.

"Luca, why don't you come for dinner on Sunday?" my mom asks. My eyes pop open, and I shake my head at him behind her back.

"I think he's busy, Mom."

"No, I'm not busy," he says. "I'd love to have dinner with you and Story."

This just keeps getting more complicated. "We'd better go," I say, and Luca gestures for me to lead the way.

When we're safely in the bubble of the Portofino, I stare at him. "Why would you tell my mom yes?"

Luca's face contracts. "About dinner? Why wouldn't I?"

"Because I'm not actually your girlfriend?"

"But your mom thinks you are. And she asked very politely."

"Luca, involving our families was not part of the plan."

"You can meet my mom if you like."

"Luca, this isn't funny!"

Luca laughs. "You are way too uptight, you know that? I like your mom. And you and I are friends, remember? It'll be fine."

I let out a deep breath. It's too late now anyway. Luca breezes us through Rome, and I try to let go of the prickly feeling around my heart.

I've never been to a gala of any kind, but I've learned enough about Luca's life to expect a red carpet. Luca knows where to stop to let the photographers take their shots. They yell questions about our relationship. He just smiles and nods before moving me along. When we get inside, he takes my hand. "Come on. I want you to meet someone."

We thread our way through the attendees. There are enough celebrities that you'd think we were at the Oscars. Luca introduces me to the endless number of people he knows and manages the small talk. Then he extracts us with the dexterity of a skilled surgeon.

"Andrew!" Luca exclaims as a guy our age comes striding over. He's got strawberry blond hair and a really nice smile.

"Luca's told me so much about you," Andrew says with a Scottish accent. "But you're even prettier than your photos."

"Thank you. You can't trust him, though."

"Well, that's something I already knew," he says. "We grew up together."

"Ah, so if anyone knows the real Luca Kinnaird, it's you."

"What exactly does that mean?" Luca asks, tilting his head.

"It means you have the real Luca, and then the Luca persona you deploy on the world. I'm never really sure which one I'm talking to, like an excellent spy."

"That is precisely him," Andrew says, laughing.

I raise my eyebrows at Luca in victory, but he just gives me a shrewd look.

"Are you sitting with us?" he asks Andrew.

"Aye, I seem to have finally infiltrated the cool kids' table."

"Good, I want you and Story to get to know each other."

Luca's attention is caught, and I follow his gaze across the crowded ballroom to his beloved. She looks like you would expect her to look, wearing a dress that Satan would blush at and wearing it exceptionally well. Her dark, dyed hair is in its signature look, tight to the face and pulled back high. Her makeup is like a mask, but perfectly set. She must have spent hours getting ready. I feel sorry for her because I can't imagine anything more boring. But it's easy to see why she's every guy's dream.

I hadn't expected her to be here, with her European tour starting tomorrow. There are enough people that it doesn't seem likely I'll have to meet her, until she slowly serpentines her way over to us, bodyguards trailing her like bridesmaids, and I catch myself picking at my nail beds. There's no way she thought the dress she sent was nice. Or that she won't say something about me not wearing it.

"Andrew, Luca," she says as she kisses each of them, "how great to see you both."

They exchange their pleasantries, and Luca introduces me. Andrew offers to get us all drinks. I have no idea if he knows what's really going on, but I wish I could go with him.

I don't want her to think I'm interested in her territory, though, so I'm extra polite. "Your voice is amazing," I say, which is true even if her music relies on swearing and sex to make it bankable.

"Thanks." She lets her gaze take in my dress. She looks around as if to see if anyone is near us and then back at me expectantly. When I don't say anything, she says, "Why aren't you wearing the dress I sent?"

"That's not the dress Jasmine gave you?" Luca asks.

"Of course not," she says with a snort.

"That was really kind of you, but it didn't fit."

"My stylist gauged your measurements from the tab photos, it must have fit. Whatever it is that you're wearing is from at least three seasons ago. You're going to be a laughingstock." She's smiling for anyone watching as if she's just made nice small talk with me.

I pull my lips in. The tabloids probably will come after me for wearing a trickle-down dress. Although how anyone cares enough to be bothered to know is beyond me. Still, what she's really upset about is that I'm the one nominally here with Luca even though she's the one Luca's protecting. Luca could have run into me in every gelateria in Rome, and he wouldn't have asked me out. The one thing Patrick has ever been right about.

"Jaz, it's just a dress, and she looks lovely," Luca says quietly.

"Well, when the tabloids are making fun of her, you'll both be wishing she'd worn what I sent. She's never going to pull this off if she can't at least try to fit in." She laughs as if we are having a completely different conversation, for anyone watching her.

"It'll be fine," Luca says. "The tabs know she doesn't come from money."

"But you come from money, Luca. They'll expect you to make sure that she looks . . ." She pauses, apparently because even she can't come up with a suitably obnoxious word. "Like she belongs with us."

I turn my head. Andrew is at the bar, being handed the drinks. The only people here like me are the servers and bartenders.

"She fits in just fine." Luca slips his hand around my back. "The tabs are getting a big kick out of me dating a . . ."

The pause hits me like a slap. I turn back. The blue of his eyes is dark, like a creek that's overrun its banks. "You can say it, I won't break. Ordinary girl."

"We'll see," Jasmine says. She smiles as if she's glad I know my place, and tells Luca, "I'll see you back at the hotel, babe." Then she floats off, her icy heart not weighing her down in the least.

Luca pulls away a little, and we stand there. "I really don't know anything about fashion," he says after a few moments.

"I guess that makes two of us."

"And I didn't mean anything by that crack about you being different from us."

I can't look at him, but I square my shoulders. "You were right, though. I'm nothing like you." I turn and go in search of Andrew.

"Story, wait," Luca says, but I keep walking. A few weeks ago, I wouldn't have thought much about people making fun of me for wearing a recycled dress or being just ordinary Astoria Herriot. But right now, my eyes sting, and I don't even know why I care what Luca Kinnaird and his diva girlfriend think.

Fourteen

ndrew comes toward me with three glasses pinned in his hands.

"Let me help you." I reach out and take mine. I can't quite meet his gaze, though.

"Are you all right?" The freckles on his face pinch together as he bends his knees to catch my gaze.

"Fine." I force myself to look up at him.

"You know, I'm his best friend, but I don't recommend falling for him."

"It's not that." So, in addition to Jasmine, Luca, and me, Andrew also knows this isn't real. So much for not telling anyone.

"Are you sure? He's an easy fellow to fall for. At least, most girls seem to."

I shake my head. "That would probably be an easier problem to solve than the fact that I really, really don't belong here. But I have to be here as long as the deal runs."

"Ah, I see. Well, I wouldn't let that get to you too much. Most of these people aren't really worth knowing. Besides, you don't strike me as someone who cares what people think."

"Everyone cares what people think. And it's not what they think, it's what they say."

"I see. Well, let's make sure we have some fun and don't hear them."

He gives me a sweet smile.

I blink back some tears. "Thank you."

"Anytime. I'd offer you my arm, but—" he says as he gestures with his two full hands, and I laugh. I take Luca's drink from him, and we find Luca on his way to our table. "For you," I say as I hand him the glass. I try to sound completely normal. Luca picks up my cue and we spend the rest of the night putting on our best show yet. I'm seated between Luca and Andrew, and they tell me stories about stupid things the other has done over the years. The people at our table are acquaintances and friends of theirs, and everyone is laughing and telling funny stories. They talk about St. Moritz and the Caymans and places I've never heard of. Luca and I dance, and I'm glad he made me get the trail runners for the hike to the abbey as he pulls me out for song after song. Then he drags me through the silent auction, asking if there's anything I want him to bid on, but the trips to Swiss ski resorts and exclusive Bali spas aren't any more real to me than being his girlfriend is, so I just say no, thank you.

Somewhere after dessert and before we leave, Andrew wins the use of a fancy sailboat for a day from the silent auction, and the two of them make plans for us to go sailing tomorrow to a small island not that far from Rome, called Ponza that a lot of locals go to in summer. I've heard Jack talk about it at school. When I tell them I've never sailed before, it's like I've given them a present.

"You're going to love it," they say in stereo.

"Are you two sure you know what you're doing?"

They both laugh. "You'll be fine, lass, dinna fash," Andrew says.

"That means don't worry. Andy's a crack sailor. I just do what he tells me."

"Not true," Andrew replies. "Luca and I both grew up sailing with my parents. When we were in academy, we always said we'd take a year off and sail around the world."

"But here we are, day tripping to an island near Rome."

"He has too many family obligations," Andrew says. I don't know how this can be true when Luca can spend his whole summer in Rome chasing a diva, but Andrew seems serious.

"All right, let's go," Luca says suddenly. Across the room, Jasmine is leaving with her entourage, and I figure he wants to get back to the hotel, since this is the last night she'll be in town for a while. When he and Andrew drop me off, they both remind me not to forget about our sailing plans.

I watch my phone the next morning as I eat breakfast at the little kitchen table that overlooks the courtyard. But Luca doesn't call with his usual tabloid recap, and it starts to feel like a cat and mouse game, as if my phone knows what they've said about me but doesn't have the heart to tell me. Finally, I look at the tabs myself.

Luca and I are there, and we look really nice, I think. Then I read the caption. *Luca Kinnaird with his latest girlfriend, Astoria Herriot, fashionably poor in an altered Christian Dior from four years ago.*

"Fashionably poor? What does that even mean?"

"What did you say, honey?" my mom asks as she walks in and grabs the teakettle.

"Oh, nothing." I finish my toast and go back to my room to read the article. I'm not exactly the laughingstock Jasmine predicted, but my wardrobe choices are still a big cause for concern in my budding romance, as the magazine asks if Luca and I are from different planets too far apart. The article doesn't say I can't fit into Luca's world, but there's enough meat between the lines to make six-foot submarine sandwiches for an NFL team. I check the other tabloids. One says I looked "vintage adorable" in my "throwback gown" and gushes about how kind everyone was to "the gala's own Cinderella," while another says that "Astoria Herriot made a good try, but she clearly doesn't have the assets to run with the jet-set crowd. This sweet, but regular, girl should give up before she embarrasses herself." Too late for that. They predict Luca will tire of me by the time the annual Rock in Roma festival starts in a couple of weeks. I guess if nothing else, this will make Kelsey and her minions deliriously happy. It may even be a good excuse to break up with Luca when the time comes. But it's still not an experience I want to re-create for the next six to eight weeks.

Despite my expectations, Luca doesn't call or text. Maybe he's too busy getting an earful from Jasmine about how I should have worn her Bride of Frankenstein dress. Or maybe he's mad at me for not wearing it. That idea bothers me more than it should.

I think about running out to buy a Chiara Ferragni swimsuit for today, but I don't have three hundred euros or whatever it would be to drop on one. I should never have gotten myself into this mess. And yet, my dad's scholarship is sitting there on my shoulder like angelic Sylvester telling me to be nice to Tweety.

A little after ten, Luca texts that he and Andrew are downstairs, so I grab my things and tell my mom I'm going.

"Okay," she says. "I can't wait to hear all about it! It's so nice to see you doing things with friends like this."

"Yes, it's great. A lot of fun." I pop out the door, hoping to drag my sarcasm with me before she hears it.

When Andrew sees me, he gets out of the passenger seat to climb in the back, but since I'm small and he's nearly as tall as Luca, I insist on taking the back seat of the Portofino.

"Don't mind him," Andrew whispers as he holds the door for me. "Jasmine was still harping on your dress this morning. She wasn't happy about that sightseeing spread the other day, either."

So that explains the designer abomination. I slip into the back seat. Luca gives me a careless hello, and the Ferrari roars off. Andrew makes a few failed attempts at conversation as we drive to a marina forty minutes south of Rome, but Luca doesn't seem to be in the mood to talk any more than I am. I'm not sure how much is because his girlfriend has gone off on her European tour and how much is because he's mad at me.

I spend most of the trip arguing in my head all the things I'd never say in real life, like how his remarkably unkind girlfriend tried to sabotage me with a dress that looks like it crawled out of Hester Prynne's local swamp, or how shallow his universe is with its fashionably poor threshold, or how none of them even have the right to critique anything about me in the first place. I really let him have it. In my head, anyway.

When we get to the marina, Andrew goes off to the harbormaster to check in, while Luca and I lean against the car and look at the bay.

"So, what kind of boat are we going out in?" I say after a few minutes. It's a beautiful day, and I don't want to spend it angry.

Luca turns his gaze to me for the first time since I got in the car. For a moment or two, he just looks at me. This is going to be a really long day. Then he wrinkles his nose and says, "Well, for starters, it's technically a yacht."

I smile. "Pardon me."

Luca chuckles. "It's an easy mistake."

"Well, at least I didn't think it was a canoe."

Luca breaks into his first smile of the day. "Actually, if I'm not mistaken, it's that one there, with the blue sail." He points to a huge boat with a bright sail wrapped around whatever beam thing they are wrapped around when not in use. He laughs when he sees my mouth fall open. "It's a French-made beauty. That's why Andrew was so keen to get his hands on it. It's a cutter rigged Beneteau Oceanis 40.1."

"How big is it?"

"Forty feet."

"And you two are going to manage all those sails by yourselves?"

Luca shakes his head at me. "It's not 1950, Story. These babies practically sail themselves. And a cutter has three sails. But, aye, we both could take it across the world if we ever got the chance. You trust me in the Ferrari, don't you?"

"I guess so."

"I know you do. You don't clutch the door anymore or push the imaginary brake pedal you wish was on the passenger side." He does a little pantomime, including pretending to brake until I laugh.

He puts his arm around me. "Story, don't be so scared of life, or you're never going to actually live."

I look down. "You sound like my mom."

"She's right. Why are you so afraid all the time?"

I glance over the harbor, glad my eyes are hidden behind the superexpensive glecks he gave me. "The world is a scary place."

Luca doesn't say anything for a few moments. Then he pulls back. "Aye, but that's not why you're scared of it."

I poke the asphalt with the toe of my Converse while he waits for me to answer.

"I don't know."

"I don't really believe that. But you can stick by it if you like."

I let out a sharp breath. "It was scary growing up without a dad."

Luca nods slowly.

"Even before he died, we were on our own for a long time. My mom had to worry every time we moved whether she'd get a safe enough duty station for a single mom and who could watch me while she was at work until she found someone she trusted. I remember being terrified when I was little that something would happen to her. There was no way my dad could have raised me. And then I learned to be scared of what people would say. Believe me, people have no qualms about telling you what a loser your dad is, and how he deserves everything bad that happens to him because he's a selfish lowlife. It's almost better that he's gone, which makes me feel like such a horrible jerk. But most people won't ask what happened when I say he's dead. And when they do, I just say he was sick and change the subject. But you're always living with this skeleton in your closet, except he's not a skeleton to you, he's your dad and you want the world to see him the way you see him, secretly, in your heart, like a dad should be, the way he could have been without the substances. But you know they'll only see the embarrassing remnants if they ever find out, so you hide." I finish out of breath, all the anger washed out of me.

Luca's been biting his lower lip as he listened. "I'm sorry, Story. I keep being a jerk to you when I really just want to be nice."

I rest my head against his shoulder. "You're not being a jerk, trust me. I've had plenty of people be jerks to me." As soon as I finish, I realize I shouldn't have leaned into him. I guess I'm so used to him holding my hand or putting his arms around me that I didn't even think. I pull back too suddenly and catch the surprise on his face before I look away.

"The thing I don't get is that you'll go and explore all those places, by yourself, like the Porta Alchemica."

"When it's daylight, after I've read enough about them and plotted the map to get there and back. I mean, I've still been harassed on the streets, like any girl, but I never push the envelope too far. I know where the boundaries are." At least, I always thought I did, before Luca came into my life.

Andrew runs up to us. "We're set. It's that one over there." He points to the boat Luca thought it would be.

Luca turns to me. "Shall we go push some boundaries, just a little?"

I nod.

"Just remember the first rule of sailing: if it doesn't seem safe, don't do it. I promise, I won't let anything happen to you."

"Aye, aye, Captain," I say, and take his outstretched hand.

Fifteen

Luca and Andrew have backpacks and a tote filled with towels, and they each grab a handle of a cooler that's stocked with food. "The yacht is supposed to be well supplied," Andrew says, "but we figured we shouldn't chance it."

As we're walking down the dock, someone calls my name. I look up, and Jack is hanging off the back of a sailboat, smiling at us.

"Hey," I say, "I didn't expect to see you here today."

Luca and Jack exchange hellos and we introduce him to Andrew. "We're going down to Ponza," Jack says.

Jack's friends come over, and he introduces us. They're all Italian boys from his team. One of them, Francesco, says they know Ponza well and will show us the best spots for snorkeling if we want. He whistles when Andrew points to the boat we'll be taking. "It's not ours," Andrew says with a laugh. "We just have it for the day."

Francesco shrugs. "It's still sweet." They make plans to rendez-vous at the northwestern end of the island.

When we get on the yacht, Andrew and Luca discuss the wind speeds and get familiar with the boat's navigation system. Luca takes the cooler below deck, and I put the food into the little fridge. The cabin is perfectly clean and bright, with small, high-end appliances. There are three bedrooms, one in the front of the boat and two in the back, each one with a full bed. There's two bathrooms with showers, too. You really could live on this thing if you wanted to, like we're on one of those *Lifestyles of the Rich and Famous* shows. When we're ready to leave, Luca teaches me the terminology as he shows me how to prepare the sails, fender the stern, and slip the lines. When we've pulled the last rope, he has me call "Lines clear" to Andrew.

"Not bad, for your first go-round," Luca says as we head for open water. "We'll see how well you can let out sails, though."

Once we're clear of harbor traffic, Luca and Andrew put the boat into the headwind, and Luca teaches me how to raise the sails. The wind is refreshingly cool, and the smell of salt-water sprays through the air. As we leave the harbor, Andrew turns the boat, and it rolls hard to the left. I lose my footing, but Luca grabs me.

"Is it supposed to be like this?" I ask, trying to mask the small terror I had that we were going to capsize or I'd be flung off.

"Aye, it's fine," he says with a laugh, his arms still around me. "You steady now?"

I nod, and he lets go.

We straighten out and skim the small waves. Jack's boat left before us, but this one is faster. We lose sight of them before long. Luca explains the mathematical principles of how to use the wind for tacking and jibing. At first, it seems like we're very fragile in the water, as we tilt to one side or the other, but after I get used to the angles, it really is fun.

"You're smiling," Luca says. "You like it!"

He goes over and talks to Andrew about knots and the map and says, "Let's take Story where there won't be any land, just so she can see what it's like." They smile like little kids.

"Why do I get the feeling you two are up to something?"

They look at each other and laugh. The beautiful Italian coastline disappears as we enter the open water.

"Do you know how to drive a car?" Andrew asks.

"Yes."

"Come on, then." He puts me behind the wheel and shows me how to steer. He and Luca banter about the best way to explain things to me. We pass fishing boats and some yachts, but then there's finally nothing, and Luca cuts the engine.

"Story, come here," he says. He takes my hand and leads me around the sails to the bow. We stand at the front of the boat, and all I can see in any direction is blue-green water, rising and falling in little crests. "Close your eyes."

I give him one suspicious look and then do it. I lose my balance a bit as the boat rocks and open my eyes to grab the railing. Luca boxes me in with his arms so I can't fall. "Go on, eyes closed."

"Okay."

"What do you hear?"

I listen. "I hear the sails flapping in the breeze."

"And?"

Luca's soft cotton T-shirt is blowing against me, and the light scent of his aftershave distracts me for a moment. "I hear the water lapping against the yacht, because this is definitely not just a boat, and I hear gulls crying somewhere."

"Port or starboard?" he asks with a chuckle.

I have to think about this. "Starboard, behind us."

"Very good. Anything else?"

I take a deep breath as we roll gently with the waves, the sun warming us while the wind keeps us cool. There is so much peace surrounding us as we float. "You're going to laugh at me, but it's almost like I hear the sunlight falling on us."

"Ha ha! Andy, we have a sailor!" Luca cries out, and I open my eyes as Andrew comes along the side, and Luca lifts me off the deck as if he might throw me overboard.

"No!" I yell, and throw my arms around his neck.

Luca instantly sets me down. "I wasnae really gonnae drop yoo," he says, with so much concerned seriousness, I feel like a jerk for having doubted him.

"Ah, come on yoo wee bairns, I've got the deck down," Andrew says. We follow him to the stern, which has a platform that drops to the surface of the water. Andrew climbs down and takes my hand to help me. For a moment, I just stand there and take it all in. Luca stands behind me and wraps his arm around me just below my neck and whispers, "Look, Story!"

while he points with his left hand in front of us. Several dolphins are jumping the waves, and one is rolling as it swims.

"Now, that's magic," Andrew says.

"I've never seen a dolphin outside of an aquarium," I whisper.

"Do you want to take a swim?" Luca asks. "They might come closer out of curiosity."

I nod. The water is warm, and we swim out a little toward the dolphins. They're watching us, but they've seen this before. It's not nearly as exciting to them as it is to me. They circle the boat a couple of times and then leave. Afterward, we sit on the platform and dry off, and then we head for Ponza. Luca smiles when he catches me watching for more dolphins.

We rendezvous with Jack and his friends. They come to our boat in a little dinghy, and we have lunch together. We've brought calzones from a restaurant, and Luca has made sure mine is vegan, without mushrooms. Jack and his friends have brought bread and salami and cheese for sandwiches. There are cookies I made and fruit and soda. Two of Jack's friends are talking about me in Italian. I don't catch all of it, but they say I'm the dark-haired Scot's charity girl, and it's not supposed to last. Then they say something about Jack and me, but I'm not sure what because they're speaking low, and not enough of the words reach me.

Francesco and his friends come here a lot, and they tell us the history of the place. The island is the remnant of an extinct volcano, filled with cliffs and caves. When Francesco gets stuck for an English word, Jack tells him I can translate and that my

Italian is better than his. The boys who were talking about me exchange a glance, but I don't let on that I heard them before. When I don't know a word, they all jockey to be the first one to make me understand, and then I translate it for Jack and Luca and Andrew. It's almost a party game, and we laugh over the misunderstandings and interpretations.

Then they talk football, as they call it. I'm beside Luca on the bench seat, his arm hanging over my shoulder, only chiming in to translate. When I reach forward for my drink, the strap of my bikini falls from my shoulder. Luca slips it into place in a single beat.

I turn to him. "Thanks."

I can't see his eyes behind his shades, but he gives me a short smile. "I got you, Herriot," he says, just loud enough for me to hear. For a moment, it seems like everyone else is far away, until Andrew's voice cuts through.

"You must be really good," he says to Jack and Francesco, "to have scholarships back in the States."

"Francesco helped me a lot when I got here," Jack says. "I just wish he were coming to Princeton with Story and me instead of going to UCLA." Jack looks over at me. "It's going to be a lot of fun."

"We should go explore before it gets too late," Luca says, standing suddenly and pulling me up. The rest of them agree and follow. Francesco's plan has us avoiding the eastern side of the island where most of the yachts anchor, and instead we go where there aren't a lot of people. We spend the afternoon snorkeling and swimming in various coves and beaches. Each spot feels different from the last. Some are sandy, while others are strewn with pebbles, and still others are a combination of the two. Sometimes we're all together with Jack's group, but we also split apart. Luca stays by my side as we snorkel and hike little trails near the beaches. Late in the day, Luca and Andrew and I are across a cove from the others when Luca grabs his sun shirt from the tender dinghy as we slip into the hip-high water.

"Your shoulders are turning pink," he says.

"Thanks."

"So, do you love it?" he asks, as he helps guide the too-big shirt over my head.

"Yes."

He pushes a damp clump of my hair back from my face. "Better than the Aventine Keyhole?"

"I don't know that I'd go that far."

He bites his lip in a smile and shakes his head. "Well, come on, then, I'll have to make it a little more fun."

"There are no paparazzi here," Andrew says as he wades past us.

"You don't know that," Luca says. He grabs me from behind in a hug and kisses my cheek, laughing. Andrew turns and gives him a serious look, like maybe he's taking this all too far. His warning not to fall for Luca crashes through my head like a baseball blasting a window to pieces. Luca and I stop laughing and follow Andrew toward the shore. Luca wants to check out a small cave, but I decide to heed Andrew's dark looks and wade over to a small tidal area while they go. I'm watching a group of reddish sea stars in the shade of a huge stone arch when Jack comes over.

"Look how cool these little guys are," I say.

We talk about sea stars, and the jellyfish Jack saw earlier. "Luca and I saw huge schools of fish swimming by those rocks over there," I say, pointing, "and it was like watching big flocks of birds all moving as if they were one big wave in the sky."

Jack reaches down to pick up a sea star. I put my hand on his arm. "Please don't, they're supersensitive, and you can give them bacteria."

Jack pulls back and smiles. "You really do love animals."

"How did you know that?"

"Ed, from school, told me."

I laugh. "Maybe Ed is the spy and not our Russian suspect."

He grins. "Maybe. He said you volunteer at a farm sanctuary in the summer. Hit me up anytime if you need extra hands."

I promised Luca not to be seen with Jack. And I really don't want to give the papers any more reason to talk about me. "I'm sure the farm would be happy for the help," I say, but the awkwardness of how I say it makes the words lose their meaning.

Jack's gaze sweeps the bay, and I feel like a total jerk for not being more appreciative. "This place is pretty awesome. I'm not sure we're going to be able to deal with plain old New Jersey after this."

"We'll probably be so busy studying, it won't matter."

Jack drops his smile. "Your boyfriend's really nice, Story. I'm sorry, I was wrong about him. He obviously cares about you."

I look up, feeling worse by the minute. Maybe someday I'll tell Jack the truth when we're at school and this is all over. But I can't imagine thinking about this moment and not being completely ashamed. His green eyes match the water. There's something really honest about Jack. Not like Luca. Or me, anymore.

"Thanks."

"I hope you don't mind that my friends and I crashed your party."

"Not at all. It's been really nice to have them show us all these places. That natural bridge was beautiful."

"They're pretty good guys."

Andrew and Luca are wading toward us. "Did you find any treasure?" I call. "Because I did."

Luca furrows his brow like he can't figure out what I mean. "See," I say, and point to the sea star colony.

"Oh, right," he says as he gets closer. He slips his arm around my waist. "Are you getting hungry? Andy, what's that ridiculous Rolex of yours say?"

"It's a little after eight," Andrew says, checking his giant watch that does everything except perform emergency surgery.

"I could definitely eat." I look at Jack. "Do you guys want to have dinner on our boat?"

He looks at Luca and me a moment and then sweeps his hand through his hair. "You know, I think we might actually be heading back soon. You guys go ahead, but thanks."

"I mean, you're welcome to join us, mannie," Luca says, but not with his usual ease.

"I think we're good. But thanks. I'll see you guys." Jack gives me one last glance before he wades across the inlet to catch up with his teammates. Luca draws his arm off my waist like a line retracting and takes my hand. "Come on," he says to Andrew and me, "I'm starving."

Andrew is watching me intently. I turn away and let Luca tow me slowly back to the deep water.

Sixteen

Back on the boat, the boys let me shower first, then we reheat pasta primavera they brought. We eat up on deck as the last of the sunset fades into the water. Somewhere out there, dolphins are settling in for the night, and I wonder when and how they sleep.

"So," Andrew says, "what are we going to do about Story's wardrobe problem?"

"Is it a problem?" I ask.

They exchange a look, like they don't know how to break it to me. "It just would be better," Luca says, "if we don't give the tabs anything to harass you about."

I'm not stupid. I understand what they're saying. But the solutions aren't as easy as they think they are. "So I'm supposed to be ashamed that I can't afford to spend thousands of dollars on a dress when there are kids in the world who are starving?"

Andrew chokes on his mouthful.

"Are you okay?"

"Aye," Andrew says between coughs. "You're just very direct."

"Take it as a compliment," Luca says without a smile. "She's only direct if she trusts you. Look, Story, you've seen the stuff they print. It might not be fair, but that's not going to stop them. And the quickest way to make them your enemy is to speak like that. They make their living by glamorizing our lifestyle."

I look around the boat. "I think you guys do a pretty good job of glamorizing your lifestyle all on your own."

Luca's jaw tightens. "I don't know why we should be ashamed of living well any more than you should be ashamed of living—less well."

"I don't have a problem with you living well. It's the complete imbalance between our worlds that bothers me, and the way your world wants to shame me for it when, if anything, it should be the other way around. I've never been poor by normal standards. But wasting huge sums of money on clothes when there's so much to be fixed in this world, it's too much for me."

They look at each other, and then Andrew settles his gaze on me. "Rich people give a lot of money to charity, Story."

"They do. But there wouldn't be tremendous poverty in the world if there weren't tremendous wealth. They don't exist on separate planes, Andrew. Society is a type of ecosystem, just like the natural world. When those with power tip the scales in their favor to create more wealth and power, someone further down the line gets harmed, whether it's intended or not."

Luca turns his limonata bottle around slowly. "She's not wrong," he says with a glance at Andrew.

"We don't create the world, Luca, we just live in it."

"We all create the world, Andrew. Some of us more than others." I'm only halfway through dinner, but my appetite is gone. I don't like being confrontational. I don't even know why I'm doing it, except that I'm angry with myself for this whole mess, and angry that spending my mom's hard-earned salary to buy a gorgeous dress isn't enough for people whose opinion of me I shouldn't need to care about. I'm doing this to get a scholarship for people their world can't even understand because when it happens in their world, people are treated differently than mine. Rowdy will be praised for going to rehab. My dad lost his law license.

"But it's people like your classmates, those girls, who buy the tabloids," Andrew says.

"Just because someone willfully participates against their own interests doesn't make it okay to take advantage of that. I guarantee you Guin and Kelsey have never thought about the impact of a click they made or a dollar they spent in their entire lives, but the people who are selling to them do."

"We're all afraid of them," Luca says, "but they keep us in power, so we keep them in business. They keep our brands and businesses flourishing by selling a dream most people will never taste. Hell, we don't even live that way. We sit here trying to run damage control and worry about how everything we do looks to a camera lens in the distance. We scrutinize every detail of our lives until we care more about what we're wearing than we do about seeing a colony of red sea stars."

We're quiet then. Luca noticing sea stars feels like a victory, but it doesn't make me happy. I push my food around on the plate and sneak a glance at him. He's staring at his limonata.

"Well, arguing about geopolitics isn't going to solve our problem," Andrew says.

Luca sighs. "Andy's right there, Stor. I mean, I actually like your"—he throws his hands around as if I'm something that can't be contained—"vintage totally-you style, but the point is that the tabs expect you to dress a certain way."

"What am I supposed to do? I don't have the money to live in your world, even if I wanted to wear thousand-dollar dresses." The breeze has cooled now that the sun is almost gone, and I shiver. Luca grabs his sweatshirt from behind him and hands it to me.

"Thanks."

"Luca can afford to buy the clothes you need," Andrew says. "I tried to warn Jasmine this was a bad idea from the start, but now that you're both in it, it's the only thing to do."

"So wait, this wasn't your idea?"

Luca's gaze darts up to mine.

"Actually, it was Jasmine's idea," Andrew says.

I don't know why I had just assumed this was all Luca's idea, but knowing it was Jasmine's makes me look at Luca a little differently. Maybe she didn't realize how much it would bother her for me to be held up to everyone as Luca's girlfriend. Or maybe she thought I'm so far beneath her she couldn't even feel jealous. Or maybe she's just a careless person, too selfish to realize the harm she causes others to get what she wants.

Whatever the reason, Luca must really care about her to have gone along with it, because he's still trying to protect me, too.

"Look, I get that in your world a credit card solves most problems, but that's not how it works in mine. My mom's going to want to know where these expensive clothes came from, and she's not going to be okay with me taking gifts like that, even if I were okay with it, which I'm not. I don't even know how I'm going to explain the scholarship to her yet. Plus, the paparazzi know I don't come from money. If they see Luca showering me with gifts, they're going to label me a gold digger. Or worse. Whatever I do, it's likely to turn out badly. Everyone's just going to have to accept that Luca is slumming for the summer. I mean, it's not even two months now. The sooner this is over, the better for all of us."

Luca is watching me intently. "The gold digger angle is a concern. I wish you'd worn the dress Jasmine sent you. Then they might not have thought about it."

"It didn't fit." I grip my fork tighter and try not to cry. This isn't what I agreed to. There's no way for me to explain that dress without sounding like I'm trying to be the star in an underbudget teen movie. She wants me to date Luca to cover for her, but she also wants me to look like an idiot doing it. I scrape up the last of my dignity. "I'll get a job. I won't be able to afford the clothes you expect me to wear, but I have some savings for school, and I can use that for now, and try to replenish it before I leave. I'll buy a few low-end designer pieces and mix and match them so it seems like it's more than it is."

"That's not right to do to you," Luca says. "What about your volunteer work?"

"And how are you going to show up with Luca to events if you have to work enough to afford designer clothes?"

I look out over the water. What Andrew's really trying to say is that the girls Luca dates don't scoop gelato or ring cash registers. They strut runways and stages.

"Maybe we should call the whole thing now. We've distracted the media from the Jasmine story, and she's off doing her thing. All you two have to do is not see each other outside of a hotel for six weeks or so. You can tell the tabloids I broke it off because I don't like being called a charity case. It would probably garner you a lot of sympathy. And then I can go back to being Astoria Nobody, and you and your Disney princess can sail into the sunset."

Luca looks hard at me and then gets up and walks to the rail. He's facing the water, but he turns his head halfway so that his profile is outlined by the dusk. "You aren't nobody."

"Just forget the donation." I wipe a tear from my cheek. "This whole thing was a mistake." In some ways, I guess I do envy her. Luca can be really thoughtful when he cares about you.

"I'm keeping my word on the scholarship," Luca says as he turns around. "But maybe you're right. It's actually been a lot of fun hanging with you, but I don't think it's fair to put you through this anymore. I can't believe I'm saying this, but I'm going to miss you, defensive sarcasm and all." He's looking at me as if my heart is encased in glass and he can see every fold of it. His phone is sitting on the bench beside me. It vibrates, and Jasmine's name flashes on the screen.

I get up and hand it to him without looking at him. Then I grab our plates and take them below. Andrew follows me.

"You know," he says as he stands beside me at the sink, "he never meant for any of this to get out of hand."

"I know. You don't have to play his fixer to me."

"Luca's right, Story. You aren't a nobody. You're actually pretty amazing, even if you do make minted guys choke sometimes."

"Thanks, Andrew." I can't look up at him.

He pats my head like I'm a good dog, and we finish cleaning up. When we go back on deck, Luca is sitting in the faint blue dark, staring at the water.

"Well, Jasmine should be happy," Andrew says. "She didn't enjoy seeing Story spending time with you."

"Actually, no," Luca says. "The press was asking her about me this morning. They keep asking why Rowdy isn't visiting her on tour, and they wanted to know if there was any truth to the rumors about us that were circulating right before my sudden deep dive into dating Story. They've been told Rowdy's in LA working on an album, but they want to know why no one's seen him."

"That's not good. At least for you and Jasmine. Story could still get out of this cleanly." Andrew says it like a warning, the way a parent tells you not to make a bad situation worse.

Luca looks at me. I can't really see his eyes in the darkness, but I feel them searching me. He clears his throat. "I was thinking, what about Dani?"

"Who's Danny?" I ask.

"My cousin," Andrew says. "She's a designer in London. She hasn't really had much success yet, she's just starting. How could Dani help this mess, Luca?"

"How many followers do you have now, Story?"

"I don't know. It was like forty-two thousand a few days ago."

"Forty thousand, Andrew. Dani could outfit Story, and Story could act as an influencer for her. It's a win-win. The paparazzi won't be able to criticize Story then, because she's getting her clothes from a sponsor based on her own following. And it helps Dani out."

Andrew's heavy breath gets carried away on the breeze. "I'm sorry, Luca. I think you should manage your own damage control on this one and leave Story out of it."

Luca has his elbows on his knees and drops his head down for a moment before looking back at us. "You're right. Forget it. I'll figure something else out." For a few moments, the only sound is the water lapping the boat.

When I do speak, my voice is smaller than I'd like it to be. "I'll do it."

They both look at me. "I really don't think this is a good idea," Andrew says.

"Probably not. But I agreed to help, so I will. Right now, though, I'm going to go raise the anchor. And if you don't want a hole in the boat," I add to lighten things up, "one of you should probably help me." The words are strong enough, but there's a sick feeling in my stomach, because this time I'm not just doing it for the scholarship. This time, I'm also doing it for Luca.

144

Seventeen

never meant to let Luca Kinnaird crawl into my heart. I'm
not in love with him, but, somehow, I feel connected to him,
responsible for him. Maybe carrying a secret together does
that to you. Or maybe it's the fact that he's sticking by his end
of the deal no matter what. Or maybe it's because, deep down,
he'd like to be a better person than he is.

Whatever the reason, I wake up the next morning with the
same heavy feeling that weighed on me the whole way home
last night. Andrew called his cousin from the car, and they
told her enough to get her on board, without telling her it was
all to protect Jasmine. "This way," Andrew had said, "if this
blows up and either of you lose influencer credit, she can claim
she had no idea and it's the truth." Whoever came up with the
tangled web analogy wasn't kidding.

Andrew gave me a mini tutorial on running social media
accounts, but I told him he could do it. The whole thing seems
like a colossal waste of time and energy. Besides, this will be

over soon. The sooner, the better. He says we have to be more regular about it if I'm going to be taken seriously as an influencer. I've never been a fan of social media, but strategizing to show a life that's anything but authentic makes me feel like I've joined the club in the worst way possible. It seems ridiculous that anyone will listen to me just because I supposedly date someone famous. When I look at the accounts of sports stars and musicians, though, their partners do become famous just by being with them if they aren't already celebrities. Although, people like Jasmine exist in their own sphere. The girl has well over three hundred million followers, and all she does is post pictures of herself that look the same. I don't get the fascination.

Luca is supposed to come for dinner at four, but he shows up at two. He's brought us a giant bouquet of flowers and a bunch of things my mom likes that he had Hodges go buy, like her favorite tea and biscotti al cioccolato. My mom gives Luca way more credit than he deserves, and he smiles smugly as if I'd challenged him that she wouldn't like him. Anyone looking in would think getting her good opinion actually mattered to him.

I show Luca around the flat. It's not very big, and we use the third bedroom as a guest room and office, so the tour takes all of five minutes. When we get to my room, Luca walks to the balcony door and looks over the courtyard. "I'm not sure you could hear me from down there, Juliet, unless I had a megaphone."

I laugh. "It's a good thing you won't need to make me any love speeches, then."

My guitar, which is sitting in its stand in the corner, catches his eye. "You didn't tell me you play."

"I figured your background check on me was more thorough than a CIA investigation."

"I did not run a background check on you. Although, clearly, I should have." He crosses to a wall of photos. "Is this your dad? You look like him."

I pad over and stand beside him. "Yes. And these are his parents. And this is my granddad from Maine."

"The one who would think my car is impractical?"

"Can you move a cow with it?"

"No."

"Then it is impractical. At least in Maine."

"Oh, wow, is that his farm? That's barry. It's right on the water, just like my parents' place."

He's pointing to my favorite picture of my granddad's farm. It just catches the edge of the white clapboard house beside the flower garden overlooking the bay, with the tattered old red barn off to the right. "The ocean's too cold to swim in, even in August, though people do."

Luca laughs. "Same, but we say Baltic." He catches my hand and fingers a silver band I wear with latitude and longitude marks engraved on it. "These coordinates are to your granddad's farm, aren't they?"

I nod. We just look at each other a moment, and then I turn, not even needing Andrew around to chastise me.

He runs his hand over my shelves, filled with books and a few old movies. "All classics."

"Were you expecting *Star Wars*?"

"No. But I suspect you have at least seen *Star Wars*."

"Some of them."

Luca pulls his phone from his pocket. "Andy says to check your latest posts."

"You mean his latest posts." I pull out my phone and open the photo app. My number of followers has jumped by at least three thousand since Andrew posted pictures of our sailing day, apparently because the tabloids somehow missed capturing our excursion, so there's a buzz of curiosity over it.

"What?" Luca asks when I just stare at it. "It's a good thing."

I shrug. "It was such a wonderful day, but somehow it doesn't seem like it's ours with all these people pawing at it."

"That's exactly how it feels. Welcome to celebrity-ville."

As I look at the posts Andrew has made, Luca suddenly grabs my hand. "Don't read the comments."

"Are they bad?"

"Not usually, but sometimes, aye. Most of the time, it's just a bunch of heart emojis or people saying stuff like what a cute couple we are or how much they love us."

"And when it is mean?"

"Nothing to believe," Luca says. "If you let strangers take up space in your head, Story, there won't be any room left in there for you."

"Isn't that the point, though, that we're doing this so that they'll say good things? How are we supposed to know if we're doing it right?"

"Andrew will keep an eye on it in case there's anything we really need to know. Most of it's out of our control. We put content out there, they get to choose whether they like it or not. Did you talk to Dani yet?"

I let him change the subject. "We FaceTimed. She has my measurements and address. She said she'd overnight some things."

"Well, that's one problem solved."

"Not exactly," I whisper. "I have no idea how I'm going to explain to my mom that her daughter is an overnight social media influencer with a new wardrobe. She's going to know I wouldn't agree to that normally."

Luca scratches his head. "Well, you can play up the angle that you're just helping Andrew's cousin out. That's not a lie. And maybe she won't think much about it. Maybe she won't question how many followers either of us has."

"I did tell her you're a little famous in celebrity circles, but she has no idea my picture is being splashed everywhere. She wouldn't be happy. She's more of a force protection, keep-it-under-wraps kind of person."

"Well, she does work for a state department. I'm not really famous outside of Europe, so that should help. There's famous, and then there's Jasmine famous."

I push my hands into my pockets. "You aren't chasing her because of how famous she is, right?"

"Wow. I knew you didn't think much of me, Story, but that's a bit lower than I realized."

"I'm sorry. I do think you like her. I just . . . I'm struggling to wrap my head around this celebrity stuff. And even you said it helps to be famous."

Luca gazes at me. "I'm not saying I've never dated any-one for the optics"—he pauses and tilts his head at me with a smile—"but that's not how this started out."

"It just seems like—" I stop because it really doesn't matter what I think.

"Like what?"

"You know, it's really not my business. I'm just going to shut up now."

Luca looks at me with a half smile playing about his lips. "While I do appreciate this momentous occasion, I'd still like to know what you were going to say."

I raise my eyebrows at his joke.

"Come on," he says with a bigger smile.

"I just wonder if it's her persona more than her. Because it seems like it's your Luca persona that likes her, and not the real you."

Luca's face slackens, and he just looks at me. I'm not sure if he's mad or surprised or what. My mom calls to us from the kitchen. We're out of gelato for the chocolate cake I made for dessert, so she sends us to get some. On the way down in the elevator, it feels as if there's an unspoken contract between us to let the conversation go, so we debate what flavors of ice cream to get instead. Out on the street, a paparazzo is hanging around Luca's car, and we wave to him as we walk by.

"We're just popping out for some gelato, mannie, but you're welcome to follow us if you think it's exciting," Luca says.

He answers something in German, and Luca laughs.

"What did he say?"

"Well, I don't know a lot of German, but I caught that. He said he hates his job."

We both laugh, and I feel kind of sorry for the guy as he drags along behind us to the gelato shop. When we get back, we run into Guin, Kelsey, and Alicia in the lobby.

I introduce them to Luca. They giggle like preteens. "I love your posts, you're soooo funny. We totally have to hang sometime," Guin says.

Luca smiles as he puts his arm around my neck. "I'm sure Story and I would love to if we get the chance. We always seem to be booked up, though I can never remember making the plans."

"Everybody at school just loves Story," Kelsey says.

"Yeah, she's the sweetest," Alicia adds.

"She is?" Luca asks. "I tend to think of her more as a fierce warrior type. You know, a ballbuster."

I crinkle my eyebrows together. "Thanks?"

"But in the absolute best kind of way," he adds with an inside smile.

"Barry," I say, and Luca laughs and pulls me in and kisses me. Not on the cheek, but a real kiss. Enough of a kiss that the softness of his lips and the scratch of his stubble sizzle on my skin. When he pulls back, neither of us is smiling. "Well, right," he says as he turns to the girls. "We'd better get this gelato upstairs before it melts. Nice to meet you."

They stand there awkwardly saying goodbye. As soon as our backs are turned, Guin half whispers, "Oh my God, he is waaay hot, but what the hell does he see in her?" Luca and I don't turn around, but he drapes his arm over me and kisses my temple, leaving his face pressed against me. His breath is sweet, like wintergreen. The elevator comes and we get in. As soon as the door closes, Luca lets go of me.

"I am so sorry, Story! I didnae mean to do that, I mean the way I did, I just wanted to teach those twits a lesson. I cannae stand how fake they are to you. I didnae mean to take advantage. I swear!"

My face has to be a violent shade of crimson from the way it's burning, and I can barely look at him. It's not that this was my first kiss, but it's up there on the list, and having it be a charity kiss is even worse than how the tabloids have made me feel.

"It's totally fine," I say, though the words come out stilted and sloppy as if they're a bunch of drunk guys careening down a street. "I was just surprised, that's all. It's not a big deal. Honestly. Like, just completely forget it." I'm waving my arm around like I'm in a *Saturday Night Live* skit. I need to go to some kind of composure school for the socially impaired.

"Story, I wouldnae ever want to do anything to disrespect you. You know that, right? I think you're incredible." He pulls me close. "You deserve someone incredible."

I look down so he can't see how hard it is for me to breathe. "It was just a silly kiss. I appreciate you trying to make me popular, but I never will be with those girls. I'm okay with that."

"Good, because they aren't even remotely worth you noticing them."

"I don't. It's cool. Everything's cool." I wish my cheeks and verbal stupidity and my out-of-control arm would stop making me an obvious liar. I am not cool. I've just been charity kissed by someone whose opinion I wouldn't have given two lattes for a month ago. And I can still feel his lips on mine.

He pulls away. "I cannae believe those fandans actually think they're better'n you!"

I appreciate he's mad enough to slip into his home accent, but it doesn't make me any less mortified. The elevator doors open. I make an awkward gesture that we should go. I don't have any choice but to act naturally around my mom, which helps calm me down. Luca goes into full Luca-on-parade mode. He couldn't be more charming, or sweeter to me, and he has my mom under his spell a lot faster than even I expected. I learn things about him, like that he knows how to fence and ride horses, which prompts me to some more "Yes, my lord," comments. He and my mom laugh, although she tells me not to be rude. He's on the crew team at university, and he played soccer in high school. His favorite color is green, and he hates coconut. Occasionally, I catch him slipping into just being Luca, and, to me at least, that's when he's at his most charming.

My mom suggests a walk after dinner, but I don't even need

to give Luca a warning glance. Instead, he asks about a pile of board games on a shelf in the living room, and we end up playing a game set in Colonial Williamsburg, which my mom wins. Luca is just competitive enough to make it funny, and it's the first time in a while that my mom and I have done something like this. It's going to be really strange to be so far away from her in the fall. Having Luca in my life has dramatically increased the joy factor, surprisingly. But there are too many expiration dates looming over me, and they're getting all blurred together.

After we play, I suggest we watch a movie and Luca gets to choose since he's the guest. He picks out *Roman Holiday*.

"Story loves this movie," my mom says.

He smiles at me. When the scene at the Bocca della Verità comes on, Luca tells her I took him there.

"Mmmm, of course she did," she says. Not long after, my mom goes off to bed, but Luca stays and watches the whole film. He seems particularly drawn to the Audrey Hepburn character, and not just because she was the most beautiful woman who probably ever lived. He asks me multiple times if they get to be together in the end, but I tell him he has to keep watching.

"Imagine if she had the paparazzi we have now?" he says, scrunched against me on the sofa as if he's forgotten we don't have an audience. Or maybe we're both so used to acting that he hasn't even noticed. It took me a while. "She'd never be able to get away with hiding out like this."

"I suppose not. Is that what you wish you could do, hide

out? Are you tired of being famous?" I sound pretty snarky, but Luca doesn't seem to hear it.

"Sometimes," he says. "Sometimes I wish my life were more like yours."

I practically snort because the thought of Luca being like me is so preposterous, but he's serious. "Well, I can't even go to the bookstore with a classmate now, so, I guess I can understand."

He turns to catch my gaze. "I'm sorry about that. You know he has a thing for you?"

"Jack? No. He's just being nice because we're going to the same college."

"Story, dai, as you say."

I ignore him and keep my gaze on the television.

We're silent then. The romantic part comes where Princess Ann and Joe Bradley have to say goodbye because they come from two completely different worlds. I guess things haven't changed that much since 1953. Different worlds are still different worlds, even if they aren't different in quite the same way.

"Well, that's sad," Luca says as Gregory Peck walks out after seeing Ann for the last time. "You didn't tell me I was going to need tissues." He's not really crying, but he also isn't exactly joking. "I pictured you as the happy ending type."

"Life isn't always happy. Sometimes, it has to be enough just to get what you need. She needed to satisfy her curiosity about what she was missing in the world, and he needed to learn how to love."

Luca purses his lips a moment. "Sounds a little too much like us, doesn't it?"

I hesitate because suddenly I'm not so sure. "I don't know about you, but I was fine missing out on the world, at least your version of it. Maybe you're thinking of Guin."

Luca chuckles and checks the time on his smartwatch. "I should go." He pulls me up from the sofa after him. I walk him to the door. He takes my hand and shakes it.

"Why are you being so formal?" I ask with a laugh.

"I'm trying to make up for earlier. I just want you to know that I think exceptionally highly of you, Astoria Herriot. And your mom."

I nod stupidly, right back in the zone of mortification.

"Good night, sweet Story."

"Good night, Luca."

I close the door behind him and listen as his footsteps head toward the elevator. I had never even wondered about missing out on the world Luca lived in before I met him, but now he's making me think there are parts of it that may haunt me long after the two of us have gone our separate ways.

Eighteen

The next morning, I rise and shine and take the metro and then a bus to get to the farm sanctuary. It's a quaint little respite on the outskirts of the city. Sycamores line the drive to the old terra-cotta-colored house that serves as offices now. Plum trees and flowering vines welcome visitors, with a stone barn and a small potting shed behind the car park and house. Three black-and-white cats sun themselves on benches and the edge of a small fountain in the garden beside the house. Bright red and purple flowers line the pathways between the buildings.

They've moved some things around since I was here last, and Elisa, the manager, updates me. She's in her early thirties, with a mass of black curly hair and some subtle crow's-feet from being in the sun too much. Afterward, I go to the barn and feed the mignon ducks, who are always happy to see anyone, and then rake the stalls. It's not Maine, but it feels close enough for now.

Around eleven, Luca texts. *Andy wants to have lunch. Can you come to the hotel?*

I'm at the farm. I won't be back until two, and that's without a shower.

Oh. Right.

I go back to brushing a little white Romagnola calf, Fabrizio. My phone vibrates, and Fabrizio shakes his head at me. Even he knows I'm in way deeper than I should be.

How do you get there? You don't have a car.

I take the metro, and a bus, and then I walk the last three quarters of a mile. You've heard of public transportation, right?

Hilarious as you say. When are you done?

One.

No dots pop up on my screen. Fabrizio is pushing on me to brush him as he tries to chew my hair. He's so cute, I wish I could take him back to Maine, where I could at least visit him sometimes. But he's another fleeting attachment to Rome that I can't really afford.

Maybe spending all this time with Luca is making me realize I'm not quite the loner I've always imagined myself to be. Or maybe I'm just being soft about everything because I have to make another fresh start, this time without my mom there to be my security blanket. Whatever is going on with me, it seems like there's a lot more danger than reward to making friends.

When I finally check the time, it's twenty past one. Luca and I are scheduled to go to some gallery tonight for a photography show, so I need to get home. I walk back to the barn and hear Elisa talking in English to someone. "She's probably here," she says. I round the corner and run into Luca and her.

"Hey, I wasn't expecting you," I say.

"I thought I'd give you a ride back to town. It sounded like a long trip what with all the walking and the bus and the metro and the uphill both ways."

"I wasn't complaining, just explaining."

Luca turns to Elisa and thanks her.

"Certo, it was a pleasure to meet you. Ci vediamo domani, Story."

"Sì, ciao, ciao."

Luca and I walk to the car park.

"So you came all this way just to give me a ride?"

He nods.

"I thought you were spending the afternoon video-chatting with Jasmine."

He shrugs. "I called her on my way out here instead," he says. "You know how to drive, right?"

"I've driven orchard and row-crop tractors since I was nine. You?"

"I forgot a farm girl would learn to drive early. Well, in Scotland, the legal age is seventeen, but my dad started teaching me around our place when I was thirteen."

"Explains your mad skills."

Luca laughs as we reach the Portofino. "I didn't think you liked my driving."

"I'm getting used to it."

He hands me the key fob.

"You want me to drive the Ferrari?"

"Why not?"

"This car is really expensive. I think you should drive." I push the fob back into his hand.

"You have a license, right?"

"International and US. My mom's very big on being independent."

"Well, then?"

"I've never driven anything this fancy. What would your parents say if I got into an accident?"

"Something like 'Why did you let a commoner drive the Ferrari?'"

"See!"

"I'm joking. They'd say, 'Well, at least you weren't driving, or it probably would've been worse.' Plus, it's my uncle's car."

"Wait, have you had accidents before?"

"You ask a lot of questions, you know that? Let's just go."

I hesitate, but he seems serious.

"Okay, but I haven't driven much in Rome, so I won't be zipping around like you do."

"Noted," he says, and walks over to the driver's side and opens the door for me. "By the way, you smell like a cow."

"I know, isn't it heavenly? All your model and diva girlfriends would be jealous if they knew."

He laughs and pushes me to get in.

I'm expecting the car to have a lot of power, but I still jerk us out of the parking space, which Luca finds extremely funny.

I look over at him, and we both say, "It's not a tractor." Once

I get the sensitivity of the pedals, though, it's not bad. "Except for Christmas back home and a couple of Vespa trips, I haven't driven since we lived in Zagreb."

"I've never been there. What is Astoria Herriot's must-see weird attraction for Zagreb?"

I don't even hesitate. "The Museum of Broken Relationships."

Luca looks at me skeptically.

"It's a whole museum dedicated to failed love. How could you not?"

"You are so dark sometimes. It scares me."

I laugh. "Well, from a statistical standpoint, it's just practical. Seriously, though, why did you pick me up? Have I sent the tabs on another spiral? Or were you just afraid the paparazzi might catch your girlfriend riding the metro and smelling like cows?"

"As far as I know, you haven't done anything *new* that requires damage control. But I'll admit the idea of them calling me out for letting my girlfriend go through an expedition-level trek to volunteer someplace was my first thought. Then I thought it's just something a friend does for another friend." He smiles at me, and I turn my gaze back to the road. He really shouldn't smile like that. Although, I guess he can't help how he smiles.

"Why didn't you just send Andy to fetch me?"

"I suppose I could have asked him," Luca says casually before he shoots me a mischievous smile. "But where's the fun in that?"

I turn my attention back to the road and try to ignore the flutter in my stomach. He should really rein in his charm, but I don't think he can help himself. It's just who he is. I carefully snake us through an S curve in the rolling green hillside. Luca reaches over and points to the gas pedal.

"That one will move you forward," he says, a laugh waiting on his lips.

"You can drive if you like."

He just smiles and shakes his head.

"Well, thanks for coming to get me, but it's not necessary. If the paparazzi call you out, just tell them I'm used to being independent."

"Story, I know none of this was on your agenda a few weeks ago, but it really would be best to make them happy." He isn't laughing anymore. "The less you give them to write about, the better, if that's your goal. Most people have the opposite goal."

He's right. "Message received. And it's not that I mean to sound like a martyr. Some of this life you lead is pretty surreal, like the yacht, and traipsing around the Italian countryside in this car. Getting a ride is definitely better."

"So, I'm hearing you might be getting used to my world, as you call it?"

I glance over and he seems almost as if he wants me to say yes.

"No," I say, as much to convince myself as him. "I won't ever belong in your world."

"Right," he says and drops the subject as he hijacks my seventies playlist.

When we get back to my flat, the box that Dani has over-nighted is waiting for me in the lobby. Luca texts Andrew to come over, and I leave Luca puttering around the living room. After a shower, I open the package, worried it's theoretically possible the clothes she sent could be worse than the witch of Salem bog dress Jasmine wanted me to parade around in. Thankfully, it's better than I expect. She's sent a sundress, a ruched floral silk cocktail dress, a short pencil skirt, a pair of cropped pants, and three tops. None of it's something I would pick for myself, but it's at least not some nod to eighties' punk or the millennial whale tail. I throw my hair up into a loose bun so I don't have to dry it, fluff on the little bit of makeup I wear, and choose the cocktail dress, hoping it's appropriate for a gallery opening, since Luca said he needs to grab a suit from his hotel. The dress has a fairly deep V cut, though, and I go through most of my bras trying to find one that doesn't show.

When I emerge from my bedroom turned fashion den, Andrew and Luca are on the sofa watching *Charade.*

"Hey, this one is pretty good, too," Luca says as he hears me pad over.

"Well?" I ask. "Am I properly elite now?"

They look up then and nod and clap as if I were on a fashion runway.

"You two are so funny."

"You look brilliant," Andrew says. "Except you need to lose that look on your face."

Luca squints a bit. "Stor, you do kind of look like you've got thong underwear riding up."

I throw him a disgusted look before I take a deep breath and plaster on a fake smile. "Better?"

"It'll do," Andrew says. "You don't have to be a professional model, just exude confidence like you're sure you're wearing the greatest thing possible."

"That's pretty much what professional models do. I don't like people looking at me. And this isn't really my style." I almost blush as I say it, afraid to move and fall out of what little coverage the dress provides.

"Andy's right, Stor. You've got to sell it. You look great. You just have to know that and it'll show."

"Well, I'm not doing any stupid poses."

They look at each other as if I'm two and just declared I'm not eating my carrots.

"No stupid poses," Andrew says. "Just you in front of some landmarks or something that looks super Romey."

"Romey?"

"Elegant and cosmopolitan, okay?" Andrew spreads his hands to ask me to give him a break.

"And I'm not doing selfies in front of bathroom mirrors. That's gross."

"Real influencers don't do that, only regular people," Andrew says.

Luca narrows his eyes. "How do you know that?"

"I checked," Andrew replies, "because someone has to."

Luca leans his head back to catch my gaze. "He's angling for a salary."

"Can Luca be in the pictures with me? I really don't want to do this alone."

"Sure," Luca says before Andrew can stop him. He wraps his hand around my fingertips. "It's the least I can do." He seems genuinely contrite, and it makes me feel guilty for complaining, when he's been so nice. I need to focus.

"And they can't be anything that's going to embarrass me out of a fellowship or getting into law school or something. I don't know what I'm doing with my life, but it's sure not this."

"Noted," Luca says, the way he always does when I try to put my foot down.

As long as I'm being treated like a child, I add one more thing. "And can we get something to eat? I'm starving."

Nineteen

We stop at the boys' hotel on the way to dinner. Hodges is just bringing the suit Luca wants to wear back from the cleaners. "It's lovely to see you again, Miss Story."

"Thank you, Hodges, it's nice to see you, too."

"Thank you, miss, for the bookstore gift card. It was most thoughtful of you, but not necessary."

"I appreciate you always making sure I'm on top of all this chaos."

He smiles and nods before he disappears with Luca to do whatever guys like him do.

"You make a ghastly rich person," Andrew says as he throws himself onto the sofa, legs outstretched.

I sit in a chair beside him and whisper, "I'm not really rich, you know. At least by your standards."

"Really?" he says, fighting off a smile. "You had me completely fooled."

"Besides, this way I stay connected to my people for when all this ends and Cinderella has to crawl back to her unlit hearth." I say it lightly, but Andrew looks at me as if all the ways this experience could spoil my happiness have just occurred to him.

"Story—" he says as he sits up, but Luca comes out, and I shake my head for Andrew to let it go.

Luca takes us to an early dinner at a tiny restaurant my mom and I love on Via Urbana. It's so early, we're the only people there, but we still ask for a table in the back.

"This place is nice," Andrew says as we sit down, chairs scraping.

"Wait till you taste the food."

The place has a trendy, modern feel that would be considered cosmopolitan in any city. Luca relaxes in a way I haven't seen at another restaurant, I guess because there's no audience. A trio of older women come in before we finish, but they sit in the front and people-watch through the windows, so we're alone except for the waiter.

"I think we should talk strategy," Andrew says.

"Can we just not?" Luca asks. "For one meal, anyway. The situation is under control."

Andrew pulls his lower lip in but doesn't argue. When I order an eggplant dish, Luca asks the waiter if they can make it vegan for me.

"Yes, of course, signorina," the waiter says.

"Grazie," I say, and give Luca an appreciative glance. When I turn my gaze back to the room, Andrew is watching us. It makes me self-conscious, as if I've overstepped some boundary listed in the fake-girlfriend codebook.

After dinner, we drive up to the Villa Borghese gardens and walk around. Andrew takes photos of us by some of the statues and follies. We manage to agree that the ones at the Temple of Aesculapius give off the most who-wouldn't-want-to-be-us vibes, so Andrew chooses those, and Luca takes a selfie of us with a tree-lined avenue in the background. Luca's followers have increased substantially since he decided to date an ordinary girl.

"Everyone's waiting to see the crash," Andrew says.

Luca suddenly spins me around like we're dancing. Andrew whips his phone back out for photos.

"I'll set these to post tomorrow morning," he says. "That way, the tabs get their scoop on Story's wardrobe tonight and won't be angry."

"I never realized how complicated dressing could be. I mean, at least since the Victorian era."

Luca laughs and puts his arm around my neck and kisses my temple, but Andrew gives me a dry look. A couple of girls around fourteen approach us. They recognize Luca and ask for a picture with him. I smile at Andrew that we aren't worth being asked, but Luca tells them they can have the picture if I'm in it, too.

"That's okay," I say, but Andrew discreetly shakes his head at me, so I glom on to Luca.

"What was that about?" I ask when the girls have gone.

"I don't want to be in pictures alone with underage girls," Luca says. "People could get the wrong idea."

"Gotcha," I say, but it's another price to fame I hadn't thought about.

"We're going to be late if we don't get going," Andrew says, and Luca holds my hand as we walk back to the car.

A swarm of paparazzi buzz outside the gallery, which is opening a show by a UK photographer whose work is mostly of African wildlife. We stop to let the tabs take their pictures on our way in, and a woman calls out, "Who are you wearing, Astoria?"

From a cluster of paparazzi, someone yells, "Old Navy?" I think it's the German guy Luca teased outside my flat. They all laugh. Someone in the back calls, "Walmart?" They can barely contain themselves, relaxing their cameras as they giggle.

For a moment, it feels like someone has punched me, and I can't smile. Then I square my shoulders and lightly toss back, "Dani Meadows." I say it with confidence, as if they surely know her name. They look at each other uncertainly. It feels good, like watching Patrick stand with his mouth open as Luca whisked me away from school the day we made our pact. Luca has his arm around me, and he pulls me a little closer. "Welcome to the Premier League, Herriot," he whispers through smiles.

"Do I get my own jersey?"

"Bloody hell, yes!"

He turns me, and Andrew opens the door for us. There are

a lot of British people, including the UK ambassador, and she introduces me to the photographer, Rishi Patel. Of course he already knows Luca. He's in his late twenties, with the handsome rough-and-tumble look of a guy who would do shaving cream commercials if he weren't a wildlife photographer. Rishi asks me which photos are my favorite when I compliment his work.

"It's so hard to choose," I say, and he seems to take that as a sign I haven't really looked, as he nods complacently.

"I love the one of the giraffe mother and baby. I'm leaving for college soon, and it makes me think of my mom and me. I'm already missing her, and that photo has the same kind of love in it, the way the mother is bending to touch her face against her baby's. And the subtle colors of pink and blue in the one of the flock of storks is gorgeous. It feels surreal and peaceful even though there's so much activity with all of them wading in the water. But I think my favorite is the zebras on the beach by the waves. That one makes me believe in all the beauty of unexpected things. I can't imagine what it would be like to see that sight in person."

When I stop, Luca is watching me intently. A hot flush spreads across my face. "Sorry," I mumble. I look down and push back a strand of hair that's escaped my sloppy bun.

Rishi laughs. "Please, don't be sorry. We live for someone to care about our work. How you describe the zebras is exactly how I feel when I look at it, too."

I catch his gaze, and I don't think he's making fun of me.

He seems genuinely happy to be appreciated, even if it is from a girl who gushes like a nerdy twelve-year-old.

"Story brings a unique perspective to everything," Luca says. "It's one of my favorite things about her." He slips his hand onto my hip and pulls me closer, nestling me against his side.

"I see that," Rishi says. "You should keep this one, Luca."

"Thanks," I say, not sure how much either of them really means what they say. Luca gives me a shrug.

A couple comes over to talk to Rishi, and we slip away to wander around the exhibit some more. I stop in front of a photo of two cheetah cubs. They're playing, but also hiding from the great and terrifying world, half-hidden beside a boulder. Luca's fingers are intertwined with mine, and he stops when I do.

"And what does this one make you think of?" he asks.

"Us."

He scoffs. "Us? Why?"

"Look at their faces. They want to just be themselves, but they have no idea how to do that in the world they've been given."

Luca studies the photograph. He absent-mindedly rubs his thumb against the back of my hand. "You know, Story," he says, so quietly it's almost a whisper, "sometimes I think you're the only person who sees me as more than Luca Kinnaird, the brand."

He looks down at me and smiles a little.

"Maybe you need to stop worrying about being a brand, and just be Luca."

He searches my eyes for a long moment until Andrew pops up behind us. "You two are going to get an Academy Award if you keep going on like this."

We break apart. "Let's get out of here," Luca says.

When we emerge from the gallery, he's quieter than usual. We stroll to a gelateria and then to a little park nearby before they take me home, paparazzi in tow.

In the morning, Luca takes me to the farm. It's rained overnight. The roads and trees are still sparkling. We're a bit late because we have to stop and get Luca tea and pastries to keep him awake, and Elisa tells him he's welcome to stay and help if he wants.

"I can't today, but I will when I bring Story on Friday." He's flying to Nice to have a secret brunch with Jasmine. It's the first time they've seen each other since she started her tour. I told him he didn't have to bring me this morning so he could get an earlier start, but he'd said we should keep to appearances to be consistent.

I laugh as I get out of the car. "Who is this masked aristocrat so ready to help?"

Luca gives me his dangerous smile. "Hilarious. I can be useful sometimes. I'll be back at two-thirty. Three at the latest." He sends me an air-kiss and takes flight.

Later, when I come back to the office at the end of the day, four Vespas are stationed across the road from the entrance to the sanctuary, each with a paparazzo. I sigh. Elisa and Ferdy, a ranch hand in his sixties, are standing outside the office, watching the spectacle. I walk over to them.

"I'm sorry, they're here for me."

"For you, Story?" Elisa asks, because I'm obviously not the kind of person people follow around with cameras.

"Well, really for Luca," I explain. "He's a bit famous in the celebrity magazines."

They nod and say, "Ahhhhh."

"Well," Elisa says as she smiles and waves to them, "maybe they'll write about us, and people will make donations."

"I hope so," I say.

Luca comes swooping in, tires crunching on the fine gravel that lines the driveway. "Ciao," he says. He seems happy, so I guess his reunion was all he had hoped it would be. The thought is like a sting to me, but it's just because I don't really like the girl. He could do so much better.

"Buongiorno," Ferdy and Elisa say.

Ferdy smiles at me. "È una bella macchina ma non puoi trasportare una mucca dentro," he says.

I laugh. "Sì, sì, Ferdy. Ciao, a venerdì."

They say goodbye as I hop in the car. Luca makes a circle.

"Can you go slow by the sign? I want to make sure the paparazzi get it in the background."

He smiles at my sudden willingness to be photographed for a good cause and then rolls the Portofino past the gate. The paparazzi shoot their photos as we drive away.

"What did that guy say that was so funny?" Luca asks.

I grab my glecks from the console where I leave them and smile as I slip them on. "He said it's a beautiful car, but you can't move a cow with it."

Twenty

On the way back to Rome, Luca fills me in on the success of our latest PR heist. Dani's followers have increased substantially, and she's gotten some trial orders from a store in London. Another small chain she already has a line with is expanding her collection.

"Wow, just from the tabloids and us posting those pictures from last night?"

"I told you social media is powerful. Just remember, it giveth and it taketh away."

"I'd be just as happy if it had never giveth to me, but at least it's helped Andy's cousin."

Andrew meets us back at my flat and brings lunch. After I've showered and changed, we sit on the floor of the living room and finish watching *Charade* while we eat spinach pie and fruit cups and they plan out which outfits I should wear as if they were YouTube stylists.

"This is getting too weird for me. Can you two just—not—"

They both laugh. Luca says to Andrew, "I think she's got this."

Dani texts me. *I can't believe this! I'll send you some more outfits.*

Please, no wide pants. I'm too short.

Gotcha. What is your style?

Don't worry, it's old school.

Tell me.

1950s Givenchy and a little boho.

OMG, I love that stuff. Audrey Hepburn was a queen. I can work with that.

I send her thumbs-up and winking emojis. The intercom buzzes. When I answer it, a woman says in Italian that she has a delivery for me. No one ever sends me packages, so I can't imagine what it is, but Luca offers to go down for it. That's when I remember the swamp dress is still shoved under my bed, so I grab it while he heads downstairs. When I bring the box out, I ask Andrew to make sure they take it with them.

"What is it?"

"The dress Jasmine sent me for the gala. I keep forgetting to give it to him when my mom isn't here."

Andrew comes over and lifts the lid. When he pulls the dress up, his mouth drops open.

"Don't tell Luca. He thinks she was being nice. Just give it to her stylist."

He lowers it back into the box and puts the lid on like he's burying something frightening.

"It really didn't fit," I say, which is more defense than she's entitled to.

"She's every guy's dream and all, but honestly." He shakes his head. "She's my least favorite of all the girls he's dated."

"She won't be the one he ends up with anyway. It will be some bluestocking heiress who runs carpool like a boss and a dinner party like Amal Clooney."

Andrew laughs, but then he doesn't. "Story, I'm worried about how close you two are getting. I don't want you to get hurt. You're a nice person, despite your proletarian proclivities."

"Such flattery, Andrew," I say with a Southern accent, "I declare you will make me swoon." He gives me a tentative smile. "Don't worry," I add in my normal voice, "I solemnly swear not to become too attached to Luca Kinnaird. We're friends. Without benefits, unless you count riding around in a Portofino." Besides, even if I wanted to be more than friends, which I don't, Jasmine is the girl he's chasing. Just like Patrick said, guys like Luca don't date girls like me. I'm just someone he's gotten used to, like that Pomeranian in a backpack I thought I'd be.

Andrew nods, apparently satisfied.

Luca comes back with an enormous box.

"What on earth?" I ask. It's from the gallery. When I open the box, it's the three prints I gushed about to the photographer. "Luca—"

He cuts me off. "I had to buy something to support Rishi, so you should have some souvenirs of this ridiculous adventure. Something besides that new wardrobe you don't really want."

I throw my arms around him. "Thank you!"

He squeezes me before he lets me go.

"He bought himself one, too. A photo of some cheetah cubs," Andrew says.

I blush, and then Luca says we're missing the whole plot of *Charade,* and we go back to watching the movie, Andrew wedged between us like a chaperone.

Afterward, they put the swamp dress in Luca's car before my mom comes home. They stay for dinner. Luca has promised Saga, his Swedish model friend, that we'll come to some club tonight, but he seems reluctant to leave. Even I know you don't go to clubs in Rome before midnight, but it's after twelve when Andrew reminds him for the third time that we should go.

The club is in Trastevere, which is the most bohemian of Rome's neighborhoods, with lots of trendy nightlife. For once, Luca doesn't have to take my hand because I've already grabbed his before we've even gotten through the door. I've always hated crowds, but it was never a problem before Luca came into my life, since I just avoided them. The club is huge. Each floor has a different theme, and the place is packed.

We snake our way through the first floor as a deejay pumps electronic dance music to sweaty people jumping up and down like elastic dolls. I stick so close to Luca, I can smell the lavender laundry detergent of his honey-colored T-shirt. A few people grab him to say hello as we go by, but you'd need a megaphone to actually talk. The bass thumps inside me as we reach the stairs.

The second floor is delivering hip-hop to the dance-hungry inhabitants, who slosh their drinks around and scream, but their words are lost beneath the vibrating amplifiers. The girls wear very small dresses. Puddled makeup and disheveled hair complete the look. Luca reintroduces me to some people I met the night of the Jamie Talon concert, but we keep moving. I recognize some American actors at the bar, but there are people from all over the globe dressed in their designer finest.

We finally make our way to the rooftop garden, and it's a thousand times cooler and quieter, even though summer in Rome is never cool and Italian pop music is blasting. Baby K is on the dance floor with an entourage, as the deejay plays her latest hit. We find Saga and her friends. She pulls me into a hug, but I don't entirely let go of Luca. I've been clinging so tightly to him that he turns and asks if I'm all right.

"Fine." He gives me a sympathetic smile and drapes his arm around me. I lean into him, and this time it isn't for show. Being in this crowd has made me realize just how much I hate them. I refuse to look at Andrew in case he's sending me warning shots, and he hovers close on my other side. Saga squeezes in between Andrew and me. She's wearing a metallic gold dress and she looks absolutely gorgeous. "Isn't this place great?" she yells.

"Awesome," I say, with as much fake excitement as I can muster. Luca pulls his lips in to hide a smile.

"We should go shopping together tomorrow," she yells. "I'll get Luca to send me your number and I'll text you!" Her blue eyes are almost as glittery as her makeup.

There's no way I can afford even the cheapest item for sale in any store where this girl shops, but, despite my many lessons at the Luca Kinnaird School of Social Event Avoidance, I can't think of an excuse.

"Brilliant!" I say instead.

Luca starts laughing. He pulls me back a bit and rests his lips on my ear. "Don't worry. She's steamin'. She won't remember by tomorrow."

Andrew gets us drinks from the bar. He hands Luca a bottle of beer and me a glass of something clear with lime.

"I figured you'd prefer sparkling water, but I can get you something else if you want," he says before he takes a swig of his beer. I just shake my head. We talk to Saga and her friends for a while.

Luca drops his head toward mine. "I'd ask you to dance, but the floor is pretty tight."

"It's fine, honestly."

"I figured you'd rather stay here." We've managed to nudge our way to the edge of the balcony. Below us, the river sparkles from city lights. There's an occasional breeze to keep us cool, and Saga tells me all about her school in Lund and her modeling and her horses.

"Do you want another?" Andrew asks us, pointing to our drinks.

"No, I'm good," Luca says. "Story?"

I shake my head.

"Saga, let's dance first," Andrew says. He grabs her hand, and she follows him to the floor. Luca and I watch them.

"They make a cute couple," I say.

Luca smiles. "Saga would decimate him. Her last boyfriend was a Qatari prince, and the one before that was a French billionaire venture capitalist. The one before that was a girl."

I smile. "And to think we max him out."

Luca laughs and takes a swig of my water. Saga's friends talk to Luca about soccer. I just lean into him, the cotton of his shirt soft against my cheek. They're pretty drunk, and most of what they say just rolls into nothingness. Then a guy in the group named Emile takes out a small vial and starts offering pills to everyone. I don't know if they're Molly or opioids or what, but it doesn't matter. Every muscle goes stiff. The worst is that I'm not entirely sure Luca won't accept, until he doesn't. I can hardly breathe.

"One of these days," Emile says in accented English, but Luca just looks at him. My pulse is pounding in my ears.

When Emile offers me one, I say no, but no sound comes out. It's just my lips moving. "Come on," he says, "it's good stuff."

"No," I say, this time with shaking sound.

"Leave her alone, min," Luca says. He pushes Emile's hand away from me.

"It's just some fun," Emile says. "Go on, have one!"

"Please stop," I say.

"What's wrong with her?" Emile asks Luca. "You'd think she just got out of convent school for the night."

Luca's arm is still draped over me, and he has a strand of my hair wrapped around his finger. It tightens. "That's not funny."

"It's hilarious," Emile says. "Look at her face. She looks like she's seen a ghost!"

Luca releases me and steps close to Emile. "Nothing's wrong with her, you tadger. Apologize to her."

Andrew runs off the dance floor and gets between them. Tears sting my eyes.

"Let it go," Andrew says as Emile and Luca stare at each other.

"I didn't think you went for choir girls, Luca," Emile says. "Or doesn't your slum rat know how to have fun?"

Luca's fist comes up, but Andrew pushes him. It's just enough for Luca to regain control.

He steps back and scoops up my hand. "Let's go." He turns and makes a wake for me to follow. Andrew trails behind us, as Saga yells at Emile that he's a jerk and someone else defends him. We thread our way back through the throng of people down to the street. Paparazzi take our photos, but they don't follow us. There are bigger fish in the club.

When we're clear of them, Luca stops. "You okay?"

I nod, my eyes glistening. "I'm really sorry."

He hugs me. "You have nothing to be sorry about. That guy would push drugs on his grandmother. I don't care what they do to themselves, but they don't have any right to manipulate other people into it." He wipes a tear from my cheek.

"He really is a bawbag," Andrew says.

"I shouldn't have taken you anywhere near that jerk." Luca squeezes me to him.

"It's not your fault. People who use want everyone to use. It makes it seem okay to them then. It justifies it."

He shakes his head. "I hoped that since the club would be crowded, it'd be okay. Saga is sweet, it's just some of the people she attracts. I wanted you to have a good time. Now you'll never want to go clubbing again."

"Well, maybe I should take you two clubbing instead?" They both look at me like I couldn't possibly be serious.

"I mean it." I sound like I'm eight.

Luca purses his lips in a smile and holds his key fob up for me to grab. "Lead on."

I drive us back toward Via Veneto to a club Anna Maria has taken me to a couple of times. It's more of a piano bar, really, but it's popular with the university crowd.

Anna Maria is with a group of friends at some tables near the small stage. She waves us over when she sees me. She introduces everyone, and one girl asks Luca if he's "the" Luca Kinnaird. I worry she might say something about the tabloids in front of Anna Maria, but there's too much commotion, and she doesn't. They pull up chairs for us while a trio plays jazz and soft Italian pop. The tables are strewn with Italian bar food like Pecorino with acacia honey and fried clams. They're making fun of the Italian government, and those who speak English switch to it for us, and the rest is a jumble of translation and laughing.

"Story tells me you've been taking her to all the most fun places in Roma," Anna Maria says to Luca.

"Actually, it's the other way around. I take her to all the exclusive places, and she takes me to all the fun ones."

Anna Maria smiles. "She's great, isn't she? It's so nice to finally meet you."

"She is great," Luca answers.

"She's right here," I say. "She can hear everything you're saying."

"We can be more critical, if you like," Luca says.

Anna Maria laughs and asks if he speaks German.

"Not really. Just French."

"Ah, my papa is from Francia," she says. "Now we can talk about her!"

"Tell me what she says about me," Luca says. The two of them dive into an animated conversation. I catch my name sometimes, but mostly I sit between them as if I'm watching a tennis tournament. I need to put French on my language-learning app. I look over at Andrew. "Do you know what they're saying?"

He shakes his head with way too much innocence. "Traitor," I say.

"I like this boy," Anna Maria tells me.

I try to think of some way to prepare her for our coming split without sounding like a total jerk, but I can't. When the band takes a break, they all come over and squeeze in with us because the drummer, Silvano, is Anna Maria's cousin.

Luca and Silvano start to talk about drumming after Luca compliments his technique.

"Do you drum?" Silvano asks him.

"Aye, but not as well as you."

"Wait, why didn't I know this?" I ask.

"You should have done a CIA background check on me," Luca says.

"I guess that's fair," I say, and he laughs.

The whole table starts talking about music, and it's as lively as their conversation about politics. Luca and Andrew seem to be having a really good time, although Andrew is often looking at Anna Maria. When the band's break is over, Silvano sends Luca up to play a couple songs. I guess I'm watching Luca too intently, because Andrew grabs my hand and pulls me to the dance floor. Or maybe he just wants an excuse to ask Anna Maria next. It's a slow jazz number, and Andrew holds me close. I have one hand on his shoulder, and we're holding our other hands together like we're in some old movie. Luca watches us as he taps out the notes.

"He can't fly fighter jets," Andrew drops in my ear.

I pull back and smile at him. "No, thank heaven for the little things."

Andrew laughs and pulls me back in. "I never know what to make of you, Astoria Herriot."

When the song ends, we clap, and Luca hands Silvano the sticks and comes over and claims his place as my supposed boyfriend, while Andrew asks Anna Maria to dance. Luca slips his arms around me and fixes his eyes on mine. He brushes some hair back behind my ear. Sometimes I wonder if he gets as confused as I do about what's real and what's not in our lives now.

It's ridiculously late, though, and I'm tired. I rest my head against Luca's chest and breathe in his pine-scented aftershave as the four of us float around the tiny dance floor of this quirky old piano bar. Anna Maria smiles at me, happy to have finally met my "cute Scottish boys," but I start wondering whether I may have made the biggest blunder yet in bringing Luca Kinnaird any deeper into my world.

Twenty-One

uca comes with me to the farm on Friday and actually stays. We unload some hay in the barn, and then he feeds the ducks. "They're so happy to see me," he says.

"It's clearly your Scottish charm and not the food you have."

"We Scots have a way about us."

"Really? You seem like a bunch of bampots to me."

Luca laughs. "You must be thinking of Andy."

"Sometimes I wonder if he's your handler or your best friend."

"Same."

"Maybe the problem is that you need a handler?"

Luca looks at the ducks. "This is how she talks to me, mannies," he says as they congregate at his feet to get their food. One of the large males stares at Luca, unconvinced he's safe.

"Look at this one's face," Luca says. "He's thinking what a dobber I am. This is worse than standing in front of the paparazzi."

"Except animals only judge you on how safe you are, not on how you dress or where you land on a Forbes list."

Luca nods with a slight laugh, and we get to work. We even stay past one o'clock to help Ferdy finish some repairs on a fence.

On the way back to Rome, Luca says he'll drop me off at my place and then go get a shower and come back to pick me up.

I shake my head at him. "There's nothing on the schedule tonight."

His eyes are dark like the afternoon sky when he glances over. "I know, it's glorious, isn't it? I have a surprise for you. So just get ready, okay?"

I try to rein in my smile. "What am I supposed to wear?" I've gotten so used to planning my wardrobe to match where we'll be that it's become my first thought.

"How about that yellow dress you wore the day we met?"

"That's definitely not paparazzi approved."

"I like it."

I watch him a moment, but he has no intention of elaborating.

When he picks me up later, we drive to a square near the Colosseum that I've only ever walked through, San Pietro in Vincoli.

"Have you been here?" Luca asks. "To the basilica?"

"No, only to the square."

He looks at me as if he's just beaten me at world-class checkers and grabs my hand to lead me inside a basilica that could totally pass for an office building on the outside. "This," he whispers as we walk through an ugly brown door to the cool quiet of the stone interior, "is one of the oldest churches in Rome."

Inside it's a whole different place, in a simple, elegant way. Luca pulls me across the smooth marble floor and down some steps below the altar to find the chains of St. Peter displayed in a glass case.

"Do I get into the tour guide union?" he whispers as we stand before it.

"Definitely," I admit. I'm kind of touched he's even trying.

"Well, just wait." He can barely contain himself, he's so happy to have the upper hand in our nerdy adventure series. But what he shows me next really is surprising. It's a sculpture of Moses by Michelangelo. An actual Michelangelo, sitting in the nave of a regular church on a backstreet in Rome.

"It never gets old to me how there's art by the most famous artists in the world just scattered in random places throughout the city like this," I say as we contemplate it.

"You have to admit I showed you something special." He slips his hand back into mine, and I smile up at him and nod.

When we step outside again, the summer sun is too bright, and we both squint. "So, I have somewhere else to take you where you've probably been before, but I still think we'll be able to find some new discoveries."

"And where is this?"

We start to turn the corner back to the car but stop when we see a bunch of paparazzi surrounding the Portofino. Luca jerks me back before they can spot us.

He groans. "They ruin everything."

"It's okay," I say, even though I'm disappointed.

Luca shakes his head. "I have an idea." He types into his phone and waits for the genie's answer to whatever he asked it. "Come on," he says, just as a paparazzo rounds the corner and shouts at us, his camera clicking in the now-familiar-to-me way. They must have spotted us after all.

"Not today," Luca says. He scoops up my hand and takes off running, and I bob along behind him with no idea how we are going to outrun some paparazzo. It feels like we're flying through the busy sidewalks. We dodge between tourists and a flower shop stand, its brightly colored buckets of roses and lilies cascading their scent along the road. We round a corner, and Luca pulls me into a souvenir shop. We duck behind a center console of T-shirts and watch through the plate-glass window as the paparazzo runs into the square. He stops to look for us as others join him.

"If our luck holds, we'll lose them," Luca says, panting a bit. "You okay?"

I nod. "Just need to catch my breath."

"Good thing you wore your Converses."

"I know to come prepared for your adventures now. Maybe this dress is unlucky, though. You seem to get chased a lot by tabloids when I'm wearing it."

"It would only be unlucky," he says, "if I'd never met you."

From behind us, a soft voice asks, "Do you want to go out the back?"

We turn. A young salesgirl is looking shyly at Luca.

188

"That would be brilliant," he says.

She smiles and gestures to follow her.

"Does this happen to you all the time?" I ask him.

He laughs. "Not to me, just the girls I'm with."

"Funny," I say as Luca hands the girl some euros and thanks her.

We come out of the back of the shop and walk through an alley to a main street. A snake charmer sits on the sidewalk doing his thing, incense burning beside him. We edge around him and keep heading in the direction Luca's phone tells us to go until we reach a Vespa rental place. Within minutes, Luca has rented us a blue scooter, and I'm trying to figure out how to artfully climb onto it in a dress while Luca waits to hand me a helmet like some knight from a modern-day fairy tale.

"Hold on," he says when he's settled in front, and I slip my arms around him. He's wearing a soft, green linen T-shirt that flutters against my skin as we zip and weave through the streets of Rome, out of the historic district and across the river. The breeze against us is cool in the late-afternoon heat, and I can feel Luca's heartbeat against the palm of my hand. He really should come with a full legal disclaimer. In writing, not just a few warnings from his trusty sidekick.

When we stop about twenty minutes later, we're at the Villa Doria Pamphili, a large park at the western edge of the city.

Luca parks and turns his head to catch my gaze. He slides off his helmet and musses his dark hair back into place. "What do you think? You can't possibly have explored this whole place."

"Believe it or not, I've never been here."

"What?"

I smile. "It was on my list, but then my plans for the summer got interrupted."

"Well," he says, jumping off the Vespa and pulling me with him, "your plans are now uninterrupted." His smile is huge.

He takes my hand, and we find our way to the place Romans call the secret garden because it sits behind the beautiful old villa that's used now as a government building. The garden is made up of perfectly symmetrical hedges in little patterns. We stop at a small bistro in the park and grab some Italian sodas. Then we stroll to the Garden of the Theatre, a pretty half-circle wall that was used as an amphitheater in the 1600s. Birds chatter around us, and stone pine trees stand like tall, skinny umbrellas.

As we walk, Luca pulls me closer. "I see why you love the animals at the farm so much," he says.

"There's something about being on the farm that makes everything clearer," I say. "We spend so much time trying to figure out how to get other people to think well of us, when the only thing we really need is to think well of ourselves. But animals never worry about that at all."

"I've spent my whole life worrying about what people think of me," he says. "My first memory, I was maybe three years old. My dad took Adaira, my eldest sister, and me to town for a meeting he had. I started to cry about something, I don't know what, probably I was bored or hungry, and my father took me out of the room, and we went and stood at a window, and he told me to look at the town below us. People were going about their business on the streets, as if we didn't even exist. And then he told me that all those people down there not only knew who I was, but expected me to be a good little boy and not to cry, because I was a Kinnaird."

"Wow, no pressure. So you stopped crying?"

"Well, no, not until Adaira called me a baby." He looks at me, and we both laugh. "But I never again forgot that people were expecting me to be a Kinnaird, and what, exactly, being a Kinnaird means."

"I think," I say, not able to look at him, "that you should only ever worry about being what you know in your heart is right for Luca."

"And is that what you were doing, before I came along and made you a public spectacle who has to wear designer clothes to help me out?"

"I suppose so." I smile at him. "Maybe a little hiding, too."

Luca is quiet for a few moments, but then he looks right through me. "You should never hide."

My face starts to burn. "I will take that under advisement, my lord."

Luca turns his gaze back to the path in front of us. "What's your earliest memory?"

"It's not any happier than yours. Worse, actually."

"You don't have to tell me, then."

"It's okay," I say. "It's of my dad. The last day he lived with us. I was four. He'd already lost his job, so he picked me up at preschool. My mom had told him to go straight home with me, but he didn't. He took me on a drug buy, first. I mean, I didn't understand that until years later. Anyway, my mom was calling him to make sure we were home, and he wasn't answering, but she didn't know where to look for us because he kept that side of his life secret. She only knew he was using at that point, but not where he got it. I guess I was lucky, because he was still in control enough that he brought me home before he used. But I remember being frightened by the dirty bar we were in and crying for my mom. When we did get home, she was standing in the driveway, frantic. She grabbed me out of my car seat and hung on to me like she was scared she'd never see me again, tears streaming down her face. She told him to pack his things and not come back until he was sober."

Luca slips his hand around my arm. "And he never came back."

I shake my head. "I saw him, every so often, on supervised visits. But it was always awkward, and I was always a little afraid of him. Not because he was mean or anything, he was very sweet with me, always so happy to see me, but because I'd seen how scared he'd made my mom that day. I didn't understand then why she was afraid, but I understood how much. Maybe that's why I'm so scared of the world.

"And then it was something I had to navigate. I got that I was supposed to be ashamed of him, but my mom told me we were the only ones who had the right to judge him. I just wanted to make him love me enough that he'd get sober and come home, but I didn't know how to make that happen. It was so confusing, how you could love someone who was completely self-destructive and who pulled you under with him. So we bought a lemon tree, and we transplanted it to a new pot, and my mom said that was where all the sorrow and things we couldn't share with other people could be at home and grow and become something better and happier than they started out as."

"Wait, you have a lemon tree in your apartment."

I nod. "She somehow managed to take all that shame and sorrow and repurpose it for me. We call it Bert. And every new place we go, she spends hours making sure Bert ships safely and gets through quarantine. And then we make lemonade to celebrate."

Luca smiles. "Your mom is pretty cool."

"She is."

He pulls me into a hug. "Her daughter is pretty cool, too."

I hold on for a moment, and then let go with a laugh. "I don't know why I tell you these things. I never tell anyone else."

"Well, you don't let yourself have friends, so who would there be to tell?"

"That's not true, what Patrick said. I have friends. I mean, only Anna Maria here, because I've only been here for a year. And it's two friends, if you count Jack."

"Aye, because it takes at least a year, so that means we can be friends next summer."

"You are so funny. Well, as much as I enjoy talking about my selective friend group, I'm very hungry."

"Aye, milady," Luca says, and pulls out his phone to find a restaurant. We find our way back to the Vespa and go to a small trattoria nearby. We sit at a sidewalk table under a bright red umbrella as the sun sets. A candle glimmers on the table, and fairy lights sparkle in potted trees around the little patio. We eat pasta and share a plate of cannoli for dessert, and we talk about all the things we would do and the places we would visit if we didn't have any constraints, like time or money or family. Or girlfriends. Luca doesn't mention Jasmine, and I don't remind him.

Afterward, we hop on the Vespa, and Luca drives us around the city aimlessly, across the river and through streets sparkling with the city's streetlights and the light that spills from shops and restaurants and apartments. I hang on a little tighter than I should and rest my cheek on his shoulder blade as all the sights and sounds and smells of Rome blur by us, and I wish this didn't have to end.

Sometimes he pulls over, and we stay on the scooter, my arms still wrapped around him as he tilts his head back toward mine as we gaze at the view or talk about a monument. And then he pulls out again and we zip and weave our way around the city like it's a magical modern fairy capital.

It's well past midnight when he drops me off at my flat.

"Thank you for today," I say as I let go of him and hop off the Vespa.

Luca catches my hand in his. "The pleasure was all mine, sweet Story."

I pull away and go unlock the door to the building. When it closes behind me, I hear the Vespa hover and then purr into the street, but I don't turn around to watch it go. Andy's right, he's an easy guy to fall for, and I need to change course before I make a complete fool of myself. He's just bored because the girl he's actually chasing, the girl he thinks is a dream come true, isn't here.

The next two weeks are filled with typical Luca Kinnaird activities, and we settle back into our usual routines except for when Luca comes to the sanctuary or has Sunday dinner with my mom and me. The paparazzi declare I'm "taming the rogue Scot." My partnership with Dani Meadows Designs has given Dani and me tons of new followers. Other companies approach me about plugging their products, but I leave that to Andrew so long as the products are vegan, organic, and ethically produced. He calls that a "great angle." Luca and I just look at each other and smile. But Andrew takes care of the business side of it as if he were a professional manager.

When I scroll through my photo gallery, it seems effortless. "You've put a lot of thought into this," I tell Andrew one day as we're waiting for Luca to get the car.

"Luca was very specific about how your brand should look."

"He was?"

Andrew nods. "Crisp, cultured, and congenial."

"Thanks," I say. "I guess you've become my handler, too?"

Andrew laughs. "You don't really need one, but I'm happy to oblige. I've had some inquiries from charities that want you to promote them for free."

"That's fine, so long as they fit the brand."

"As you wish, Yankee hippie," he says, but he smiles.

My mom has noticed the new wardrobe, so I have to explain that some people are following me because of Luca and I'm helping Dani out by wearing her clothes. She shakes her head as she packs her lunch one morning. "I don't understand any of this influencer culture your generation has."

"Me neither, honestly. Andrew just thought it would help his cousin, so I said yes." I know I should leave it at that, but I've never been good at lying through omission. "And it helps me, too, because then people don't criticize me for not being able to fit into Luca's designer world."

"Story, you know better than to get caught up in that kind of nonsense."

"I know, but I don't want Luca to have to deal with people making fun of my clothes."

She stops peeling an orange and looks at me. "How many people follow this boy?"

I shake my head. "Not that many. This isn't forever, Mom. I'll be at Princeton next month, and Luca will be back at Oxford. It will all be over."

"Are you sure this is just a summer fling? You two seem pretty connected."

"We'll always be friends," I say, and there's truth in that. We'll end our business arrangement as friends. We just won't stay in touch. She looks at me skeptically, but she doesn't say anything. I try not to think about how much my life without Luca seems—less full. Less everything. But at least maybe this friendship angle will be the foundation for telling my mom about the scholarship when the time comes.

The tabs are off my back, and some of them even comment on what a proficient influencer I'm becoming, although I'm "still no Chiara Ferragni." Elisa is happy with me because the sanctuary has gotten some free publicity, and donations are up. Luca is more relaxed than I've ever seen him. Even Andrew is pleased, as he tells me I'll need to hire an accountant about what taxes to pay on the endorsement income he's started to deposit into my checking account. It's not nearly enough to pay for a year of school, but it's more than I ever expected. We're more than halfway through this insanity, and I'm finally pulling it off to everyone's satisfaction. Except my own.

And Jasmine's. She calls Luca one afternoon when we're in his hotel suite having lunch with Andrew. I can hear her even though he doesn't have her on speaker.

"What the hell is she doing, babe? She isn't supposed to be transforming into an influencer. She's just a plus-one to take the heat off our relationship. Can't that stupid wannabe do anything right?"

I'm sitting cross-legged on the sofa with my plate on my lap. Andrew is on the other end of the sofa, and Luca is in a chair next to me. I glance at Andrew. He must be able to hear her because he pulls his face into a long, awkward arrow toward the balcony. I get up and walk past Luca. He grabs my wrist as I go, but I don't stop and he lets me slip by. His face is flushed, though.

"Jasmine, you aren't being fair," he says. "This was your idea and she's doing great. Yeah, I am saying everything's under control." He lowers his voice. "Don't talk about her like that."

Sunlight is beating down on the balcony as Andrew closes

the door behind us. We chat stupidly about Via Condotti. "I don't know how anyone manages this heat," he says after a couple of minutes.

"They don't. The street is practically empty."

"Except for that diddy down there with the camera watching us."

I don't look, but Andrew and I aren't standing too close or acting weird, except for being on a hot balcony in the middle of the day in July in Rome.

"Listen, for what it's worth," he says, "I'd pick you over her any day."

I laugh. "Only because you know what she's really like."

"Aye, she's right hackit in her soul."

I let out a deep breath. I just need to focus on how close we are to the finish. Billboards for Rowdy and Jasmine's album started going up around town two days ago.

"I thought a couple weeks ago that he might break up with her. But it's complicated."

"What do you mean?" If it's possible for hearts to do cartwheels, mine just might have.

Andrew shrugs and gets vague. "He'll usually walk away when a girl brings this much drama."

If Luca is putting up with all her drama when he doesn't like it, he must really like her. Luca and my mom are right, I need to get some real friends. Maybe when I get to Princeton. Maybe Jack can help with that.

Luca pushes the French doors open and steps out. He's in bare feet, and he jumps at the hot marble.

"I'm sorry about that, you can come back in. Jings, it's blazing out here."

"We're being watched," Andrew says. "Two o'clock street level."

Without missing a beat, Luca wraps his arms around me and puts his chin on my shoulder. He leans his face against mine, so close I'm in a haze of his aftershave. "We need to go in before I melt."

Andrew and I laugh and start toward the door, but Luca pulls me back. I look up, and he slips a strand of my hair behind my ear, one arm around my waist.

"She didn't mean any of that. She's just stressed about the tour. They had some security issues, and there was a problem with the sound system at the Oslo venue, and two of her dancers got food poisoning."

There's a camera lens pointed at me. Along with Luca's eyes, which are the color of a stormy ocean. "It's no big deal." I force a smile. "I wouldn't want to have to see us together in photos all the time if I were her."

I look down because the way he's searching my eyes feels like he's found the secrets of my heart that I don't even know. He could have at least picked a diva who wasn't hackit in her soul. Whatever exactly that means.

"I just wish—"

I don't let him finish. Whatever he wants is probably best left unsaid. "Dai," I say as I pull him back inside. "If you melt, she'll blame me for that, too."

Twenty-Two

hat night, we go to dinner at a trendy restaurant not far from Via Condotti with some business associates of Luca's dad who are in town. Luca and I are the only people at the table who aren't adults, but I'm used to being around my mom and her friends, so it doesn't feel awkward. They ask lots of questions about what we've been doing all summer, and Luca recites his many social events like it's some sort of social page checklist. I talk mostly about Princeton and moving back to the States so it won't come as a surprise to them when we break up.

Afterward, Luca walks me home. He takes us the long way, past the Trevi. We split a vegan chocolate gelato, sharing it back and forth between us.

"You were pure barry tonight. I don't usually like these dinners, but this one wasn't bad at all. It's my dad's way of checking up on me when I go abroad."

"I can't imagine why he'd think he needs to."

"Hilarious. Even before you tamed the roguish Scot, though, I wasn't really that bad."

"It's not about what it really is, it's only about how it looks."

"Ah, I've taught you well, Astoria Herriot."

"It still seems pretty backward to me."

"So you are teaching me."

When we get back to my building, it's only about ten o'clock. "Do you want to come up?" I ask.

"That's a good idea. We won't have to put on a good-night show for any paparazzi."

I nod, because that's how I should have been thinking, not like I was, just that I should soak up what little time is left.

We wait for the elevator. When it opens, Jack steps out.

"Oh, hey," he says.

Luca stops and shakes his hand as we exchange hellos, and then he looks at me as if he's wondering what I'm thinking about Jack.

"Patrick is at Alicia's with the girls, but I decided to cut," Jack says as if he's apologizing for having been with them at all.

Luca nods. "We're just going up to Story's for a wee bit, do you want to come?"

Jack looks from Luca to me. I smile stupidly, not sure why Luca thinks this is a good idea.

"Yeah, sure," Jack says. Luca gestures for me to go first, and I stand between them in the elevator like we're three mismatched garden gnomes. When we get to the apartment, my mom is reading in the living room.

"Jack, it's so nice to see you," she says. "I'm always telling

Story she should bring her friends around more, and now that she's almost ready to leave, she's finally started."

"Thanks, Mom," I say, but Luca already knows why I'm solitary, and Jack witnessed my humiliation firsthand, so it doesn't really matter.

Jack looks a little embarrassed as he says, "I wish I had gotten to know Story better during the school year, Mrs. Herriot."

Luca nudges me, but I ignore him.

My mom says good night, and I go to the kitchen to get us some lemon waters. When I come back, Luca is leaning forward on the sofa toward Jack. "I'm serious. You'll look out for her, right, min?"

"Of course," Jack says before he looks up and sees me.

"What's going on?" I ask as I set the glasses down on the coffee table.

"Nothing," Luca says. I look from him to Jack.

"Luca just wanted to make sure that I'll be around if you need anything at school," Jack says. "I'd ask the same thing if I were going to be a continent away from my girlfriend."

I frown. "Luca worries too much." I sit beside Luca on the sofa, but he doesn't put his arm around me like he usually would when we're performing our vaudeville show.

"Story's very resourceful," Jack tells Luca. "She picks her friends wisely. If the girls in her class are shallow, then she'll make friends with John Keats instead."

Luca tilts his head at me.

"How do you know about that?" I ask Jack.

He laughs. "I thought you had a job there at first, because I'd see you leaving when I was heading home from soccer practice."

"Oh, I saw you once or twice."

"I came up the opposite side of the street, going in the other direction, and you were always lost in thought."

"Sorry. I can't believe you never said anything."

"I wasn't sure you'd want me to." The way he looks at me makes me think I've never realized how much he was paying attention to me all along.

"What are we talking about?" Luca asks. He leans forward and puts his hand on my leg, but then he pulls it back again with a glance at Jack.

"Anna Maria works at the John Keats's house. It's where we met."

"Ah, I should have known you'd be soft for Keats." Without another beat, Luca recites one of my favorite Keats's poems.

The sonnet sounds so beautiful with his accent. I almost forget Jack is there until Luca finishes. "I would have guessed you could recite 'Bright Star,' but not 'When I Have Fears,'" I say. "You always know how to surprise me." The specter of lost love from the poem weaves its way into my heart.

Luca laughs. "Scots are a morbid bunch."

"You're both over my head," Jack says. "But I got into Princeton on math, not English."

"Well, Story doesn't think I actually speak English, so—"

"I dinnae ken whit ye mean," I say.

Luca looks at Jack and points to me with his thumb, as if to say *I told you so.* "Haud yer wheesht," he tells me.

"That means shut up," I translate.

Luca throws his arms around me and pulls me into him, but then stops himself just as quickly. He lets go of me and his laugh at the same time.

Jack smiles, but then he stands up. "I'd better go and let you two fight this battle without me."

I expect Luca to say he's going, too, and we all walk to the door. Instead of walking out with Jack, Luca just looks at him. "You won't forget, Jack, right?"

Jack looks him in the eye. "No, man, I won't forget. I'll look out for Story. I promise."

"Thanks, min." Luca shakes his hand like they've just struck a business deal.

"No problem, good night."

When I've closed the door, I turn to Luca. "What the hell was that about?"

"What?"

"Why are you pushing me on Jack? I don't need your charity matchmaking."

"That's not what I was doing," Luca says, and slips his hand around my waist. I pull away and go sit on the sofa, and he sits beside me.

"Look, I know you're just trying to be nice, but I don't need you to get me friends. Or a boyfriend."

"Story, you have one friend, and Jack."

"So?"

Luca shakes his head as if he doesn't understand how he hasn't already explained what's wrong here.

"Luca, if and when I need more friends, I'll handle it." I so need more friends. So many friends that I never have time to think about him again.

He glances down. "I'm sorry. That guy really likes you, and it would make me feel better if you had someone watching out for you. You know, after all this. . . ." His voice trails off a bit, and he looks at me without looking me in the eyes.

I don't like the idea of what my life will be like when this is over. And I really don't like Luca feeling sorry for me. "I'm not some pathetic charity case, and I don't need you to become my dating app." My tone is ferocious, but I'm whispering so I don't wake my mom.

"Stor, I don't think you're pathetic, that's ridiculous. Any guy would be lucky to be with you."

Any guy but one who has a Disney princess, apparently. "If that were true, then you wouldn't be setting me up." My eyes are stinging. Someone should slap me.

He pulls my hands into his and squeezes them. "That's not—" His phone starts to buzz. It'll be Jasmine calling after her show.

"Go ahead," I say. I tug my hands out of his grip. He frowns as he checks the screen. "I'll see you tomorrow."

"I'll call her back," he says, but I've already stood up. He follows.

"There's no need." I push him toward the door.

He clicks Accept, but his eyes are on me. Jasmine starts yelling at him, but none of the individual words come through to me. I nudge him into the hallway. He gives me a small wave as he walks away. I close the door behind him and hope that autumn comes a lot sooner than I think it can.

Twenty-Three

'm not even awake when my phone starts shimmying across the nightstand. The clock reads 7:16, and I groan. It's Luca.

"Pronto?"

"Story, TMZ broke the news that Rowdy is in rehab."

I push my hair back and sit up. "Is that what she was screaming about last night?"

"You heard that?"

"Just that she was mad about something." But then, she usually is.

"After her gig, she was asked about Rowdy, and if he went to rehab after hearing the rumors about Jasmine and me."

"Nobody needs to go to rehab just because their significant other might be cheating. That's a stupid question. And he's not even in rehab anymore, you said he transferred to the step-down care."

"Aye, he's been in sober living for at least a week, but the tabs call it all rehab. And it might be a stupid question, but she still has to answer it."

I yawn. "So this is actually a good thing. It gives her a chance to put some distance between her and Jeremy that has nothing to do with you. She can just say she will always love and support Rowdy, but, right now, they're focused on his recovery and she's giving him the space he needs to do that. If they ask about you, she can just say she isn't ready to even think about what's next for her, or whether or not it includes Rowdy. That leaves the door open."

"When did you get so savvy? That's really good."

I shrug even though he can't see it. "I guess Andrew's rubbing off on me."

"Unfortunately, they caught her off guard and she doubled down on her commitment to Rowdy."

I don't say anything. How does someone with a publicist get caught off guard about anything, let alone about news she's been worried could, and most likely would, leak? I guess the same way they send a freak dress to someone who is supposed to be catching their boyfriend's eye. This girl wants everything without sacrificing anything.

"Story?"

"Yes?"

"What do you think?"

"Does it matter what I think? She's already told the world she's all in for Jeremy."

Luca doesn't say anything for a long moment. "Andrew thinks we should be seen together all day."

I sigh. I don't know how we're supposed to save a girl whose ego makes her sabotage even her own schemes. We're already scheduled to go to an afternoon lecture by a visiting Scottish professor at Università di Roma. For a girl who doesn't want me around her boyfriend, she sure finds ways to make it necessary. I need to stand up for myself. But right now, Luca wouldn't believe me even if I told him Jasmine isn't worth his time.

"Okay. When should I be ready?"

"Pick you up at twelve-thirty? I'll take you somewhere nice for lunch."

"You mean somewhere visible."

"That doesn't mean it won't be nice. Somehow, even when you're ballbusting me, it ends up being a good time."

I lie back down. "You can turn off your charm faucet. I'll be ready."

"Story, I know how to work a crowd, but I'd never do that to you. You know that, right?"

"Of course," I say strongly enough that I hope he drops it.

"That's why I asked Jack to watch out for you. I want you to be happy, even if it's not—"

"I'm fine. I'll see you later." I hang up before he has the chance to finish whatever humiliating platitude he's about to offer.

At twelve-thirty, I'm downstairs in a Dani Meadows sundress that actually seems like me. Kelsey, Guin, and Alicia come in together, their hands filled with shopping bags.

"Oh, it's you!" Kelsey says as if it's surprising I'd be in the lobby of the building where we all live.

"Hi," I say. "Looks like you guys had a good morning."

"How crazy is the news about Rowdy Funkmaster?" Guin says. "Is it true he went to rehab because Luca was hooking up with Jasmine? Cute dress, though!"

"Is that true, Story?" Kelsey asks. "Jasmine is so beautiful, what guy wouldn't want to be with her?"

"I don't know," Alicia says, pushing back her dark curls. "I think Luca and Story make a cute couple."

Kelsey's eyebrows arch up as she turns to her. Alicia looks down and shuffles her feet.

"Jeremy's been in rehab for weeks, actually," I say.

"How do you know that?" Guin asks.

"Everyone's known." I shrug as I say it, and the reaction is immediate. Kelsey's eye twitches, and she's clearly perturbed I run in circles she can only dream about. I shouldn't enjoy it, and karma will probably come for me with a vengeance, but I'm so tired of them.

The Portofino pulls up. "Gotta run. Enjoy your day." I sail through the glass entry.

Luca comes around to open the car door. He grabs me around the waist and pulls me to him.

"They're watching, aren't they?" I ask.

He smiles and whispers, "Aye."

I smooth his hair on the side they can see, and Luca bends down and dusts his lips against mine, letting our noses touch. It all feels a little too real. I slip into the car, and he closes the door. I don't look back, as if I've forgotten the Dip Squad even exists.

Once we pull away, I tell Luca what they said.

"I figured, with that lot."

"If this blows up, I think them knowing the truth would be the worst of it. That's so stupid of me. It's not like I want their good opinion. I just don't want them exulting at my failure."

"It's hard not to let people get under your skin when they wish you'd fail for no reason, so don't beat yourself up for that. I don't know why you let them jab at you."

I don't say anything.

"Story?"

"I think it's better to take the stupid jabs instead of the ones that could really hurt. I'd rather they didn't know me well enough to know where to punch."

"They're just jealous of you."

"Why on earth would they be jealous of me? I mean, now that I'm supposed to be with you, yes, but not before."

"Story, you have no idea what you have going for you. You've got your own vibe that's completely genuine. Of course, girls who need influencers to tell them how to look and act would be jealous."

It doesn't make sense. I don't fit in. Not in Luca's world, and not in mine. I've accepted I don't fit in. But maybe that's it. People don't like what they can't control, and I've always done my own thing, even if it meant going it alone. "I guess we all see ourselves through a perspective that isn't any more real than the way other people see us. It's just a snapshot of a moment, and then we're something else the next, anyway, but we see ourselves as if we are only that one snapshot. It's all just invented perception, like the photos the tabloids take or that Andy posts of us."

"It's not all invented," Luca says. "You and I really are friends. Aren't we?"

He seems genuinely unsure of what I might say.

I nod, probably a little too slowly, and hope he doesn't see how I really feel.

"Besides, I'm not going to let this perception blow up."

I don't know how he's going to do that when his girlfriend seems determined to sabotage us. Then I think about Jack. Lying to the Dip Squad is one thing but lying to someone who is nice to me is something else. I can't even think about how I'm lying to my mom.

Andrew meets us at the lecture. It's on the influence of Romanesque architecture on British castles, and how it gives them their massive walls, round arches, and large towers. After the lecture, Luca gets pulled into conversation with the professor, so Andrew and I walk into the courtyard.

"Jasmine saw those pictures of you two on the balcony."

"We were just putting on for the camera you spotted, you know that."

"That's what Luca told her, but she said it looked way too real."

I can't meet his gaze. "I thought this was the whole point, that it looks real?"

"I'm just saying, Story, she's pretty jealous. I know you've both gotten used to playing the game, but maybe you should tone it down a bit. Maybe you've gotten too good at it."

I hope there weren't any paparazzi when Luca picked me up, or she's going to really give him an earful after our little display for Kelsey and company. "I don't know what the girl wants. She's the one he's doing it for, not me."

"Just be careful, Story." He starts to turn away but then looks back at me. "And that speech sounds a wee bit bitter."

I want to fling some flippant retort at him, but his face shows he really is concerned about me. "Noted," I say instead. He's right. Being around Luca has become dangerous to more than just my reputation.

Andrew has some perfume I need to hawk, so when Luca joins us, we go take pictures around the university. "It meets all of your requirements," Andrew says as he hands me the bottle.

I take a sniff. "It's not bad."

"She'd rather have L'Air du Temps or Ma Griffe," Luca says.

I turn toward him. "How do you know that?"

"You have them on your dresser," he says. "And I love it when you wear Ma Griffe."

Andrew looks up sharply, first at Luca and then at me, as if it's my fault Luca notices details.

"Let's take the pictures," I say, "and get it over with."

Andrew takes the shots as I pretend to spritz myself with the proper amount of delight. "Okay, that should do it. Now let's go shopping," he says. "Tabloids love seeing minted people spend money, and you two can help me find a present for my sister's birthday."

We hit the busy Via Condotti, packed with wealthy summer tourists, and it doesn't take long to be picked up by paparazzi.

There's the German guy who made fun of my wardrobe and a woman with dyed-purple hair who calls me Astrollee whenever she yells my name. We wander in and out of trendy designer shops until we find a cute purse in Prada for Andrew's sister.

"I bet she'd be just as happy with something a lot less expensive, if it came from the heart," I say as I search aimlessly for a price tag because rich people aren't supposed to care how much things cost.

Luca and Andrew laugh. "Not Kenna," they say together.

"Story is sentimental," Luca says as Andrew pays. "She'd pick a plastic ring over Cartier if it had meaning."

"Are all progressive women like that?" Andrew asks with mock incredulity.

"Most of them," I say. "See what you're missing?"

Andrew laughs and opens the door as we step into the street. We pass a coffee bar, and the whole sidewalk is filled with the scent of fresh brewed espresso. We've only taken a few steps when a group of four girls walking in the other direction spot Luca and start talking excitedly to each other, obviously trying to decide which one is going to stop him for a photo. They're barely old enough to drive. When they reach us, a dark-haired girl gets shoved toward us by the others and blurts out in English accented by French, "Can we take un photo weeth you?"

We've already stopped. Luca moves over by the wall, out of sidewalk traffic, and pulls me toward him. The girls are all chattering to each other in French, and Andrew and Luca start to laugh.

"What's so funny?" I ask.

"They don't want Luca," Andrew says. "They want you, Story."

"What?"

"They say I'm hot, but they don't know why I think everything is about me," Luca adds. "They think I must have a big ego." He smiles at me, barely able to keep from laughing at himself. When the girls realize he can speak French, they start apologizing from what I can tell, but Luca just tells them, "Ce n'est pas un problème," and steps away with a gesture for them to join me.

Suddenly I'm surrounded by these girls as Andrew takes pictures of us with each of their phones. One of them is crying, she's so excited to meet me.

"Please don't cry," I tell her. "I'm just a girl like you." Luca translates for me, and I think he adds on, because it seems like a lot of words, but soon she is smiling shyly and nodding. I give her a hug.

Afterward, they thank me in a mix of French and English and go on their way, squealing as they check the photos. Andrew and Luca are biting their lips not to burst out laughing.

"Neither of you say a word!"

They shake their heads at me, but their smiles let me know how funny they think it is. "It was actually really sweet of you," Luca says, squeezing my hand.

"Dai," I say, "I don't want to talk about it," and start walking. Rush-hour taxis and cars jostle each other along the boulevard, and I lose myself in the noise of it all. When we pass by Tiffany's, I slow and browse the windows. Luca has his fingertips laced in mine, so he slows, too.

"Wait," he says, "isn't there an Audrey Hepburn movie about Tiffany's?"

I nod. *"Breakfast at Tiffany's."*

"Come on," Luca says, and pulls me into the store.

We peruse the glass cases. Most of the jewelry is too modern for me, but some of it's very pretty. Luca tries to guess which designs I like the best, and he hits it pretty well.

"Story could use some diamond earrings," Andrew says.

"Which ones do you like?" Luca asks.

I point sarcastically at a big pair that look hyper expensive.

"Those ones," Luca says to the girl.

"Oh, I wasn't serious," I say as the lady says, "These are twenty-three thousand dollars."

I cough.

"They're a bit large," I add to cover my shock.

Luca nods very seriously as he looks at my ear. "Something classic," he tells her. "These are conflict-free, correct?"

"Oh, yes, sir. We have very stringent standards."

Luca smiles at me to get credit for checking.

"These are very classic, and less expensive," the saleswoman says as she pulls out petal-shaped earrings. My comment about not wanting large earrings clearly didn't fool her. "Would signorina like to try them?"

I shake my head. "Oh, no, thank you."

"You'd like something else? The vine ones are nine thousand four hundred. They're very popular."

"Oh, no, those are lovely, it's just, I'm not shopping for diamonds today."

She arches her brow at me because who says that in a Tiffany's?

"Wrap a pair up," Luca tells her.

She smiles and nods at him.

"Luca," I whisper as fiercely as I dare. He pulls me away from the counter. "It's no big deal," he says. Andrew joins our little meeting.

I turn my back to the windows in case any paparazzi are watching. "Are you pazzo? Those are diamonds. Did you see how much they cost?"

"I'm getting off easy, you could have liked the nine-thousand-dollar ones. Or the twenty-three-thousand-dollar ones, for that matter." He laughs.

"It's not funny. Andrew, explain it to him."

Andrew looks at me blankly. "Story, just take them, you've earned them."

"I can't take those!"

They look at each other and shake their heads.

"Sir?" the woman says. Luca goes to the counter flashing his credit card like he's 007 on a mission.

"Andrew, you know I can't accept them."

"Story, you should have diamonds if you're going to be an influencer and look like you belong with the Lucas of the world."

"Luca! One Luca! One and done. I won't be an influencer after this is over. And it's almost over."

Andrew frowns. "If it really bothers you, you can pay him back. You've got enough income from the influencer ads. But honestly, I think you should let him buy them. He asked you to do this, not the other way around. He can afford it a lot more than you can."

I just stare, because Andrew is supposed to be the sensible one, the one who keeps Luca in line. He's also supposed to be the one who doesn't worry about lower classes needing a leg up.

"First of all, that's way too egalitarian a thing for you to say. Second, he doesn't owe me anything, Andy. He's already doing the scholarship, which is a lot more than I ever expected from this deal. Plus—"

"What?" Andrew asks when I hesitate. I take a deep breath.

"He's given me dolphins and wildlife prints, and he helps at the farm, and the dinners, and flowers, and just everything. He's been my friend, Andrew. It's not right."

He looks at me for a long moment. "You're one in a million, Astoria Herriot. Do you want me to make sure they're returned quietly?"

I nod. Luca comes over and hands me the little blue bag. His smile is huge, and his North Atlantic eyes are gleaming. "These are going to look gorgeous on you. And I have somewhere for you to wear them."

I glance at Andrew. So much for returning them. "I'll pay you back. Andrew says I have enough now."

Luca laughs and throws his arm around my neck and kisses my temple. "Oh, sweet Story, you just did. You just did."

Twenty-Four

When we step into the arid heat of evening, Andrew says he's taking us both to dinner.

"That's good," Luca says, "because Story just cleaned out my wallet."

"Not funny," I say while they laugh. "I will pay you back."

"Haud yer wheesht," Luca says. "It's just a present among friends."

"Friends buy each other smoothies. Or fuzzy socks. Or, if they've been best friends since fourth grade, maybe sterling silver jewelry."

Andrew makes a face at Luca like he's just tasted sour mayonnaise. "Her world sounds horrible, doesn't it?"

"A nightmare."

"You two should have your own late-night show." Luca links a pinkie into mine because it's too hot to hold hands. We walk to a restaurant down the street and get an early seating. I put the Tiffany bag on the table in front of me to keep it safe, which amuses Luca. We spend a long time over dinner, the way Italians do.

After dinner, Luca wants to go to the overlook that's on the way to Villa Borghese. We stop at his hotel, and he asks the valet to get my Converses, which are in his trunk, and bring them to his room. The paparazzi are waiting across the street. They'll think we've ordered the car.

Luca tips the valet when my shoes arrive. Andrew says he's babysat us enough for one day, so Luca and I leave him and slip out a back entrance. Somehow, though, Andrew's parting warning look comes along with me. We navigate a few small alleys and emerge not far from the Spanish Steps. The evening has suddenly cooled to almost normal, the way it can in Rome, and there are lots of tourists for us to get lost among. A ballerina dances in a square for spare change by the light of souvenir shops. We sidestep pigeons begging for snacks and listen to a girl playing a cello and drop some euros for her. Children chase each other in the piazzas as their parents chat. The scent of roasting tomatoes and chicken in basil follows us around a corner.

"Most people go to the Terrazza del Pincio," I say, "but I think the Viale della Trinità dei Monti is nicer."

"Then let's go there."

"We can do both, if you like. They aren't far from each other. But Pincio will be more crowded."

"No crowds tonight. I just want to be." He takes my hand.

He pulls me in whenever there are people passing too close or the way narrows. By the time we climb the hill to the Viale della Trinità, though, the crowd has thinned considerably. A few couples and small groups cluster along the wall on the hillside. I watch Luca's face for his first view of the city from here and smile when I see his surprise at all of Rome spread before us. We find a spot away from others and gaze over the Eternal City as golden shades fall across terra-cotta roofs. Venus's Belt has wrapped around the skyline in violets and pinks.

"You weren't kidding."

"Everyone should see this at least once in their lives."

Luca pulls out his phone and takes a photo, and then a selfie of the two of us with the view behind. "'I found Rome a city of bricks and left it a city of marble.'"

"Are you testing the tour guide? Augustus Caesar said that."

Luca laughs. "How about this one? 'Rome is the city of echoes, the city of illusions, and the city of yearning.'"

"I've never heard that one. But it's definitely true. Who said it?"

"Now I've forgotten." He looks it up on his phone. "Giotto di Bondone. Crivvens, what a name."

"Anatole Broyard said, 'Rome was a poem pressed into service as a city.'"

"Oh, that's magic."

"But my favorite quote is from Edmonia Lewis, an American sculptor: 'I thought I knew everything when I came to Rome, but I soon found out I had everything to learn.'"

Luca gazes at me until I look away.

"But I think Rome is like someone who steals your heart while you weren't even paying attention."

He pauses before he replies. "That may be the best one yet." He contemplates the city as the stars throw off their daylight veil. After a while he says to himself, "I soon found out I had everything to learn."

"You okay?"

"Aye," he says. "I just wish I knew how to be me and still be me."

I slip my hand around his arm.

"I guess that makes no sense," he says, shaking his head slightly.

"No, I know you feel pulled to be what your family wants even though you want something else."

Luca looks down at me until I nudge away and lean my back against the wall.

"Listen," he says, "there's something I need to tell you. I have to go home for a few days this weekend, for my grandmother's seventy-fifth birthday. There's going to be a big party at the house, black tie and all that."

"Oh." I turn and lean my forearms on the wall, still warm from the sun, to hide the pang that skitters across my face. "I hope you have fun."

"Well, the thing is, I'm hoping you'll come with me?"

I look up, pretty sure I'm channeling Andy's cautionary face. "You want me to come home with you and meet your family? As your girlfriend? That seems a bit extreme, don't you think?"

"Well, they already know about you from the tabs. That's why my dad asked his business friends to check up on me."

"Right," I say, and I'm a bit thrown because it hadn't occurred to me that his family would know about any of this, but it should have. Of course they'd be watching the tabs to see what mess Luca got himself into next. They weren't just checking up on Luca. They were checking me out, too. They're probably worried I'm a gold digger, but I wonder what they'd think of Jasmine strutting across the stage in some dominatrix outfit as she belts out how many ways she knows to please a guy.

"They'll all be expecting you, honestly, and Andrew thinks you should come, since everyone's asking about Rowdy's recovery. You can ask Dani to send a dress to my parents' place. Your mom won't mind you going, will she? I can assure her that, after five kids, nothing goes on in our house that my mum doesn't know about."

I laugh a little. "I don't see why she'd mind, considering I'll be leaving for college in less than a month. But I don't like lying to your parents, especially as a guest in their house? It doesn't seem right, even if it is Andrew approved."

"It's no big deal. They think I go through girlfriends faster than I go through cars, so they won't be expecting you at Christmas anyway. They'll be very polite and hospitable, and then they'll have a rousing pool on how long you'll last. Somehow, my mother always wins."

"Ooh, can I get in on that?"

Luca laughs and pulls me in and kisses my temple, I guess out of habit. "I can't wait to show you how bonnie it is at home."

"Is this why you and Andrew said I need diamonds?"

Luca exhales. "You need diamonds because they're classic and so are you."

I let his evasiveness pass. We're silent together for a few minutes.

"And I was thinking that, when we get back, we should take your mum up to my uncle's place on Lake Como for the weekend. We could take her sailing."

The Colosseum shimmers in a golden glow as if there were thousands of candles around it instead of electric floodlights, while St. Peter's dome has faded into darkness. The delicate scent of flowered window boxes that decorate the apartments behind us drifts to the ground. I wish he didn't always have to live in the moment, as if we'll be friends forever. It would be better for me if he could just be realistic for once. He and Andrew won't even remember they met me six weeks from now.

"That sounds really nice, Luca, but I don't think it's a very good idea. We'll only have a couple weeks left of this by the time we get back, and I don't want my mom to fall for you any harder than she already has." Jasmine and Rowdy's first single drops in less than a week.

Luca shakes his head. "I guess you're right. Now that you don't despise me, I keep thinking summer is going to float on. There are so many places I want you to see, like Edinburgh and Amsterdam. You'd love those cities."

Sometimes I wonder if Luca just loves the one he's with. It's Jasmine he should be thinking about taking everywhere. But then I think that's a jerky way to think. He's just trying to share his overabundant world with his little Cinderella friend.

"I never despised you." It's unsettling how much I'd like to see these places with him. To take my mom sailing with him.

"Oh, I think you did."

"I just didn't think I was going to be able to stand your company. But I never despised you."

He grins. "That seems like the same thing. And now?"

How do I answer him?

"You often surprise me."

He nudges closer to me. It's hard to breathe. "In a good way?"

I stare at the azure-washed city below. "Aye."

He pulls me into a hug. A friendship hug, not a hug for show. I think. I want to see where Luca grew up, but I don't want to make Jasmine any more jealous. Maybe she's smarter than me. Maybe she knew that sooner or later I'd fall for him, just like everyone else does. This whole idea seems to be tempting fate a bit too much, like some Shakespearean drama.

"Luca, you don't think Jasmine would intentionally sabotage this, do you?"

Luca pulls back and studies me. "What do you mean?"

There's no way for me to tell him what I mean without telling him what she's already done. "I don't know. I'm just worried she might get mad about me being in Scotland and tell people enough that it gets out or something."

"Jasmine has the most at risk of any of us. She wouldn't do that."

I don't say anything. Luca isn't going to see her as she really is until he's ready.

"You don't think so?"

I shrug. "She's the most famous, so, in a sense she has the highest stakes. But that also insulates her to some degree. At least half of her fans would defend her no matter what she does, which is still a significant fan base. People will keep buying her albums, even if it's just for the confessional songs she'd write. I see a lot of ways she could spin this to her advantage if she decided to."

"And to your detriment?"

I keep my eyes on the sparkling lights of the darkened city. "The longer this goes on, the more I see how badly I look in all of it. But she could hurt you, too."

"She's not like that."

I'm not sure he really believes this. I should let it go, but I can't stand him defending her.

"Look, Luca, she's like you, she has a public persona and a private one. Her public persona is sugar sweet, but her songs show she'll do what it takes to be on top. How much do you really know her? I mean, *really* know her, and not the persona she struts around in."

Luca shuffles. "Story, I know Jasmine can be harsh sometimes, but it's just because of all the pressure."

I nod. More for his sake than because I believe him. "I get that she doesn't want this to blow up, but if it does, she's got a nice cushion to work with."

Luca stares into the blue. "She knows what's at stake. I promise I won't let you lose anything in this."

"That's not a promise you can keep."

"What are you saying, Story?"

"I checked Princeton's rules about offers. It seems unlikely the school would come after me for something that happens off campus unless it's an actual crime, but Harvard rescinded a bunch of offers a few years ago over some social media memes. Anything that reflects poorly on my honesty or judgment is fair game. It would probably come down to how badly the tabloids make me look and how much blowback the school got for my role in it. She's more than just a big star, Luca. She's at the epicenter of the music industry."

His face clouds up. "You have a backup plan, right?"

"I've already had to decline the other schools I got into. Besides, if Princeton won't take me, why would they?"

He shrugs, but not with his usual confidence. "Some schools would fluff it off as celebrity nonsense. Where else did you get in?"

"Brown, Tufts, and Oxford."

"Oxford? We could get the band back together!"

A couple walks past us a little too closely, and I lower my voice. "There is no band, Luca. And, by now, they've given away my spot, even if they were willing to overlook whatever fallout might come."

"There's always someone who doesn't show up. And Oxford could hardly blame you for all this. They'd be more likely to blame me."

"Great, we can both get kicked out, except I'm not actually in at this point."

"Look, Story, you worry too much. We're lying about something that no one has any right to expect us to tell the truth about."

I don't say anything.

"Story?"

"All I know is that I'm helping Jasmine lie to her fans, and she's going to make a fortune because of it when this album drops. Otherwise, the label wouldn't have made her keep it a secret in the first place. Her fans aren't just buying her music. They're buying her whole lifestyle. It feels like fraud, and I'm at the center of it."

He shakes his head, but I'm not sure if it's at me or at himself. "Jasmine doesn't owe anyone the details of whom she dates."

The girl literally traffics in boyfriends by selling songs about them. But I don't throw that in his face. "A lot of people wouldn't be happy about her lying to them, which gives her a lot of incentive to make it someone else's fault. But," I add to make him stop frowning, "I'm happy to see that you know the difference between 'who' and 'whom.'"

He shakes his head. "Crivvens, where did I find you?"

"In a gelateria off the Piazza di Spagna. I made the mistake of wearing yellow that day."

Luca laughs and pulls me into him. "Dai, we have a big day tomorrow. I'll keep Jasmine under control. I promise."

I slip my arm around him, and we walk back down to my flat as if we're the lovers we pretend to be, wishing Luca's promises were as solid as he wants them to be.

Twenty-Five

Andrew's father sends a private jet to bring us to Scotland, and, like everything with them, it surprises me how easily it all comes. There's no line at the counter, no long shuffle through security, no need to pull up a confirmation number on my phone, no worry about getting a taxi on the other end. Luca's sister is to pick us up at the Oban Airport.

The small jet has a set of club chairs facing each other with a table in between on one side, and a long bench on the other. Andrew gestures me into a window seat and sits down beside me. Luca takes the seat opposite and then takes a picture of Andrew and me.

"Are you putting that on your feed?" Andrew asks. "People might think I'm trying to steal your hen."

"No," Luca says. "Some pictures are just for us."

The flight is a little more than four hours. In the early afternoon, Luca takes me over to the bench seat to show me Glasgow when the clouds break. Luca's family has a residence in Edinburgh, but we're going to the house he actually calls home. The terrain below becomes more remote as we head northwest. When we begin the descent, Luca pulls me back to the club chairs and puts me on his side by the window.

"Isn't it gorgeous?" he asks as he leans in, and a tiny airport next to a large bay comes into view.

Andrew takes a picture of us looking out the window. I look over at him.

"Some photos are just for us," he says with a slight smile. When it pops up in my texts, I mouth, *Thanks*. He gives me a small shrug. Maybe he knows how much I'm going to miss them.

Adaira is waiting by the tarmac when we pull up outside the tiny white bungalow that serves as the airport's terminal. She and Luca have the same beautiful lines to their faces, and the same dark, soft hair. Her eyes are more green than blue, though, and when she smiles, there's a lot more determination to it than I've ever seen with Luca, even when he's using his public persona.

"It's so great to meet you," she says, pumping my hand up and down. "Luca has told me so much about you."

"It's lovely to meet you as well." All the practice I've had with Luca over the summer meeting people doesn't help me feel any less nervous with his sister. Or guilty. We hustle our luggage into her Mercedes SUV, and Luca offers to drive, but Adaira says she wants to make it in one piece.

"I've become a very responsible driver, haven't I, Story?"

"He actually has."

Adaira laughs and swings into the driver's seat, and Andrew rides shotgun. "Well, I'm glad to hear it!"

We skim through remote landscapes. Lush greens sparkle under huge puffs of blue-gray clouds. Adaira asks me a slew of questions.

"So where did you two meet?" she asks, catching my gaze in the mirror.

I look at Luca, not sure what to say.

"In a gelateria near the Keats-Shelley House," he says.

"I can't believe Luca even knows there is a Keats-Shelley House, how did you manage that?"

"My friend works there," I say.

"And how long have you lived in Rome?"

"Almost a year."

After a few more questions, she meets my gaze in the rear-view mirror and winks. "Sorry, he'll always be my little brother."

"It's fine. Andrew thought I was a wee bit of a chancer at first, too."

Andrew looks back at me with mock confusion, and Luca laughs.

When we get near Oban, Luca points out landmarks with the excitement of a little boy.

"You'd think you'd been away for years," Adaira says. "Was Rome so bad?"

"No," Luca says. "Rome wasn't bad at all."

I turn my face to the window then, already knowing Andrew is giving us his disapproving face. But I let myself imagine how wonderful this would all be if it were real, even if it's only for a few moments.

"Addie, take a turn around town before we drop Andy off. I want Story to see how bonnie it is," Luca says.

Adaira takes us through the heart of Oban. Victorian architecture slopes up hills away from the blue bay. Sailboats line the harbor, and there's something that looks like the Colosseum at the top of a nearby hill.

"That's McCaig's Tower," Luca says. "It was probably supposed to be a museum and art gallery, but when the owner died, his family contested his will and construction stopped. It's a park now. I'll take you there. I know how you love follies."

"You're not a bad tour guide," I say.

"I learned from the best."

We head back out of town, along pretty country roads. We turn into a driveway and follow it to a hillside with views of the town and harbor. I lean my head down a bit to take in a substantial old stone mansion. Adaira pops the back hatch, and Andrew turns and says, "Well, I'll check on you kids later. Don't do anything I wouldn't do." He looks straight at me as he imparts this wisdom.

He hops out and retrieves his bags from the trunk before he bounces up the front steps. Adaira pushes the button to close the back hatch.

"I see Andy hasn't changed," she says, smiling at us in the mirror.

"Andy will never change," Luca says. "It's one of his charms, like a reliable club chair."

Adaira and I chuckle. Luca grabs my hand, but when I look at him, I don't think he even realizes he's doing it as he's watching the scenery fly by. We drive on for another ten minutes or so, and then Adaira pulls into a one-lane road. We follow it through twists and turns, trees lining either side.

We make a turn, and ahead of us is a stunning white house that has a kind of castle appearance to it, with circular towers built on either side, framed by blue water behind and rolling green lawns in front. I expected a lot, but this is beyond even what I had imagined.

Adaira follows the gravel drive around the house to the back. The view of the bay is almost too perfect to be real, and I'd forget to get out of the car except that Luca is tugging me. There are garden beds all around the house with miniature seas of pink and coral and blue flowers. Seagulls cry over the water, and a soft breeze is blowing.

"The weather is going to be great for sailing tomorrow," Luca says. "Come on."

"Shouldn't we get our bags?"

"Hodges will make sure your things get to your room."

He pulls me up across a terrace into the back entrance of the house, which shines with dark woods and white ceilings and walls. It smells like lavender and mint. The hallway opens to a large, fancy kitchen, and there's a back staircase at the end of the hall. An older woman in a chef's uniform smiles at us.

"Welcome home, sir! It's been too quiet without you." She's kneading dough, her hands covered in flour. "And welcome, Miss Herriot."

"It's a pleasure to meet you," I say.

"This is Iona. When you get hungry, just tell her. She knows you're vegan."

I suddenly feel stupid over the three bottles of water and handful of vegan protein bars in my luggage.

"That's right, miss, anythin' you want, just let me know. I've got plenty of plant-based staples in for you."

"Thank you, that's so thoughtful."

Adaira wanders down the hallway. "Mother, Luca's here."

We follow her, but then Luca stops me. "Are you nervous?"

"Why?"

"You're squeezing the blood out of my hand."

"Oh, sorry." I slacken my grip.

He smiles. "There's nothing to worry about. I promise." He pulls me on as if I'm really his girlfriend about to meet his mother.

There's a bisecting hallway and then an entryway at the front of the house with soaring ceilings. A grand staircase swirls upward to a balcony hallway. Off this entryway are several rooms, and Luca follows the sound of Adaira's voice into an elegant sitting room. It's large, with long casement windows that sweep the two outer walls like dancers holding their positions. Blue and white fabrics, with splashes of color and fresh flowers on a credenza, make it one of the happiest rooms I've ever seen.

"Hello, Mum," Luca says. He drops my hand and goes over to kiss her.

"Luca! I've missed you." She's a tall woman with fashionable blond hair and Luca's straight nose. Adaira is also tall as she stands beside her mother, and I feel like a gorse bush surrounded by oak trees.

"I'd like to present Miss Astoria Herriot to you."

I think Luca forgot to tell me I'm supposed to bow or something. This is not average rich-people stuff. "How do you do, Mrs. Kinnaird?" I hold out my hand.

"Oh, sorry!" Luca says, slapping his palm to his forehead. "I forgot to tell you, it's 'Your Grace.'"

My mouth drops open, and I feel just like I did the first night we met. All that's missing is stracciatella dripping off my tongue. "I'm so sorry, Your Grace, forgive me." I look at Luca to see if I'm supposed to curtsy or something.

"Oh, darling, it's fine," she says as she gives Luca a quick side-glance. Her voice is serene, though, as if she could convince grizzly bears to do yoga. She takes my hand, but not like a handshake. Instead, she cradles my hand between both of hers as she looks into my eyes, probably calculating how long she thinks I have left before Luca moves on and why I'm so stupid that I don't know to say "Your Grace" instead of "Mrs. Kinnaird."

"Thank you for having me. Your home is lovely."

"Thank you, dear," she says as she lets my hand go.

I wrestle a jar of blueberry preserves from my little backpack. "I brought you this. It's from my grandfather's farm in Maine. He doesn't actually make the preserves, a lady in town does, but they're his blueberries."

She takes the jar from me, and I'm glad it's got a pretty little watercolor label from Mabel's Stoneground Organic Kitchen. "Thank you, Astoria, how thoughtful! We'll have it tomorrow with breakfast, this looks delicious. We're delighted you could be with us."

"It was very kind of you to include me. You can just call me Story, if you like."

"I'm looking forward to getting to know you, Story, but you'd probably like a chance to freshen up. Luca, why don't you take Story up to her room and help her settle in? We'll have an early dinner so we have time to relax tonight and catch up. I want to hear all about Rome. It sounds like it's been very interesting." She gives Luca a playful smile.

"Aye, Mum." Luca puts his hand on my elbow and steers me out of the room as Adaira adds, "If you need anything, just ask."

"Thank you," I say. I look back and they're watching me curiously, probably wondering how Luca managed to bring home an ordinary girl who isn't a model.

I follow Luca upstairs and along the balcony hallway into another hall. "I had them put you on the bay side so you have the view."

"Thanks."

He smiles. "What do they say in Italian? Certo?"

"Sì, certo."

The room looks like it belongs in a BBC show, with glistening vistas of the water and a large, four-poster bed. My suitcase is on a luggage rack, and puffy towels are stacked in the adjacent bathroom. It's like staying at a five-star hotel, which I wouldn't know except for having seen how Luca's hotel treats him. There are even chocolates on the pillow.

"So, what's going on? Are you royalty or something?"

I kind of expect him to laugh, but he bobbles his head from side to side as if to say *Sort of.*

"Luca?"

"My father's a duke."

I stare a moment as this settles in my head. "And you didn't think to mention this to me at any time since we met?"

"Well, I did, but it never seemed like a good time. I knew you'd frown, just like that."

"I'm not frowning." I try to smooth out my face.

"And you apparently never Googled me, so—" It even sounds stupid. "Googling" someone.

"Buyer beware?"

Luca smiles tentatively. "Something like that?"

From now on, I am definitely Googling people.

"So what are you?"

"Well, technically, I'm a commoner, just like you. At least until I inherit my dad's title. But I have the honorary title of marquess."

I put my hand around a post of the bed. "Why didn't you tell me?"

Luca shuffles on his feet. "Well, at first, I didn't tell you because I didn't know you well enough. I mean, most people know this about me, but you were so innocent of it, I figured

I'd get to know you better first, in case you weren't what you seemed. A good cardplayer never shows his hand and all that. And then, that day at the Porta Alchemica—"

"I made fun of the Marquess of Pietraforte."

"You kind of said we were all crazy, so I figured I should wait until you knew me better because you were just starting to tolerate me, and I didn't want to give you a reason to dislike me any more than you did."

That day was the first time Luca and I had fun together. "I'm sorry?"

Luca laughs. "I was going to spring it on you on the plane when I had Andrew there to shame you into accepting me with his upper-crust pride. But then I got too focused on showing you Oban and forgot."

"So is Andrew royalty, too?"

"No. He's just a spoiled rich brat. I'm a spoiled rich brat with a title."

"So that's what you meant when you said the eldest son had certain expectations to meet in your family?"

He nods.

"And you can't disappoint your family."

The smile leaves his face. "Come here." I follow him across a plush carpet to the window. The view is like something out of a travel magazine. Luca slips his hand into mine. "It's not a terrible price to pay for all this."

Small white crests rise and fall, and a road of sunlight sparkles into the horizon across the water. Shorebirds glide on currents of air above the pebbled beach. "I guess we've both had expectations guide our whole lives. Now I get why you were so interested in Princess Ann in *Roman Holiday*."

He pulls his hand from mine and slips it around my shoulder, his hand resting gently against my neck, and holds me close, his lips resting on my temple. I feel like Psyche must have when Cupid raised her from her deathless sleep, my heart skittering all over the place. I look up, and his lips brush my nose. For a second, I think he's about to kiss me for real.

"Well," he says, pulling away from me as he clears his throat, "I should let you have a few minutes to yourself before the grilling begins. You're going to be charred like a swordfish. Let me know if you forgot anything. I can get the messages or send someone."

"Get the messages?"

"Oh, that means go to the store, because, you know, someone writes the list up and leaves it on the fridge and then someone goes to get the messages."

"That is the cutest saying I have ever heard. How did you guys *not* conquer England?"

"Ah, hen, I ask myself that all the time." He breaks into a huge smile. "I'm so glad you're here."

I laugh. "I wouldn't have missed it for the world."

Twenty-Six

A half hour later, Luca texts. *Would you like a tour of the ancestral heritage that leads to my peerage?*

How could I possibly say no?

He knocks on my door a minute or two later and offers me his arm.

"Andrew wouldn't approve of you making fun of your title."

Luca shakes his head. "Definitely not. He takes this all very seriously. Which is good because if people like Andrew didn't take it seriously, it wouldn't exist, and we'd need to find new ways to be relevant, rather than relying on the mad warrior skills of my ancestor, the first Duke of Dunrobin. He vanquished a bunch of heathen keelies at the Battle of Haddon Rig in 1542. There's a portrait of him in the library. I'll show you. I have his chin."

He says this last bit with mock seriousness in his best home accent.

"Poor Andy. No wonder he's so invested in protecting the sanctity of the realm."

"Someone's got to do it."

Luca starts our tour in the uppermost part of the house, which isn't exactly a watchtower, but is a kind of attic widow's walk. "When we were kids, Addie and my other sister, Lillias, and I would come up here and pretend to be guarding the place from invaders. Usually English, but sometimes French or Viking. Lil would always cry because I'd say we should offer her as a sacrifice."

"That's terrible. And did you win?"

"Did we win? We're Kinnairds! We have the mad warrior skills of the first Duke of Dunrobin in our veins, you daft American."

"Of course," I concede. "I think I would have imagined this to be a magical castle."

"Well, Princess Astoria, you would have been a great ruler."

"Thank you, my lord."

"I mean it." He studies me. "I think I'd trust you with the fate of the world more than anyone I've ever met."

"I doubt I have your mad warrior skills, though," I say, blushing a little at the compliment.

"No," he says. "But you have a pure heart. And that, sweet Story, is worth more than mad warrior skills any day."

I'm not sure what to say, so I don't say anything. But I wish I could tell him how grateful I am to have known him. He touches his fingertips to mine, and for a moment we just look at each other. Luca opens his mouth to say something, but then he turns away.

"Come on," he says. "It's a huge house and we are expected at the table at precisely six o'clock."

I start to follow him but then pull back. "I'm dressed all right, aren't I?"

"I mean, it's fine if that's all you brought." He shrugs.

I hesitate. "You're teasing me, right?"

"Aye, Stor, I'm kidding. This isn't Buckingham Palace. And you look beautiful." He turns, and I could swear I hear him add, "Really beautiful."

Something about the way he says it reminds me of his charity kiss, and my face gets hot no matter how much I will it to stop.

We continue the tour. His room is on the other side of the house from mine, and also faces the bay. It smells like him, a kind of earthy pine I love now. There's a desk across from his bed. The cheetah cubs photo from the gallery opening hangs above it. We stand at the window. Someday, he'll bring Jasmine here. I'm not the one who's supposed to be sharing this view with him. For the first time in my life, I envy a celebrity.

"It must be hard to grow up in a house like this. You'd never get to redecorate your room."

Luca smiles. "I bet every place you've lived in you've had a different theme to your room."

"Guilty," I say. The word settles on me like a mist because I'm not Jasmine. "We'd better keep moving if we're going to be on time."

We make our way downstairs. He shows me the library with the portrait of the first duke. Luca stands beside it and sticks his chin out until I assure him that I see the resemblance. When our eyes meet over the laugh, I have to turn away.

I run my hands along the books, soaking in their titles. "This room is gorgeous."

"I knew anyone who appreciates the Keats house would appreciate this."

"I could live above it." There's a little cushioned window seat with leaded panes glinting in the late-afternoon light, and Luca points to it. I nod. That would definitely be my spot, and it's like we have our own secret language, we know each other so well.

We wander down a corridor to a large hall, with wide plank floors and dark paneling. At the far end, a drum set, piano, and several guitars are clustered together.

"Oh, jings," I say.

"You spend too much time with Andy and me." He goes to the drum set and sits down, then nods at me to take a guitar.

"What should we play?" he asks.

"He mostly plays pub music," someone says, and I look up to see a boy of about thirteen standing in the doorway. He looks like a younger, blond version of Adaira.

"Story, this is my brother, Will."

We say hello, and Will sits at the piano. "Do you all play?" I ask.

"Just Will and Lillias and me," Luca says. "She's a better drummer than I am."

"But Luca plays at the pub in town," Will says.

"When Craig's band is home, they let me mess around a wee bit. That's all."

I suppose being on tour like Jasmine, or maybe even with her, is the thing Luca can't do because of his title. It makes him feel even farther away.

"Will," Luca says, "can you play 'Where the Heather Grows'? You had it down really well before I left for Rome." It's the biggest hit Craig's band has had. Luca looks at me. "You can play it, right? You sing along to it in the car."

"I think so," I say.

Will finds the music for it, and Luca and I study the notes before handing it back to him. I have to tune the guitar a bit, and it takes us a couple tries to get together, but then we do.

"Will, you are amazing," I say.

"Thanks," he says with a slight blush.

"Story, will you sing it?" Luca asks.

I've told him way too many things about the inner workings of my heart. The song is about a boy who starts out using a girl until he ends up falling for her and asking her to stay in Scotland with him, where the heather grows. Luca's not trying to make me fall in love with him, and I'm not the girl he can't lose. But he's always just a little more than you expected him to be. He and Will join in on the chorus. When the last note sounds, there's clapping. Adaira is standing just inside the door with an older man who must be Luca's father.

Luca sets down his sticks and steps out from the set. He shakes his dad's hand and introduces us.

"It's lovely to have you here, my dear," the duke says. He's tall like Luca, and a bit stern looking.

"Thank you, Your Grace."

"We can dispense with formalities tonight, I think," the duke says as he lets my hand go. "Except for the party, this weekend is just about family. Let's go into dinner, shall we? Luca, will you escort our guest?"

Luca offers me his arm. "See how quickly you picked up the royal lingo?" he whispers.

"I'm not a total bampot. I've seen a few princess rom-coms in my day."

"Well, that's good, because you're going to need those mad skills to make it through dinner with my family."

I glance up at him, but as we enter the dining room, I'm not entirely sure he's joking.

I meet Luca's other brother, Camden, at dinner. Lillias and her husband are coming the day after tomorrow from London. Camden is fifteen, and he and Will excel in telling stories of the stupid things Luca has done growing up, like the time he got his finger stuck in a metal grate in a store, or the time he fell from the barn loft making out with a girl. Luca takes it good-naturedly, and I suspect this isn't the first time the family has been through this performance for one of Luca's real girlfriends.

Dinner has a lot of courses, and I watch Luca to see what

silverware he uses for each so I don't look like I just crawled out of a blueberry patch in backwoods Maine. Anytime someone asks me anything vaguely personal, Luca follows up my answer with something that takes the conversation in another direction.

After dinner, we have dessert on the terrace. Luca brings me his Oxford crew hoodie when he sees me hugging my arms. Will starts a fire in the outdoor fireplace. The sunset over the bay completes the fairy tale. Luca must have told them about me because they tactfully stay away from asking about my dad. But the dinner gloves are off, and they ask lots of questions about where I've lived and about Maine and Princeton and the rest of my family and what I want to do with my life. It's almost like a job interview.

Luca chimes in enough to not seem distracted, but he keeps texting and then watches me contemplatively, which makes me more nervous than the dissection his family is giving me. The only time he's really animated is when he talks about Rome. He fills his parents in on the social obligations he's completed, but he also talks about the fun things we've done.

"Luca volunteered at a farm sanctuary?" Will asks with a snort.

"Luca loves animals," his mother says.

"Mum," Adaira says, "riding horses is not like taking care of real farm animals."

"He's actually a lot of help," I say. "He'll even rake the stalls."

A collective cry of disbelief and joking follows this report.

"You know, you lot don't know as much about me as you think you do," Luca declares, but he's laughing.

When the evening's over, he walks me to my room. At the door, he takes my hand. "Story, I know I promised you sailing tomorrow, but could we postpone it a day?"

"Sure, we don't have to go if you need to do other things."

He glances around. "I need to run to Edinburgh tomorrow. Jasmine is in Manchester for her tour, and she wants to hop over to meet. It's actually perfect timing."

There's a huge tug on my heart as reality straightens it up. Somehow, though, it's still leans like the Tower of Pisa. "Of course." I slip my hand from his. "The boys want to take me riding while I'm here, so I'll just pal around with them for the day."

"Well, you need to come, because my parents aren't going to believe I'm just abandoning you here for a jaunt to Edinburgh. Andy said he'd come, too, and he can show you around the city, and my family will just think we're taking you sightseeing. We can leave in the morning, and we'll be back by dinner. It's only a two-and-a-half-hour drive."

I picture the ride. I imagine Luca anticipating his hookup with his scorching diva the whole way there, and then I see him missing her already on the way back. It stings a lot more than it should, which seems like a just punishment for not having listened to Andrew. I did plan to follow Andrew's advice. Or, more accurately, I never even thought I needed his advice. But, somehow, opening the door to Luca as a friend has led to my whole house being blown apart. I thought I had built it out of bricks, but I seem to be the little piggy who used twigs after all.

"Sure, whatever you want."

"It's just, I need to see her, in person, you understand?"

The arrow hits my chest, and he doesn't even know he's holding an empty quiver. Luca and Jasmine haven't seen each other in almost a month, not since the day trip for brunch. Of course he wants to be with her. I just wish I'd realized how close she would be so that it could have occurred to me, rather than standing here like a blindsided groupie. I dig down into the bottom drawer of my pride dresser and pull out a smile.

"Of course, I understand. I'd love to see Edinburgh."

He looks at me a moment, and I'm not sure how much longer I can manage without tears coming. "Thanks," he says. "You've been the greatest fake girlfriend any guy could ask for. I know you never wanted any of this. I don't deserve you."

I want to tell him he doesn't, but I don't have any right to be mad. Playing the dutiful sidekick is what I signed up for.

"I mean that," he practically whispers. "I hope—"

He stops, his lips hovering just over mine, and I'm not sure when or how we got so close, but I'm pressed between Luca and the door to my room, and all I can think of is when he kissed me before, even if it was just a charity kiss.

I can't hold his gaze while I wait for him to tell me how he hopes we'll still be friends after all this. I look down. We stay like that a second, and then he pecks my forehead almost as if I'm a bird he's worried of frightening away. He turns down the hall toward his side of the house. "Sleep tight, sweet Story," he says over his shoulder.

I close the door and go to the window and listen to the wind over the bay, and, still wrapped up in Luca's hoodie, I let myself have a really good cry.

Twenty-Seven

Luca and I have breakfast with his parents and Adaira. If they're upset about us running off to Edinburgh for the day, they don't show it. I just hope they don't think it's my idea. Not that it matters if they like me, but I don't want them to think I'm rude.

We take Luca's dad's Land Rover and pick Andrew up a little past eight. "That gives me time to go with you guys for a while," Luca says, as if he's a little kid, afraid to miss anything. "I don't have to meet Jasmine at the hotel until one."

I concentrate on the scenery. It's ridiculous that he's seeing his diva and still worried about what fun Andy and I might have without him. He's getting more like her, wanting every-thing while sacrificing nothing. Luca and Andrew point out landmarks from time to time, and I just listen.

"You okay?" Luca asks, reaching his hand over to my arm when we're getting close to the city. "You've been really quiet."

"Yes, of course," I say. "I can be quiet, sometimes."

"I hadn't noticed," Andrew chirps from the back seat. I turn to send him a dry look, but they laugh, and it distracts Luca.

We stop at the Kinnairds' town house in a fashionable neighborhood that could be a posh section of London. Long rows of stone buildings line wide streets. The house is four stories of Georgian splendor, and it's like being in a beautifully curated museum.

"Do you like it?" Luca asks as he finishes showing me around.

"It's gorgeous. No wonder Andy is afraid of us ordinary folks wanting a slice of your life."

Andrew grabs me in a bear hug and rubs his fist into my hair, but not hard. "I cannae stand this hen, Luca."

Luca laughs. "Dai, let's get an early lunch before I have to go."

We walk to a pub a few streets over that Luca says is his favorite in the city. It's an old, dark hiding place, away from tourists and high achievers. "No paparazzi here?"

"Oh, Story, there's no paparazzi in Edinburgh unless they're following a big star," Andrew says, both of them amused at my naivete.

"You'd find them in Kansas before you'd find them here," Luca says. He stops. "Which is a place no one really goes, right?"

I shrug. "I mean, it was good enough for Dorothy." They give me a confused look, and I shake my head. "Never mind."

When we're settled at the table, Luca gives Andrew specific instructions about where to take me. He's even made a list on notebook paper that he pushes across the table. Andrew shakes his head at the small, neat print.

"Buy Story a pretty tartan skirt in Princes Street," Luca tells Andrew, "Something classic. I'll pay you back."

"That's not necessary," I say.

"You'd look beautiful in one," Luca says.

I wish he weren't so used to dropping compliments as if they were pennies in a fountain.

Our food comes, and we're still eating when Luca checks his phone. "I guess I should go," he says, as if he's going off to some dreaded chore instead of seeing his girlfriend.

"You can stay with us if you want," Andrew says with a laugh.

Luca drops his money on the table to pay the tab. "Some things you have to do in person," he replies. Andrew and I glance at each other, and Andy pulls his eyebrows up and presses his lips together.

Luca shakes his head at us. "A couple of bloody nuggets, you two are. I'll text you later to meet up. Just make sure Story has a good time. And buy her anything she wants." He tosses Andrew the key fob to the Land Rover, but I can't watch him go. Someone at the bar calls goodbye to him. I look up just as the door closes.

Andy picks up the list of places we're supposed to visit. "Crivvens, we'd need a week to do all this."

I try to smile. "He means well."

Andrew looks at me, and I have to look down. "He's a mad bastard to mean well, though, isn't he?"

I force out a little laugh. "Yes. Yes, he is."

"You'll be all right."

"I know." I need to pull myself together. I should have stuck to the agreement. My head knows all this, but my heart seems to have its own opinions on everything these days.

"Honestly, though, even with all your social-justice happy-karma-wheat-grass stuff, you're the best thing that's ever happened to him. He's a better person because of you."

Andrew's steady gray eyes are serious. Mine are swimming.

"Thank you."

"I mean it, Story. He's a lot more mature since you came into his life. He even thanks me now for the things I do. And he's so happy. I've never seen him just be himself with anyone he dated for real like he does with you."

"I guess when there's nothing to prove, you don't need to try so hard." My voice is a bit scraggly.

"Maybe."

"You can say I told you so, if you want."

"I don't want."

I press my lips together and pull the list over. Sometimes Andrew is really wonderful. "Edinburgh Castle first?"

He nods. "Definitely. Come on. We'll go have a barry time and forget all about that bampot."

"Sounds good," I say, and I'm proud of how normal it sounds because it's taking all of my energy right now not to dwell on what's about to happen at the Balmoral hotel.

Twenty-Eight

We meet up with Luca a few hours later as we're walking the Royal Mile, a group of streets that link Edinburgh Castle to the Palace of Holyroodhouse. I expect him to be glowing from basking in the arms of his diva, but he seems subdued and distracted instead. It must be getting harder to leave her.

He scans the shopping bags I'm carrying. "Did you get a tartan skirt?"

"No, we didn't get a chance," I say, but the truth is I veered Andrew away from the task. I don't need any more reminders of Luca than I'm already carrying.

"We could still grab one," he says.

"I think we're already late. I don't want your parents to hate me."

He nods. "Where's the car?"

"You already asked me that," Andy replies.

"Oh, yes, on Calton Road." He checks the time on his phone. "Story's right, we should go."

"Are you okay?" Andrew asks him.

He nods. "Aye, everything's proper."

On the way back to Oban, Luca insists on hearing our sightseeing details, although he makes us repeat ourselves so much that Andrew sends me questioning glances from his perch in the back. It's hardly surprising the guy would be distracted, though, considering the bedroom gymnastics his girlfriend is always singing about. So I talk inanely about the scarf and shortbread cookies I bought for my mom on Princes Street, and the views from Edinburgh Castle.

"I'm not gonna lie, though, we kind of had to run through the Royal Botanic Garden to hit even half of your list."

Luca doesn't even laugh. "Hmmm?" he says.

I come up with something else to say then so he doesn't have to pay attention. It's exhausting after a while, but it's better than imagining the details of what has him lost in thought. I console myself with thinking I wouldn't want to be Jasmine even if it meant having Luca. I'd still rather be ordinary me, sour grapes and all. That works really well, as long as I don't look over at him and catch the tender edges of a pensive smile. Every time I do that, my heart becomes the muddy blue puddle that watercolor brushes are soaked in.

Luca's grandmother has arrived, and Andrew's been asked to dinner, so he comes back to the house with us, which is a good thing. Lately, being alone with Luca has been too much like a forbidden indulgence. Despite Luca's best attempts to career us over a cliff, we reach the house by dinnertime. Luca introduces me to his grandmother, who is as sweet to me as the rest of the family has been. She's a spry, tall woman with colored-blond hair and perfect makeup. The boys want to know what I thought of Edinburgh, and Luca's grandmother wants to hear what he and Andrew have been doing in Rome. Luca sits beside me, but he's quiet, except when he's answering questions or checking if I have enough to eat.

"I'm fine," I tell him. "Iona's made plenty of vegan options."

He smiles then as if we're something more than we are, the way he always could turn it on for the cameras, and I'm glad when Camden interrupts to ask if they took me to any of the haunted cemeteries.

"No," Luca says, draping his arm over my chair. "You aren't going to top Story's haunted tours of Rome with a few ghost stories of Gallowglass mercenaries."

"Ooh, will you take us if we come?" Will asks, and the family erupts into a debate about whether a trip to Rome could be squeezed in before the end of summer. Luca stays out of it and gets vague when the boys press him, and I have the sense he's not sure how much longer he'll be in Rome. Once he and Jasmine are out in the open, he can go with her on tour, at least until he has to be at Oxford. Rome is going to feel empty without him. I promise myself to dive into planning for Princeton.

At the end of the night when Luca walks me to my room, I realize it's the first time we've been alone today. It's a start, anyway. It will get easier. I hope. If not, well, there aren't many days left together anyway.

"So, sailing tomorrow?" he asks as we stop by my door.

"If you have things to do for the party, we don't have to."

He shakes his head. "Mum and Addie have this thing running like clockwork. We'd just be in the way."

"Sure, then."

He gives me his dangerous smile, but he's not doing it intentionally. It's who he is. Dangerous, just the way Andy warned me at the beginning. We look at each other, but it's awkward, like he wants to say something.

"Good night," I say.

"Right, good night." He turns but then swivels around again. "There's something we should talk about tomorrow."

"Okay. Do you want to tell me now? You can come in."

He looks at me and furrows his brow. "No. It can wait until we're sailing. I want you in a really good mood when we talk about it." He gives me a wan smile. "Sleep tight, sweet Story," he says and turns for real this time.

As he walks away, I let out a heavy breath. Whatever idiotic thing Jasmine wants me to do now must be a real doozy.

Twenty-Nine

Luca texts me a little past six. *Get up sleepyhead. We already don't have time to see everything I want to show you.*

I don't tell him I've been up since dawn, trying to push thoughts of him away. *See you downstairs.*

I get ready and grab my things. Part of me is dreading today, and part of me wants to live in it forever. No wonder there are so many stories about love. It's a mess.

When I get to the kitchen, Luca is already there, putting food and stainless-steel bottles of water into a small cooler. The only other person there is Luca's grandmother, who shares her steaming Earl Grey tea and lemon-poppy scones with me.

"They're vegan," she says. "I checked with Iona."

I smile and slather on some vegan butter.

"My dear," she says, "I hope you're looking forward to tonight as much as I."

"I am, thank you," I say, even though I'm pretty sure coming here has been a terrible mistake. I would've been a lot better off if I'd never had this glimpse of Luca Kinnaird in his natural habitat. Having him in my mind's eye as he is now, leaning against the black AGA stove with his blue T-shirt snug across his shoulders and a hint of stubble on his smile, is just going to make him harder to forget. Impossible, really.

"Did your dress come yet?" Luca asks as he downs some orange juice.

"No, but Dani said she was overnighting it to be here before three."

Luca nods, and we clean up our breakfast things and set out. When we get to the garage, Luca gives me a choice.

"So, do you want to take my dad's 1966 Aston Martin or my Vantage?" He points to a modern convertible. "Oh, and my dad's car has been converted to an electric engine, so no worries there. See how well you have me trained to think about these things?" He grins at me.

His dad's coupe is really cute, but I choose Luca's car because it's his. I might as well be a glutton.

"I thought you'd pick the classic."

"Another day," I say. But then I hesitate because the back seat is nonexistent. "There's no place for Andrew to sit."

"I didn't ask him. I thought it would give us a chance to chat." His eyes dart about.

Jasmine's latest demand is apparently going to take some serious explaining. So much for not being alone with Luca.

"Is that okay?" He looks concerned.

"Of course." I don't think he believes me any more than I believe myself, but he nods and opens the door for me.

We drive to a marina on the southern end of Oban. It's much smaller than the marina in town. The views across the secluded little harbor of Loch Feochan are so pretty that I take pictures just for me.

The Kinnairds' sailboat looks like something out of a New England travel brochure. "Do you like her?" Luca asks as he pulls me onto the deck. "She was built by a company in Maine."

"Really?"

"Aye. A town called Boothbay?"

"Oh, that's north of my granddad's place, on the way up to Acadia."

"Well, if you ever invite me to Maine, we'll rent a boat and go exploring."

I smile, but it takes so much effort.

"It's not a yacht, though," he adds apologetically.

I channel Kelsey's most annoying tone. "Hashtag 'slumming in Oban.'"

Luca cracks up, which makes me laugh, too.

We stow the food and other supplies in a little cuddy toward the bow. He explains how the rigging works and all the main features. "June's the best sailing weather of the year, but July's still good. We'll never get as far as we could have yesterday, though. I really wanted to take you around Mull. I'm sorry."

I nod, trying not to think about his escapades with Jasmine. "I've never seen any of it, so whatever we see will be awesome."

He smiles and tugs my baseball cap into place. "We'll go up toward Tobermory, at least, and see the puffins and seals. But we won't get far enough for whale watching."

"Puffins and seals are perfect."

We navigate out of the little harbor to the channel that will take us to the Sound of Mull, just north of Oban. Boats are everywhere, and Luca yields to the big ferries and cruisers taking people to and from towns like Oban. He sails us past Lismore where there's a pretty, white lighthouse set into what looks like a fortress, framed by blue mountains. We pass shores with hillsides of variegated greens and rocks, dotted with little inlets at their bases. Luca knows exactly where he wants to go, and sometimes we dip into quiet little coves and wade about in the cold water. But he doesn't bring up Jasmine, and I don't make him. I'm enjoying these "just us" moments too much.

The morning passes quickly. The sailboat skimming through the water is how I imagine flying must feel to a bird. Luca has me steer sometimes, his arms guiding mine through the narrow places. I thought I was so used to him being near me, touching me, that it couldn't matter, but today I notice every tiny vibration as if I've suddenly developed bat senses. An eagle follows us for a bit, and we anchor and watch a puffin colony cascade into the water from volcanic cliffs. They catch their shiny, silver fish in clumps and take them up high to their pufflings, who are almost ready to fledge. Then Luca takes me to a place where a colony of common seals comes every summer to raise their young.

"You won't see gray seal pups until autumn, so you'll have to come back then," Luca says, as if it could happen. I'd like to bring my mom here, someday, but right now, I can't imagine when it wouldn't hurt. We take too many selfies and photos and eat cucumber sandwiches with vegan cream cheese, and Luca tells me all about the seals. It's like we're both making the most of our last hurrah.

"I don't know why my family acted so surprised I'd help you with the farm sanctuary. I volunteer with the local marine conservation groups here to help with research and rescue efforts every chance I get. It's like they believe the tabloid version of me more than the one they know."

"You never told me about volunteering."

He laughs a little. "I should have. Nobody else really cares."

So he tells me about that and the food chains and basking sharks and Minke whales, and even about the shelves and banks that form the gravels and sands of the seagrass beds. He knows a lot about the islands.

It's almost three o'clock when we stop at the Tobermory harbor. Colorful buildings anchor the town to the water in pinks and oranges and blues. We stroll along the harbor road for a bit, window-shopping. Luca pulls me into a sweet shop to pick out chocolates for his grandmother, and we decide to get ice cream.

"It's not gelato," Luca says as we consider our options, and he falls into our old patterns from Rome, wrapping his arms around me and looking at the glass cases over my shoulder, the edge of his cheek resting against my temple, the soft woodsy scent of his aftershave blanketing me. He pulls back suddenly.

"Sorry," he mumbles. "I forgot there's no one watching us here."

I don't tell him it's fine, the way I normally would.

"We should start for home," he says as he pays, checking a waterproof watch he's wearing.

We return the way we came. The clouds are heavier now, but they're like big, puffy clowns floating above us in oversized shoes. As we get near the end of the channel, Luca steers us into a little cove. "This is my favorite place," he says. "You have to see it."

A long, pebbled beach lies at the bottom of a gently sloping hill. Streams of wildflowers cascade over the rocks and through the grass toward the water. I snap a photo, but Luca's attention is drawn to the far corner of the cove. Seagulls hover over something on the beach that looks like a lump of clothing washed up.

Luca pulls us as close as he can. A furry animal lies on the rocky sand.

"What is it?"

"Otter." He slips his phone into a plastic bag, and we anchor the boat and climb down. We wade to the beach, but the otter doesn't move as we approach. There's blood on the sand around it.

"Holy crivvens," Luca says. A large gash cuts across the lower part of the otter's body. Its eyes are alert, but it's breathing hard.

"What can we do?"

"I'll call the conservation office and get a vet out here." Luca crouches down, but the otter doesn't even attempt to get away. "It's going to be okay, little one."

He pulls out his phone, while I go to the boat to get some fresh water and something to put it in. When I get back to the beach, Luca is still answering questions from the vet as he rocks on his heels near the terrified animal. "Aye, the bleeding has mostly stopped, but it definitely needs to be stitched up. Aye, aye, I'm afraid to move it. Should I put anything on it from my first aid kit? Aye. I'll wait for you, then." He shoos a fly from the wound as he hangs up.

"Ramsey, one of the local vets, is up on the north part of Lismore, so he's going to run down. But we'll be stuck here for a wee bit."

"That's okay." I put the water into a shallow plate and set it by the otter. Then we step back but sit close so the gulls get the message and we can swipe the flies away.

"These aren't actually sea otter, like you have in the States," Luca says after a few minutes. "They're just inland otters, but they've moved into the coastal waters over thousands of years. They're protected now. This area has always been a stronghold for them because the water is so clean. They've struggled in the lower UK with pollution and habitat loss."

"How do you think it got injured?"

"That looks like a propeller gash to me, and from its size, it's a younger sow or boar. But I guess it could have been a predator. It's such a clean tear, though." He shakes his head and squints up at the gulls.

"This is it, isn't it?" I ask.

"What do you mean?"

"You said there are things you can't do because of your

family obligations. I didn't know what you meant, and then I thought you wanted to be touring with some band like Craig's. But it's this."

Luca stares at the otter, his glecks resting on his forehead. "Aye. If I could do anything, it would be what Ramsey does, sailing around these islands and researching them, being a vet. I can't think of any greater thing to do with your life."

"So why don't you?"

Luca shakes his head. "Have you ever seen a duke puddling around saving otters and seals?"

"I can't say I've ever seen any duke at all before your dad."

Luca laughs. "Fair."

"What does your dad do, anyway?"

"He manages the investments and everything related to the royalty, the working farm that's part of the estate, things like that."

"Which is why you're a business major instead of a biology major?"

Luca nods.

"Well, I've never seen a duke who was a wildlife vet, but I have seen a prince who was a combat pilot marry an American actress."

Luca gazes over the water. "It's not that simple, Story. It costs a lot of money to live this lifestyle. I couldn't do it on a vet's salary."

"Well, you could still manage the investments and the farm, you'd just need to delegate some of it. And maybe you couldn't be a full-time vet, but that doesn't mean you couldn't do it at all. In some ways, the privilege binding you also gives you more choices."

Luca leans forward and chases another fly from the otter's wound. "You're an optimist, you know that?"

"I don't believe your love for your family has to mean you sacrifice who you are for them, or for tradition. The world changes, whether we try to keep it the same or not. I get that you need to embrace your family's heritage, and you should, but it can't be some box you get put into that can only look the way it's always looked. Besides, hasn't all this bad-boy image stuff been your little rebellion all along?"

Luca opens his mouth, ready to disagree with me, but then his face relaxes.

"Luca, you light up when you talk about your science classes, just like you light up over being out here. And maybe, in a way, this would be an even greater service to the traditions you're trying to honor."

He gazes at me a moment. "When did you get so wise?"

"I don't know. In Rome, I guess. Anna Maria says you can't let anyone keep you from living the life you want." Of course, her advice is totally worthless when it comes to unrequited love. "It doesn't work for everything, though."

He nods but is quiet. The otter seems to have accepted that we don't want to hurt it. Or maybe it thinks we're just like the gulls, waiting for it to die. Luca pushes the dish to it, and its little whiskered nose pokes at the edge. I pour more water onto the plate.

A soft breeze comes and goes, scented with wildflowers, as

tiny waves roll onto the shore. I need to face things as they are. "Luca, you said last night there was something you wanted to talk to me about?"

He looks at me and pulls his lip in.

"What's Jasmine mad at me for now? You can tell me."

His face clouds over. "Well, I mean, she definitely blames you."

"You mean about TMZ finding out Jeremy was in rehab? Why would I tip off the press about that? Unless she thinks I'm trying to sabotage you two, which you know I'm not." I may not be able to stand the girl, but she's still the one he wants.

"What do you mean?" He tilts his head at me. "Wait, yesterday when we were at the pub, did you and Andy really think I was there to hook up with her when I said some things you need to do in person? Is that what you thought I was saying?"

"What else would we think?"

"Oh, crivvens, I'm so stupid!" He closes his eyes a moment and breathes. "Story, I didn't drag you there so I could hook up with her. I would never do that. I broke up with her."

My mouth drops open, and so many thoughts are running through my mind that it's like a wild horse stampede. I can't grasp one before another is racing in front of it.

"Wait, are you serious?"

"Aye, I thought you knew that's why I had to see her in person?"

I shake my head slowly, trying to take it all in. "Um, no."

"Oh man, I thought you were both mad at me for bailing before the end of the charade. Andy's been scowling at me for weeks, ever since I told him what a mistake this all was. But then he said that whatever I did better not hurt you. And I didn't see any way out that wouldn't hurt you except to plow through."

I shake my head. "He's just been worried I was going to get hurt in all this." I hesitate, afraid he might pick up on what I really mean. "You know, that maybe I'd get too used to the way you live."

Luca looks at me, but I can't hold his gaze.

"You must be ragin' after everything I've put you through to keep this stupid secret."

I shake my head. "No, I'm not. I'm actually relieved."

"You can be honest with me."

"I'm glad, seriously. I don't really think she's a very nice person."

Luca scoffs. "That's an understatement. Everything you said at the overlook, and then some. I was afraid if I broke up with her that she'd come after you. I didn't want to believe she was like that. But then I started to realize she is, so I convinced myself it wouldn't be so bad to wait until the fall and then do it. After you were safely out of it."

"Wait, how long have you wanted to break up with her?"

"I don't know. Since before Nice probably. But, I mean, I've never really taken any relationship seriously." He shrugs.

"So what made you break up with her now?"

"She did. She got so jealous about you being here. Honestly, I almost stayed with her yesterday, just to protect you. She threatened to divulge the whole thing. But staying would have given her more ammunition later. The other night on the terrace, she was the one I kept texting. She wanted you to keep being my supposed girlfriend, but she wanted to have her PR team orchestrate everything. What you wore, what you said, everything. More people would have known, and who knows what they'd have put you through. From the way she was talking, it was going to be ridiculous. I knew I had to call it before it got any worse. When she said we should meet up in Edinburgh, I figured you and Andy would be expecting it. I mean, you both knew I hadn't made any attempt to see her since Nice."

"We didn't know." At least I didn't. Maybe Andy was afraid of getting my hopes up. "Andy says she's hackit in her soul, but I'm not exactly sure what that means."

He chuckles. "It means ugly, like an old crone. As usual, he's on the money. I just thought he was mad at me for all of it. It got so complicated. I didn't know how to protect you and get free. I'm so sorry."

"Don't be. It's okay." I am happy he's free of her, but just because Luca's broken up with his hackit-souled diva, it doesn't mean he wants to be with me. I swallow. "I mean, I get her blaming me. You and I have spent a lot of time together, all of it looking like the perfect couple."

And feeling like it, too. At least for me.

"Aye. We've looked like the perfect couple, and this is the hard part, Story. I've been screwing up my courage to say this to you."

My breath catches. No wonder he's been putting off breaking up with her. He's afraid I'll expect something from him if

269

he's not with Jasmine. He knows I've fallen for him. If I thought his charity kiss was mortifying, this is a thousand times worse. "You kept your end of the bargain," I say. "You've definitely treated me like a princess. I don't expect anything else."

Luca throws up his hands, his palms on his head like it might explode. "No, I've been such a jerk to you! And I know that everything I'm about to say is going to fit right into your whole perception of me as a spoiled brat who thinks he's entitled to anything he wants."

"I don't think you've been a jerk to me."

"But you do think I'm entitled. And I deserve that. But, Story, I can't imagine my life without you in it. Every time I picture my future, you're there. All the places I want to go with you, all the things I want to do with you. I know I don't have any right to ask you to care about me, and if you want to just be friends, I'll take that, because honestly, you deserve someone a lot better than me, like Andy, or that Jack kid—that guy is a ridiculously good guy. But if you'll give me even a little chance, I swear I'll make it up to you."

I wrap my arms across my stomach and try to believe I'm not dreaming this.

Luca raises his eyebrows. "Could you say something, please? 'Cause I'm having trouble breathing here." His eyes are glistening.

"How long have you felt this way?"

"I don't even know. Probably that first night, when you nerded out over Rome." He laughs in a choking kind of way. "You were so different from anyone I've ever met. And then at

Ponza, when we almost called it, I didn't want to stop spending time with you. So I doubled down, telling myself it was all for Jasmine. But it was you I looked forward to seeing. You were the one I thought about when I went to sleep. That day on the Vespa, I was gone. The only thing that kept me in this charade was protecting you. And being with you. I didn't want it to end. And at the overlook, when you started talking about how this was almost over, all I could think about was what a mess I'd made of everything and how there was no way you'd ever forgive me. Especially if I let this blow up. Story, I've never begged a girl for a chance before. But you came sweeping into my life—"

"I did not come sweeping into your life, you grabbed me and dragged me into it!" The words are combative, but I'm smiling now.

Luca breaks into a grin. "That's fair, but after I grabbed you and dragged you into my life, you upended it like the bloody *Titanic*."

"I think you mean like the iceberg that struck the *Titanic*." I'm trying to stay calm, but my eyes are wet.

He slips his hands around my waist. "And that sounds so bad, but, honestly, instead of sinking me, you make everything right." He leans his forehead against mine. "I haven't had a steak in three weeks. I'm worried about conflict diamonds and whether the Aston Martin is electrified. I know how to brush a cow and fix a fence. And I wake up every morning, and the only reason I'm checking the tabs is to make sure they haven't said something mean about you."

I shake my head, still not able to believe this. "I'm not sure another marquess would consider these good things."

He slips a strand of my hair off my cheek. "I'm thinking about how I could go to vet school and still get a business degree. And I've never felt so purposeful in my whole life."

I just look at him. It's as if all the moments we've spent together, all the little things that have made me love him, are suddenly reflected in the blue-gray of his eyes.

"Story, if you give me the chance, I promise I won't mess up again. I've never felt anything like I feel for you."

A tear rolls down my cheek. I don't know how to tell him how much I feel for him, or how miserable I've been thinking he wanted to be with someone else. Or how I can't imagine my life without him, either. So I kiss him instead. And this time when he kisses me, it's not even remotely like a charity kiss.

Thirty

"So, what now?" I ask as the otter stares up at us, still wary. I want it to be as happy and safe as I feel.

"Well, for starters, tonight we don't have to lie to my family. I guess it's a good thing they like you. They're going to be shocked when you're still around at Christmas."

"Is it too late to get in on the betting?"

He laughs before he stops. "I mean, if you want to be," he says, suddenly shy, and he's never been cuter. I dust my lips against his so he knows it's a plan.

"What about Jasmine?"

He scrunches his bonnie face. "She's not happy with either of us." He takes a deep breath. "The fact that you've become an influencer because of this really sets her off."

"The dress she sent me for the gala? It was intentionally ugly. And I mean horror-show ugly. Ask Andrew if you don't believe me."

"I believe you."

I slip my arm through his. "What if she tells?"

Luca sighs. "I think I've convinced her that it wouldn't be a great look for her. Everyone expects me to be bad. And it makes her look like such a jerk to Rowdy's fans after she doubled down for him. Her ego is bruised, but she cares more about being the Queen of Pop than she does about any guy. This way, no one has to know. She'll move on to the next sap, and it will look like she tried to make it work with Rowdy and supported him through rehab."

He kisses my temple. "If she does go public, I'll do everything I can to protect you, Stor, but she could make both our lives pretty miserable if she wants to."

"She was already making my life miserable. I couldn't stand seeing you making excuses for her."

"My priorities were completely messed up. I was so stuck in living some fake life. Meanwhile, everything I thought was fake is the only part that's real. I don't know how you don't hate me."

"It's your title," I say, and smile as the vibration of his laugh rumbles through me.

A small motorboat pulls into the cove.

"There's Ramsey."

The boat pulls up as far as it can, and a girl of about fifteen and a man jump off, carrying supplies as they wade to shore. Luca runs down and takes the things the girl is carrying.

"Story, this is Ramsey MacCloud and his daughter, Erin. This is Story Herriot."

"Oh, I was hoping we'd get to meet you," Erin says, her blue eyes lit up. Her wavy hair is the color of flames.

"Haud yer wheesht," Ramsey says to her, but he seems more embarrassed than angry.

"It's okay," I say. "I know I'm a local curiosity. How do you do?"

We shake hands, and Ramsey turns to the young otter. "Aye, probably a year old. Healthy, though, before the injury. It's a nice weight, good coat, bright eyes." He kneels and grabs some latex gloves from a backpack. The otter makes a hissing noise as he touches its flank. He takes out long, protective gloves and hands them to Luca. "Hold it, will you?"

Luca holds the otter while Ramsey triages and Erin assists, handing him antiseptic bandages to wipe the wound clean enough to see it. "Looks like a little girl," Ramsey says. "I'm just going to wrap the wound for now and take her back to the station and we'll anesthetize and stitch her there."

"What are her chances?" Luca asks.

"This is fresh. Maybe she got too close to one of the bigger vessels and was struck. But a good clean-out, some stitches and antibiotics, and she should make a full recovery. I don't see any ligament or bone damage. But she's had a close call."

"Thanks, Ramsey."

"We could use another vet around here. You should go to school for it," Ramsey says.

I smile at Luca.

"I'm actually starting to think on it." He glances at me like it's a kiss.

"Good, good."

Luca goes to Ramsey's boat and retrieves a crate. Then they wrap the otter in a giant towel and put her into the crate and carry her through the water. Erin and I follow with the supplies. "Good luck, little one," I tell the otter as Luca and Ramsey hoist the crate onto the boat. Ramsey and Erin have pulled out of the cove by the time Luca and I are ready to start back. He puts me at the wheel and wraps his arms around me and kisses me.

"So, are you ready to go to a party? There'll be fireworks."

I laugh as we steer for the headwinds. "Luca Kinnaird, I wouldn't expect anything less from you."

Thirty-One

It's almost six o'clock when we get back to Luca's house. Dani's dress has arrived, and I hurry to take a shower. Of all the "dates" Luca and I have had, none has ever given me flutters before. There's so much relief in my heart. Relief he isn't wasting himself on Jasmine. Relief he cares about me. Relief I'm not lying to his family anymore. Or mine. I don't know how Luca and I are going to make being on separate continents work, but tonight, I don't care. I just want to be with him.

The Kinnaird women have brought in a beauty stylist, and the girl stops by as I'm getting ready. "Would you like me to fix your hair, miss?"

"That would be really nice, but please, you can call me Story."

"I'm Lainey," she says with a shy smile. "How would you like to wear your hair, miss, I mean Story?"

I pad over to the box Dani sent to see what the dress looks

like. When I lift it out, we both gasp. It's reminiscent of the white gown Audrey Hepburn wore in *Sabrina,* but Dani has updated it. The strapless taffeta sheath is set off by an organza overskirt that hugs the skirt and barely trails the floor. Embroidered navy flowers cascade diagonally down the skirt from the waist and flit across the overskirt, and there's an extra band of fabric at the top of the plain bodice to give it depth. Navy elbow-length gloves in satin contrast it. I grab my phone and text her.

Dani, I could kiss you! Thank you!

She answers immediately. *I'm glad you like it. I've been nervous all day! I want pictures!!*

Promise.

"Lainey, could you put my hair up?"

"I know just the thing." She sets to work, and when it comes time to fasten my hair, she pulls out a beautiful pearled comb.

"That's not real, is it?"

Lainey shakes her head.

"Because you never know with this family."

She laughs. "We've all been wondering what you were like. Everyone here follows the celebrity magazines for the marquess."

"Well, there's no telling what he'll do next."

Lainey smiles and places little diamond-looking pins in my hair, running from above and behind my temples to the back twist.

"I can do your makeup, too."

"Thanks," I say, "but I'll do that." Luca once told me he liked the way I did it, not plastered on in thick coats like the girls he dated for real.

When Lainey leaves, I toss my makeup on and spritz Ma Griffe across my wrists and neck and slip on the dress. Every measurement is perfect. Dani has even sent navy-embroidered white satin pumps. For the final touch, I add my diamond earrings. I gave Luca a check for them, but he hasn't cashed it yet. I'll fight with him about that when we get back to Rome. I take a selfie and send it to my mom. *Can you believe this dress?*

She texts me right back. *Oh, Story, it's perfect. Are you having fun?*

Yes, everything's been wonderful. Can't wait to see you on Monday! I want to tell her that Luca loves me, that we're *together,* but she already thinks we are.

Same. It's so quiet without you.

I send her a bunch of heart emojis and kisses. I send the picture to Dani, too, and someone knocks on the door.

Luca is in his tux. He just stares at me for a moment.

"You cannae move a cow in that dress."

"Thanks."

"You look beautiful." He checks the hallway to make sure no one is near and pushes me back into the room and kisses me.

"When we get back to Rome," he says as he cradles me, our foreheads touching, "I don't want to go anywhere. We'll sit on your sofa until your mum charges me hotel fees and watch old movies and kiss every time the couple in the movie does."

"What about when they break up? There's always a point where they break up."

"We can kiss then, too. And when they do something noble for each other."

"So the whole movie?"

"If you insist," he whispers, and kisses me again. I understand why people call it butterflies, but to me it's like thousands of little stars, and they're swirling through me as they light every last cell.

Adaira's voice suddenly pops in. "Luca! Story! Come on," she says. "Wow, you two look fabulous, but we need to be downstairs. Now."

Luca smiles and offers me his arm.

The music room is set up as a ballroom, with white and salmon roses cascading from vases set out on tables scattered around the dance floor. A band plays classy soft pop, and Luca's grandmother receives her guests at the doorway. Luca and I each kiss her and wish her happy birthday. She fusses over how well we look, and then we move on and I meet Luca's sister, Lillias, and her husband. Luca's parents tell us how nice we look and ask how the sailing went.

"Luca rescued an otter," I say.

"He's always loved puttering around the islands with the animals," his mother says, looking at him lovingly.

"Well, tell us, then," his father says, and Luca launches into the story and gets most of the way through before someone comes and interrupts to speak to his dad.

Luca introduces me to his aunts and uncles and cousins. Andrew comes in and gives me a big hug.

"Luca told you?"

"He mentioned something about you both having stopped pretending to be pretending, since you weren't pretending. I wasn't sure when he'd pull the trigger with her, whether it would be before you were clear of the fallout or not, but I was hoping you'd forgive him when he did. You look gorgeous."

I smile and we say at the same time, "It's the diamonds."

"I cannae stand you two bampots," Luca says. He grabs my hand and whisks me away to meet some family friends. Everyone wants to meet me, since they think I'm Luca's latest. And, suddenly, they aren't wrong.

"You must be starving," Luca says when the buffet is announced. "I ate when we got back. I couldn't wait."

"No, I'm too happy to be able to eat."

"Then let's dance. I want to hold you."

We're on our third dance, and I've forgotten that anyone else exists, when Andrew comes over and pulls at Luca's arm.

"No, Andy, you can't dance with her. She's mine tonight." He snuggles me closer.

But when I look at Andrew's face, it's as if I'm Cinderella and midnight struck while I was still dancing with the prince. Andrew can't even find the words.

Luca stops and shuts his eyes. "It's out, isn't it?" I can feel his panic as if it's an electric pulse from his fingertips to mine.

Andrew nods. "Every tabloid is on fire with it. Rowdy, the

charity, the whole shambles. Everyone here thinks you two are just a show and that you've been chasing Jasmine all summer, or they will in a few minutes."

Around us, people are feverishly whispering and a few scroll their phones. Luca's grandmother stands in the doorway watching us, bewildered. Even the band stops playing. From across the room, Luca's parents are heading straight for us, and I'm not even sure which one of us I feel tremble.

The duke and duchess ask us to come to the library with them. "You'd better come, too, Andrew," the duchess says. "I have a feeling you've been supervising all this."

"Yes, Your Grace."

She gestures to the band to start playing. Her lilac evening gown swooshes as she leads the way out of the room while the guests stare and murmur. Luca squeezes my hand.

Luca's dad closes the library door and strides behind the huge mahogany desk. He's so angry, he doesn't say anything at first, he just straightens things on the desk and then pulls up to say something but stops himself and starts the process again.

When he does speak, he aims a laser glare at his son. "It's just one stunt after another with you. I really thought you had grown up this time. What the *hell* is going on?"

"This is not Story's fault," Luca says.

His father shuts his eyes. His whole face freezes up as if he's using every ounce of grace he has not to lose it on us.

"Start at the beginning, Luca," his mother instructs, as if she's used to having to be the voice of patience in these debacles.

So Luca recounts the important parts of the fiasco. It sounds really horrible when I hear it as a play-by-play.

"Story tried to call if off when we went to Ponza, but I convinced her to stay in," Luca says, halfway through.

"I went along with it," I say.

"No. Involving Dani was my idea. Even Andrew tried to warn me," Luca says quickly.

The duchess pinches the bridge of her nose. The duke bangs his fist on a shelf.

"And this wasn't about the money for you?" the duke asks, turning to me.

"Of course, it started out about the money. But the money isn't for me. It's for a charity, that I don't run or benefit from in any way, except it will be in my dad's name. And if you don't want Luca to give the money to them, then I understand."

"I've already transferred the money," Luca says, looking at his dad. "It's my discretionary account, not yours. Story hasn't wanted a dime from me for anything in all this outside of the charity, which is a really good cause."

"Continue the story, please," the duchess says with a dryness that could evaporate the Mediterranean.

Luca swallows and continues. Sometimes Andrew interjects, or they turn to him for confirmation. The first Duke of Dunrobin stares down with a disapproving glare.

The only part of it I can stand to hear is when Luca says, "Story has made me see I could be more than just the future

Duke of Dunrobin, that I could actually make a difference in the world and still fulfill my family duties."

His father looks at me, but he doesn't seem pleased. "Go on," he says.

So Luca continues. He tells them about the threats Jasmine made to reveal the whole disaster and why he thought it was still better to walk away. When he's done, they stare at us.

"Do any of you have anything else to say for yourselves?" the duke asks, as if he's about to sentence a gang of murderers.

"I'm really sorry to have brought scandal to your family," I say, though my voice is shaking. "I didn't think about the consequences you'd all suffer if anyone found out that Luca and Jasmine were dating. I only thought about Luca and Jasmine and Rowdy and me. It seemed like we were taking the risk. Now I see your whole family was. And I'm really sorry. I wanted to do something good in my dad's name, and at first, honestly, I just thought Luca was a spoiled brat with more money than sense, and so it didn't matter. But he's not that at all, and I've made a huge mistake." My mouth is so dry.

"This is my fault, not yours," Luca says.

"Andrew, Story, would you give us a moment alone with Luca," the duchess asks, her voice razor edged. Andrew and I nod and slip into the hall.

"Come on," Andrew says, taking my hand, "let's get back on the horse before it gets out of the corral."

"I can't go back in there. No way!"

"Sure you can. Give yourself a moment and then join me. This will blow over. Eventually."

I'm just another in the long list of Luca Kinnaird mistakes that eventually blow over. Andrew kisses my cheek and goes back into the party. I want to run up to my room and hide, but then I think maybe I should wait for Luca. Maybe the Kinnairds will want to talk to me again or want me to leave their house. So I wait outside the library. Luca's mom's voice suddenly becomes clear.

"That girl is shockingly inappropriate, Luca! What in God's name were you thinking?"

I step away so I'm not eavesdropping, but before I even can get far enough, Luca says, "It's pretty clear I wasn't thinking, isn't it, Mum?"

My mouth drops open, and for a moment I can't breathe. But maybe she means Jasmine. Luca surely means Jasmine. Their voices drop and I back away, but then his mom yells, "Bringing a girl like that into this family, this house! And with your grandmother's party tonight! How could you? You were raised better than this. We have obligations that other people don't have, Luca!"

"I know! I didn't mean to ruin tonight! I should never have risked it."

"Of all your nonsense, Luca, this is the worst," the duke exclaims. "How you could have even *thought* she was possible is beyond my comprehension, let alone expecting us to accept her!"

A small sob escapes me.

"Believe me, if I could change things, I would!" Luca's voice drops again, and I turn and run upstairs to my room. I'm not shocked that Luca's parents would think so badly of me, I deserve it. But I didn't think he'd give up on us quite so easily.

I struggle out of Dani's dress and toss it on the bed. I throw a pair of jeans and a T-shirt on and shove my things into my bags. I run down the hall to Luca's room and, my hands shaking, practically rip the earrings out. I leave them on his nightstand.

All I can think about is getting home. At least at home, I won't have to face the Kinnairds again. I run back to my room and text Andrew.

Can you give me a ride to the airport? Now?

He must have his phone in his hand because he answers right away.

The airport's closed at this hour. What's going on?

Can you take me to Glasgow? I'll get a flight somewhere and be in Rome by morning.

Does Luca know about this?

Andy, I'm begging you. I need to go NOW.

Okay, I'll come help you.

Meet me by the kitchen. I'm packed.

When I come down the back stairs, the catering staff stop and stare. Andrew walks in, and they start to work like choreographed performers, heads lowered but eyes raised. He takes my suitcase and puts his hand on my back. We head for the door when someone calls my name, and Andrew and I both turn.

It's Will. "Where are you going?"

"I—I need to head back to Rome, Will."

"Does Luca know you're going?" He walks over to us.

I can hardly breathe. "It's for Luca. Your parents are really upset, and I don't want to make it any worse for him."

"But you're the first one of his girlfriends I ever liked," he says.

I bite my lip and give him a hug.

"I really loved meeting you, too. But I need to go."

He pulls back and nods, but he doesn't look at me.

Andrew and I step outside, and he sends a valet for his car. I can barely stand still as we wait, afraid the Kinnairds will come out and tell me to my face how disgusting I am. Or worse, that Luca will find us and pretend he didn't just tell his parents he would change meeting me if he could.

As soon as we're out of the drive, I burst out crying. I cry so hard, I can barely breathe, and I think I'd be sick if there were anything in my stomach to throw up.

"Hey," Andrew says, "it can't be that bad."

"It's worse."

"Story, what the hell did Luca and his parents say to you?"

I can't even tell him. Choking sobs rack my body. Andrew doesn't say anything else. We drive in silence, except for my sobbing and sniffling. When I wipe my nose on the back of my hand, Andrew pulls a small packet of tissues from the console and hands them to me.

I don't know how long I cry, but, at some point, I just shudder and get quiet. Andy's phone has been blowing up, but he doesn't reach for it. Mine is shut off.

"This is crazy, Story. Just come back to my house and you can talk to Luca in the morning."

"There's nothing to talk about." Luca's parents are never going to forgive me. They expect him to be with a girl from their world, and I can't even blame them after the way I lied to them.

"There aren't going to be any flights to Rome at this hour. There may not be any more flights tonight at all by the time we get there."

"That's okay. I've slept in airports before." You don't travel to Maine at Christmas without getting stranded. The lights of houses and towns roll past us, but I don't really see them. All I see is the way I picture Luca's face as his mother berated me and he told her how sorry he was that he'd made such a mistake.

When we reach the airport, Andrew insists on coming in to make sure I can get a ticket. He carries my suitcase and backpack. Several of the smaller airline counters and ITA are already dark for the night. I try British Airways, but their last flight leaves for Heathrow in an hour and is already full. KLM wants to send me to Krakow for three days, while Ryanair would take me to Shannon just to get to Heathrow on Monday.

"Story, come back and stay with my family. Tomorrow we'll go talk to Luca and his parents, together."

"They don't want me there, Andrew. Let's try Air France. The French are chaotic enough to have something." I just want to go home. And I need to face my mom before she finds out from someone else.

The lady at the counter says they have a flight leaving for de Gaulle in twenty minutes and she can get me on it. They'll send me through to Rome on the red-eye, and I'll be home by sunrise.

"Book it, please." The desperation to get away from Scotland before I have to watch Luca make excuses for why we can't be together is growing with every passing minute. Of course he would choose his family over me. I just didn't think it would cost him so little or happen so easily.

"Check your bag at the gate," she says, and calls them to say I'm coming through. Andy grabs me and gives me a big hug. "I'll see you in Rome, later this week. I promise."

I pull myself up on my tiptoes to kiss his cheek as if I believe him, and then I take my backpack and bag and run to security. Luca felt like home to me, but right now, all I want is Rome.

Thirty-Two

The sun rose somewhere over the Dolomites, but I can't push through the darkness surrounding me. At Fiumicino, I drag myself to the taxi stand. Paparazzi run down the narrow sidewalk toward me as they shout, "Astoria," and cameras flash. Luca's name batters me. The early-morning air is warm and dry and smells of gasoline. The man who organizes the taxis looks curiously at me. I ask for one, speaking in Italian. As soon as he hears his language, he takes my suitcase and signs for the next in line to come forward. He shoves one of the cameramen away and opens the door for me before he puts my bag in the trunk.

I hand him some euros through the window. "Mille grazie."

I give the driver my address in Italian. He answers in heavily accented English. "You need to get away, no?"

"Yes." I root around in my backpack for Luca's glecks I forgot to leave and hide my eyes as cameras flash just outside the window.

"I get you there," the driver says as he pulls away with a big smile. He tells me he's from Senegal and chatters to me about how much I'll like Italy. It's Sunday morning, so traffic is nonexistent, except for people heading to mass at the Vatican. I scratch at my head and realize the diamond-style pins are still in, so I pull them out. I stare through the window and think the CIA should use paparazzi to find terrorists, since they seem to know everything, while the driver jabbers just outside my thoughts. I'm slowly filling up with an overwhelming sense of emptiness, as if my soul has become the inside of the Grand Canyon. Luca was the first person I've really let in since my dad died. Now it's like Luca's been swept away from me in a flash flood. Here and then gone, so suddenly it feels as if I'm drowning. The familiar grip of grief washes over me, and I have to remind myself Luca's still here, somewhere, living and laughing, even if it's not with me. I want to be angry with him for giving up on us so easily, but I can't. Being in Scotland with his family has shown me just how formidable his duties are. If all he gets out of this is vet school, at least I'll have that to be grateful for.

When I step into the flat, my mom is sitting on the sofa with her feet under her, reading her phone. She looks up as I drop my backpack and shuffle toward her. I can't meet her gaze, and I'm crying again.

"Oh, Story," she says, and folds me into her arms like an origami doll. "What on earth have you been up to? Why didn't you answer my texts or calls? I was getting frantic."

I sob until I'm exhausted by myself. She hands me tissues

from the end table and, when I finally quiet down, goes to make some tea.

"Drink," she orders as she slips the hot mug of chamomile into my hands.

I take a sip, and she brushes tears off my face with her fingers.

"I'm so sorry."

"I see that. Why don't you tell me how much of what I've read I should believe?"

So I confess every last detail. This must be why Catholics like confession, because the more my crimes spill out of my mouth, the less my heart feels like it's drowning. I didn't even realize how much it was all pressing on me. Especially lying to her. I keep saying I'm sorry and she says, "I know," or, "I can see that." She bristles that the Kinnairds would think I'm inappropriate, and then she smiles and says, "Who do they think they are, royalty?"

I give her a weak smile and shake my head.

"You're right, too soon." She gives me a bear hug and holds on. "You really fell hard for him."

"So, so hard."

"Me too. He's easy to fall for. Even without the title and the Ferrari and all the things I didn't know about. But it won't always hurt this much."

"I'm just not sure how to survive until then."

"Oh, my darling, you will."

After a while, she says we should watch a movie. Her hand skims over *Roman Holiday* and settles on *Now, Voyager.* We spend the rest of the day on the sofa, while she tries to get me to eat a little bit of this or a tad of that, and our movie marathon retreats into my favorite kids' movies.

When evening rolls in, she asks if I'm feeling any better.

"You can yell at me now."

"I think you already know everything I'd say."

I groan. "If it's not something you'd tell your mom, then you shouldn't be doing it." That's been her motto since I was little.

She raises her eyebrows. "Now you know why I say it."

She slips her arm around my shoulders. "These weren't the best choices, but you went into this with an open heart for a good reason. You haven't really hurt anyone but yourself. Luca and Jasmine can take care of themselves, I suspect. And while I don't approve of lying, especially with this whole influencer aspect, you didn't lie about anything anyone had a right to know about. Plus, this Jasmine girl sounds horrid."

"She is, Mom. So incredibly horrid."

"I wish you had taken pictures of that swamp dress."

I laugh and sniffle.

"It might not have been her who revealed your little secret, though. It could have been someone who works for her."

I shrug. "At least now I have nothing to hide."

"Did you even see the reports?"

I shake my head.

"Well, pretending they don't exist isn't going to make it go away. You should check your phone."

She goes to make us dinner, and I reluctantly pull my phone

out and turn it on. The notifications are like a fireworks show. All my social media is lit up, along with texts, voicemail, and email.

Andrew has texted, worried I haven't told him I'm home safely. Anna Maria has texted, because she's somehow seen it, and she tells me to ring if I need anything. Two of my cousins have sent messages from the States. And Elisa has called from the farm to tell me I don't need to come in this week if I'd rather not. I can't tell if she's worried about me, or the bad publicity it could bring the sanctuary.

There's a string of texts from Luca, which show me his reaction in real time. First, he can't find me and is asking where I am, then he sees I'm not in my room and my things are gone, and he keeps asking where I am and if Andrew is with me because he's missing, too. Then he finds the diamond earrings on his nightstand and the texts stop, except for one that says, *We need to talk.*

There's a text from Jack, telling me I've got a friend in him if I need one. Kelsey has texted *OMG, Story, you must be SO embarrassed. I WOULD DIE,* and Guin has texted to tell me she can't imagine how stupid I feel right now. There's irony in that and I suppose it would console her to know it's way past stupid.

The worst, though, is when I open my email. My admissions counselor at Princeton has sent a message that my presence is required Tuesday afternoon for a private teleconference. I'm to report to my high school at three o'clock.

I text Andrew to tell him I got in safely. *Thanks for everything.*

I'll always remember you. I wait a few moments, but he doesn't reply.

Then I text Jack. *I'm sorry I lied to you. I couldn't tell anyone. Looks like I'm probably getting my Princeton offer revoked in a couple of days, so you'll have to be a tiger for both of us.*

The idea of losing Princeton feels like some nightmare I can't quite wrap my mind around. All the years of planning and working and worrying about every grade, every extracurricular, every test now seem to be completely pointless. I wonder what my dad would think, and if he'd be disappointed or if he'd just welcome me to the screwup club.

Jack texts me back, full of worry, so I give him the details of my summons.

Do you want me to go with you? I mean not into the meeting, but at least to it?

That's really generous considering how I've treated you, but I need to do this on my own. Thanks, though.

Listen, Story, I don't know what went down between you two, but I can tell you one thing. That dude is crazy about you.

Maybe, but not crazy enough to stand up to his family's disapproval, so it doesn't matter.

Well, his loss IMO. If you need to talk or change your mind and want me to go with you, I'm here. Keep me posted.

I send him a purple heart emoji. Then I text Anna Maria and explain as much as I can. *Well,* she says when I've answered her questions, *don't let anyone keep you from living the life you want.*

I'll try. The life I want has Luca in every corner of it, though.

What I really need to do is learn how to change what I want. I try to picture us together, if he had stood up to his parents, but it doesn't work. Maybe that's why it was so easy for him to cave to them, because he could already see how impossible it would be for him to be torn in two directions like that.

Keep me posted.

I set my phone down, grateful for the people who still care about me but already exhausted at the idea of keeping them "posted" on my long spiral down. Andrew hasn't texted back, but for once, he probably doesn't know how to handle a situation. Luca hasn't tried to reach me since he found the earrings. I didn't expect him to, but it still stings. He's probably relieved he doesn't have to explain I'm not suitable enough for a marquess after all. At least he loved me a little bit, and at least Andrew is there for him. I close my eyes and feel Luca's lips on mine, warm sunshine above and cool sand between my toes, and my heart starts to splinter and crack like a sailboat breaking apart in a storm.

I check the tabloids next and fall into a rabbit hole of *hoo boys* that keeps getting deeper. Sources close to Jasmine say she and Luca were in the gelateria that day just as friends, and I offered to cover for her so I could get my "hooks" into Luca. According to the source, Luca was chasing her because Rowdy was already in rehab. She only started seeing Luca after Rowdy broke up with her, but they kept up the charade so her fans wouldn't blame Rowdy. She just wanted to protect Rowdy because she'll always love him.

Another tab reports sources close to me knew all along this

couldn't be real because I'm not the type of girl Luca Kinnaird would ever date. There were several other girls from my school whom Luca asked to play the part, but they all declined because it seemed wrong, so he was stuck with me. The sources also say I've always been a social climber and wannabe influencer, but the whole thing has shocked my former BFF, Guin Behringer, who has ended our friendship now that she knows the truth about me. I consider this last bit of news the silver lining.

Another tab reports Luca paid me to do this, citing sources close to Jasmine. According to this one, Luca bought me a Tesla and has started a charity for people in halfway houses because my dad died of a meth overdose. "It was heroin, but whatever," I tell my phone.

One Russian tabloid says I'm really a twenty-six-year-old American CIA agent who came here to infiltrate and destroy the British royal institution. It would be funny except I find it deeply concerning that someone somewhere is reading this and believing it. I decide whatever else the tabs have to say, I don't want to know.

When I check my social media, things really go downhill. There are messages of support. People who can't believe it or excuse or defend Luca and me. Some feel sorry for me that I've been used by Luca and Jasmine so horribly. Most of the comments, though, are from the Jasminers, her die-hard fans, and they range from disparaging to frightening. The names they call me are pretty vile. There are two death threats. One person named Steve9742 invokes a voodoo curse on me.

My mom brings two soup bowls over with rolls, and I hand

her my phone. When she's done fuming, she contacts the platforms to make them take the threats down, letting them know my mother's contacting them and I'm a minor, even if it is just for a couple more weeks, and she's an attorney who will "sue them into oblivion so that every regulator in the Western world will take action" if they don't. Then I pull up the email about my summons to Princeton, and she frowns. "I'm not really surprised. Most likely they just want to scare you into behaving better."

I want to tell her how sorry I am, but it all seems so pointless. She brushes some hair back from my face and reads my mind, the way she's done most of my life.

"Don't you dare say you're sorry. They have no right to judge you. Between what they do with the NCAA to college athletes and the parade of clowns they've matriculated who have gone on to wreak havoc on US politics, you owe them nothing."

"You wouldn't be mad if I couldn't go there?"

"Oh, honey, no. I should never have pushed it on you. It's just that's where your dad and I were happiest, when he was playing hockey and we were young and in love and planning such a wonderful life together. I guess it felt like a connection for all of us if you went there, too. But you can go anywhere you like."

"I want to crawl into a cave in Acadia and go to cyber school and major in how to become a Sasquatch."

"I think you'd have trouble getting Wi-Fi. Listen, you'll lick these wounds and face the day tomorrow. It will all work out as it should. If you want Princeton, then fight for it. If you don't, then tell them to take their concern for your welfare and—"

"I get it." She kisses my temple, the way Luca used to. Or I guess Luca kissed me the way she always has. "I really lucked out in the mom department, you know that?"

"I do, and I've been waiting many years to hear you say it." She squeezes me. "It's going to be rough for a while. But it'll get better."

I wish I had her confidence. But as I sip enough of the soup to make her happy, the only reason I'm convinced the sun will come up tomorrow is to give me sunburn.

Thirty-Three

I spend Monday hiding in our flat. Jack fights his way through the cameras out front to commiserate with me. He insists we plan a strategy for tomorrow based on different tactics the school might take, and I think he and Andy would make a great team. He brings a pint of vegan chocolate gelato and cheese-less pizza, and we spend the afternoon coming up with remorseful and mostly ridiculous platitudes for me to spout like it's a dysfunctional party game. But it makes me laugh a little.

After Jack leaves, Andrew texts to tell me to report the threatening posts, and I let him know my mom is already on it. I start to text him to ask how Luca is, but then I delete it. Two of the brands I've hawked products for DM to tell me to delete the posts associated with them, but other companies are asking to partner with me. Even though I've lost a lot of followers, I've also gained some, apparently the same people who rubberneck at car crashes.

Dani texts to let me know Andrew has explained it to her.

I'm really sorry, I tell her.

It's okay. I know how persuasive Andy and Luca can be. You really helped my business get off the ground and I won't ever be able to repay you for that. I feel so bad. I'm just afraid to say anything that could backfire on me. I've worked so hard to get here. She's really made sure she's the victim.

I understand. You need to protect the business. It's not going to help me if you turn the Jasminers against you.

What a stupid name, she replies with a rolling eye emoji.

I mark her text with a laugh, and she sends me a purple heart.

When I go to bed, I can't sleep. I reread every text Luca ever sent, and even the stupid ones have taken on some nostalgic glow. I scroll through my pictures despite fully understanding that this is obviously a bad idea. By the time I'm done, I'm more in love with him than I was when we were dancing at his grandmother's party. Then I cry myself to sleep.

Tuesday morning is the longest of my life. Sources close to Jasmine say she's broken up with a distraught Luca now that she sees he was taking advantage of how vulnerable she was after Rowdy, and she's "taking a break from dating to heal and center herself." The source also reports she's been spending a lot of time with some Hollywood A-list actor, but they're "just friends." The hypocrisy seems to be completely lost on the reporter, and I'm sure the audience. Everyone's favorite diva has also been writing a lot of new songs as "therapy." That can't be good news for Luca or me. At least I know Luca's heart isn't breaking over her. Then it's finally time to go.

The Eternal City is sweltering at three o'clock in the afternoon in late July. I take the metro because my high school is across the Tiber River. Sensible Romans are resting from the heat, so I'm surrounded by tourists. I hear their chatter as if it's on the other side of a door, muffled and incomprehensible even when English is spoken. I walk from the metro to the little building I didn't think I'd have to see again, and the day Luca came to offer his deal feels so long ago it's like it happened in ancient Rome. I follow the familiar halls to the office of my guidance counselor, Mr. Lackland. He's a young guy who usually finds his job an inconvenience to the hipster expat life he's carved out for himself in Rome.

The place smells of old leather and ink. I knock on Mr. Lackland's open door.

"Ah, Astoria, come in," he says. He wears a close beard and a striped short-sleeve button-down.

There's a television set up across from the doorway. On the screen is an empty conference room somewhere on the campus of what was once my future college. He gestures for me to sit on a small leather sofa across from his desk.

"The Admissions team and an attorney for the school will be coming on momentarily. My role is just to facilitate a place where you could meet confidentially that would be neutral territory, given the distance. I have no say in their decision-making process. Though, I am here to help you with any decision that might need to be made." He looks extremely uncomfortable as he ticks a pencil against his notepad. I was one of his prized college entries, along with Jack and our valedictorian.

Some response is necessary, so I nod. If they have their attorney coming, then I'm in for a scolding before they take my offer away. Awkward silence fills the room. "Should I have brought my mother?" I ask. "The email didn't say anything about anyone but me, and she had a big meeting at work today."

He shifts in his chair. "I think this is fine."

I nod again and check my phone. It's now 3:04. Another minute or so goes by. I pick at my nails. Then there's a small commotion, and three people come into view. They say hello to Mr. Lackland and thank him for hosting us. My admissions counselor, Ms. Golding, says hello to me and introduces the others. There's an attorney named Ms. Liu and a Mr. Miller, who is Ms. Golding's boss.

"Ms. Herriot," Mr. Miller says, "we're here today because of the disturbing reports that reached us this weekend about your personal life. There seems to be a new tabloid revelation every hour. Normally, such reports of off-campus behavior would not concern us, but the high-profile and international standing of those involved, in conjunction with the deceitful nature of the accusations, are deeply concerning. As you know, this is a prestigious institution, and we are very selective in our admissions process. Our reputation is something we take very seriously."

My mother would have a full cross-examination ready for them about that if she were here, so it's probably best she's not.

They spend the next half hour talking about the high moral expectations they have for their students and what their process is for disciplinary proceedings. I'm apparently a novelty in their grab bag of behavior to find alarming. I don't say anything unless they ask me a question. They spend a lot of time telling me they're not there to attack me, only to make sure the best decision is made for everyone involved. This implies me, too, but they don't seem concerned about what I think is best for me.

Then they talk about the fact that I'm a double legacy, "despite the unfortunate circumstances of my father's passing," and my impeccable record up to the "disturbing reports of my conduct." They ask if the reports are true.

"Aspects of them are."

"Would you care to elaborate?"

I'm suddenly not sure that I do. There are good colleges in Maine and Massachusetts, places that might not be so afraid of some bad publicity, I suppose.

"No," I say. "I wouldn't like to elaborate. I was just trying to help people to not have to live in a fishbowl. Especially when one of them was in rehab."

There's an awkward silence for a few minutes. Then Mr. Miller asks me to excuse them, and they turn off the video and mute the feed.

"Ms. Herriot," Mr. Miller says when they come back, "your behavior has brought a lot of negative attention to the university, as I'm sure you can imagine. However, we understand that, as a fan, you would have been swept away in this world of fame and fortune, and we're willing to allow you to come to campus in the fall. It will be a probationary admission, subject to your being able to keep your name out of these celebrity publications and avoid further deceptive practices."

The room seems to grow distant. I think about the day in the restaurant when Luca and I made our pact. This moment, just like the moment I knew I would help Luca, is the defining one. Even though I'll never see Luca again, their assumptions about us are too much. What we had was real, whatever the rest of the world believes. What I feel for him now is real, even if I can't fit into his world. But I don't say anything because I'm too angry.

"Ms. Herriot?" Ms. Liu says. "Is something wrong? This is a very generous offer."

I stand up. "Thank you for your generous offer. However, I'm declining." I can't believe I'm throwing away the college I've worked toward my whole life.

"Ms. Herriot," Ms. Liu says, "I think we deserve an explanation, don't you?"

I take a deep breath to stop the shaking. "I've worked really hard for years for a chance to go to the school where my parents met. There was a time when it meant everything to me. But I've done nothing to be dragged in here like this. You've insinuated I did this for personal monetary gain and fame when I'm the last person to have done it for either reason. You don't know Jasmine. You don't know the Marquess of Dunrobin. And you really don't know me. What I did was shield another woman from scrutiny she shouldn't even have to put up with. It's not anyone's business whom Jasmine dates. Or Luca. But, because Jasmine has a beautiful voice and the audacity to make a living off of it, some large segment of society thinks it owns the rights to every detail of her personal life. And what about Jeremy?

305

What I did was shield someone in rehab from tabloids wanting to dissect his most vulnerable moments for a circus show.

"When I met Luca Kinnaird, I didn't even know he was royalty. I don't follow Jasmine, and I'm definitely not her fan. She's not even a nice person. But that doesn't mean her privacy should be invaded the way mine has been for the last two months, and it's way worse for her. Luca Kinnaird never publicly called me his girlfriend. Yes, we let the tabloids think we were dating. But they didn't believe us even when we denied being a couple! Instead, they took lies from people who have no authority to speak for us, who aren't close to us and don't know the truth, and printed them as facts. We're human beings, not commodities.

"My whole life, I've been the new kid, the outsider, which was made a thousand times worse by not wanting anyone to comment on my father's substance use disorder. I've kept my head down so no one would even know about him, and believe me, people say really mean things when they do. But you think I was motivated because I wanted to glom on to Jasmine's celebrity? You think I enjoyed being stalked twenty-four seven by strangers who took my photo without my permission, photos I have no control over, while they yelled and printed insults about me? If you think anything I've done is less moral than that, then my disturbing behavior isn't the problem here."

I finish, out of breath and trembling. Behind me, someone starts to clap. I turn around. Luca is standing in the doorway.

Thirty-Four

"**W**hat are you doing here?" I can hardly breathe.

"Well," Luca says, "I came to stand up for you because I didn't think you'd stand up for yourself. But that speech was pure dead brilliant."

It hurts so much to see him, it's like the last bit of wind has been kicked out of me.

I turn back to the screen. "I need to go." I nod a thank-you at Mr. Lackland and rush past Luca.

"Story, wait," he calls, but I can't. He runs after me and grabs my arm in the hallway.

"Why won't you talk to me?"

When I look up at him, it's like trying to grab sunlight. He's right there in front of me, but he's not mine.

"Luca, I appreciate you wanting to help, but I'm begging you not to make this any harder."

Some janitors are coming down the hallway, and Luca looks up at them. I pull away and throw the front door open.

Paparazzi line the narrow sidewalk. I push through them to the familiar whir of cameras and my name being shouted as my tear-filled eyes adjust to the daylight. Jack is coming through the crowd toward me.

He motions at a cab he must have just left. We run to it and jump in. The driver peers at the paparazzi surging toward us. "Avanti," I say, and he nods and hits the gas pedal. I look back, and Luca is standing on the sidewalk watching me go.

Jack gives the cabbie my address. The man asks who I am.

"The most famous girl no one ever heard of until two months ago," I say. I look at Jack. "What are you doing here?"

"I got worried about you. I thought I should at least come and see you home."

My phone vibrates. My mom is calling. Luca is calling. Anna Maria is texting me.

"Yeah, Mom?" I say as I tap Accept.

"How did it go?"

"I'll explain later, but I won't be going to school there."

"Okay, I'll be home as soon as I can."

"Okay."

When the cab pulls up to my apartment building, Jack asks if I'm going to be okay.

"I'll be fine," I say, wiping tears from my cheeks. I can tell by the way he looks at me he doesn't believe this any more than I do. What I really mean is I'll be fine *enough*. For the foreseeable future, that will have to do. "Thanks for the getaway car. I really owe you."

He squeezes my hand, then tells the driver to take him to the embassy as I step out.

When I walk into the lobby of the apartment building, they're there. They've probably been hanging around in the hope of catching me.

"Oh, my God, Story," Guin says, "you look awful! Are you okay?"

"I'm great, Guin."

Kelsey laughs. "You are so pathetic."

"Honestly, Story," Guin says. "You really are."

I look at Alicia to see if she's going to chime in, but she bites her lip and shuffles on her feet. *I'm sorry,* she mouths.

I push the elevator button and turn around. "You know what? I may be pathetic, but at least I'm not mean. I never did anything to any of you, and you've treated me like trash since I got here. Well, Kelsey and Guin, you have. Alicia, you should find nicer friends and stop following these two because I don't think you enjoy making other people feel bad. And I may not be Jasmine, but I do know one thing, because he told me. Luca Kinnaird wouldn't give any of you five minutes of his time."

Kelsey and Guin drop their jaws, but Alicia looks away as if she's embarrassed. The elevator door opens.

"Have a nice day," I say as the doors close.

I guess this is why people stand up for themselves. It actually feels good. I mean, losing my school and having people hate me for no reason and, most of all, losing Luca is absolutely horrible. But at least I'm standing up for myself as I go down in flames, and that feels really good.

When I get in the apartment, I decide there's one more place I need to stand up for myself. Social media.

I choose the platform for pretty pictures. I pick a photo of Luca and me that's never been shared, one I've treasured because Andy took it when we didn't even realize, and there's just so much joy passing between us. We were in the Rose Garden near the Circus Maximus, and Luca was teasing me about the lack of occult attractions in the garden when a bee came and hovered in front of his face before flying off. We both cracked up. I write:

> *This post is using all the hashtags, as the #MarquessOfDunrobin told me to do in my first ever post about us. Two months ago, I was grabbed outside of a gelateria near the #PiazzadiSpagna by an impossibly handsome and entitled #ScottishRogue and asked to cover for the #SuperStar he was secretly dating. He told the #Paparazzi I was his tour guide, and I reluctantly played along and took him to the #Trevi. I gave him an almost impeccable history of the fountain, and then took him back to the Via Condotti, where we said goodbye, never expecting to see each other again.*
>
> *That night, I was stalked by paparazzi. They showed up at my school the next day, determined I must be the new girlfriend of this #ScottishRoyal. So we let them believe that.*

*This supposed bad boy was simply trying to protect
the girl he was dating. He also wanted to protect her
ex-boyfriend, who was in rehab and needed some space.
My dad died of an #Overdose, so I wanted to protect her
ex-boyfriend, too. Ever since I lost my dad, I've wanted
to start a memorial scholarship in his name, because
everyone likes to forget people who die from overdose. The
Marquess made that happen for me, and he never cared
if I kept my end of our agreement. He did it because it's a
good thing to do.*

*Somewhere along the way, I didn't need to pretend
anymore. I didn't tell him that, though, because I thought
he wanted to be with someone else. Meanwhile, he
discovered the person he was dating wasn't actually the
right person for him, so he broke up with her. It turns
out he wasn't pretending anymore, either. We shared
a few barry hours where it seemed like we might be
#HappyTogether.*

*Then the news broke, and things that never happened
were reported by people who are supposedly #Insiders.
Some of us had to be #Victims and others #Villains. None
of us is really either. We're just people trying to live our
lives, with impossible expectations. No one should have
to sacrifice all their privacy, or live being hounded, or
have to hide just to spend time with other people. No
one should have the right to take your photo and use it
to make up stories about you. No one should think that
the most precious moments in your life exist for their*

entertainment just because you haven't successfully hidden them from a telephoto lens.

In our #Digital #OnDemand culture, it's easy to forget that celebrities are people who need to get to know each other to decide if they even want to date, without everyone expecting to know every awkward moment, every intimate laugh, or every bumpy tear.

I'm really sorry for having misled anyone. I didn't realize how this would involve so many people. I'm very grateful for the bonnie people I've met, and for everyone who is standing by me.

I don't know what's next for me. I only know that I love Luca Kinnaird more than I ever thought I'd love anyone, even if we can't be together. The last two months have been a fast sail on a perfect day, and I know now that the world is meant to be tasted and felt, and not just wondered at. The world is still scary to me, but it's okay to be scared because the things that are true can't ever be really lost. Rome taught me to love, and love taught me to believe.

The story of Story Herriot is now beginning. It starts like this: Once upon a time, I met a bonnie marquess who taught me how to stand up for myself. . . . #Love #BelieveInYourself #AllRoadsLeadToRome

I click Post, and, while my heart's still broken, I feel better than I have since I left Scotland.

Thirty-Five

shut my phone off. I'll have to deal with the response at some point, but not now. Instead, I sit in the quiet and think about how dashing Luca looked as he stood in the doorway in his misguided attempt to rescue me. He had on the same midnight-navy suit he'd worn to the opera, the night a princess taught me to love Puccini. His thin, dark tie brought out the deep ocean tones of his eyes, and the tiredness around them and two days of stubble let me know all this at least cost him something, too. He thought he needed to come and rescue me, but he'd already given me all the tools I needed to rescue myself. I used to be the girl who stood at the window and watched the world go by. I'm not that girl anymore.

I'm still daydreaming of a different ending to our story when my mom gets home. "I come bearing gifts," she says as she sets a tote bag of takeout down on the table.

"Please tell me it's potato gnocchi al pomodoro from Le Belle Notti."

She smiles. "And fried zucchini flowers, and vegan chocolate caramel gelato."

"You are the best mother ever. Does this mean I'm not grounded?"

She laughs. "If you weren't too old, then I would ground you. But I think in this case, the consequences are worse than any punishment I could come up with."

"They are."

She comes over and hugs me. "Come on, let's eat and you can fill me in."

So we have dinner and I tell her. She's proud of me for standing up for myself, and Jasmine and Luca, but when I tell her about Luca riding in on his black stallion to save me, she doesn't comment.

"Maybe I could take some classes at Università di Roma and get a part-time job as a tour guide for this year."

"Well, there's time to think about that tomorrow. Today, let's just hide away in the baking show, shall we? We'll think better after a little distance from all this."

She goes to change her clothes, and I go to my room to put on sweatpants and a T-shirt. I'm pulling them from the drawer when I hear a strange sound outside. It seems like my name, but weirdly muffled and amplified. I peek through the gauzy curtain. Luca is standing in the courtyard with a megaphone.

"Astoria Herriot, please come outside."

I pull open the door and step onto the marble porch, warm from sunshine. Windows start opening all around the courtyard.

"What are you doing? Are you crazy?" I say it as quietly as I dare, but I still have to almost shout for him to hear me.

"I once joked that I'd need a megaphone to make love speeches to you like Romeo from down here, and you said, 'Well, it's a good thing you don't need to make me love speeches, then.' It turns out, though, that I do."

I glance to my right, and my mother is on the dining room balcony watching. I shake my head to let her know I have no idea what he's doing. The three amigas have come outside on Guin's floor, and other people I recognize from the embassy and lots of people I only know from the elevator or not at all have also come out. The whole building seems to be home for this spectacle. A few Italian residents yell encouragement to him in Italian. "Go on!" and "Tell her, young man!"

"Do you know how hard it is to find a megaphone in Rome?" he asks. "I had to have this dug up from the basement of the UK embassy."

I grip the railing. "Why are you doing this?"

"When you left Scotland, I thought you were mad at me, and I couldn't blame you. And then, today when I saw you, I really thought you hated me. But then I read your post. Why are you so convinced we can't be together?"

He lets the ridiculous megaphone fall and stares up at me. The last rays of the long July day are fading across the courtyard. I forget for a moment that anyone is watching until someone yells in Italian, "Answer the boy!"

"You know why, Luca! I heard what your family said. They're never going to approve of me."

Some of the Italians who have understood me boo him.

Luca leaves the megaphone on the ground, and he has to shout. "What did you hear, Story? I'll admit they were mad at first, but once they calmed down, they realized they were being unfair!"

I shake my head. There's no way they would ever accept me after what I heard them say.

"I don't know what you heard, but my family isn't against us. In fact, they said I haven't been this mature for my age since primary year one when I was five! My mum told me to come and make things right. Adaira says I'm the biggest idiot since Hamlet. And even Andy said if I don't get you back, he's dumping me to be your best friend."

"They did?"

"Aye! Can you please come down here and just talk to me? Please, Story?"

I look over at my mom, who is mouthing *Go!* at me as if I'm the Pink Panther and a giant piano is about to drop on my head. Across the courtyard, people shout at me to go down, some in English and some in Italian. One old lady yells in Italian, "Give the boy a chance, stupid girl!"

I duck back into the flat. I run out of the apartment shoeless into the hall and down the stairwell. When I come into the courtyard, Luca is watching for me. I stop running and walk over to him.

We just look at each other for a moment. "Hello," he says.

"Hello."

"Do you want to tell me what you heard?"

I nod. "First of all, I wasn't trying to eavesdrop. I just waited outside to see what I should do. I thought maybe your parents would want me to leave or have more questions for me. Then I heard your mom say I wasn't at all appropriate and they didn't know how you could have brought 'a girl like me into the family.'"

Luca's Atlantic eyes pop. "Crivvens, Story, she was talking about Jasmine!"

Tears sting my eyes. "I hoped that at first. I really did. But you didn't bring Jasmine there. You brought me home, Luca. I was the one at your family's party! She specifically said *at* your grandmother's party."

He locks his gaze on mine. "She meant I brought Jasmine into the family, into our house, in the tabloids, by linking our names! She was furious with me. When the rumors ran around that I liked Jasmine, she checked her out, and hoo boy! But when she thought I started dating you, she wasn't worried. Especially after Hodges and my dad's friends told her you were absolutely great, and not like anyone I'd ever dated before."

I put my hand to my mouth because this can't all be true.

"But she was so angry at me."

"She was disappointed. She even wondered if she'd been wrong about you. But when I told her how you wouldn't take any money from me for anything, how I had to force you to even let me buy you a pair of cheap trail runners, she knew you'd only do anything this crazy for the right reasons. And when I told her how much you made me think about the world, and my place in it, she was sold."

317

"But I ruined your grandmother's party."

"Story," Luca says, moving closer, "they know this was my fault. And my gran said it wouldn't have been a party without me causing a riot."

A sob escapes me. "So you don't have to choose between your family and me?"

Luca laughs. "No, you raging American dafty! But, just for the record, I would pick you. Every time." He slips his fingers through my hair and wraps his other arm around my waist and pulls me in. "Story, the last few days I've been gawn off my heid withou' yoo like I was steamin' the whole time." A tear falls onto my right cheek. He leans down and kisses it.

Cheers and shouting fill the space around us. Someone pops a bottle of prosecco and the bang of it breaks us apart and we laugh as the cork lands behind us. I look up at my mom, and her cheeks are glistening.

Luca picks up the megaphone. "For anyone who wants to report to the paparazzi hanging out front, or if they can hear me, I love Astoria Herriot. I love her madly, deeply, irrevocably." He looks up at my mom and adds, "And reverently, Mrs. Herriot. No worries there. I love her reverently." He turns back to me.

"You didn't mention 'truly.'"

The megaphone falls, and he smiles. "And truly. As truly as Cupid loves Psyche."

The whole building is cheering. Well, most of it. Kelsey and Guin have gone back inside, but Alicia waves a thumbs-up to me. A man yells for me to kiss the boy.

"I don't usually take unsolicited advice," I say.

"No, you don't."

I shrug and wrap my arms around his neck. "But when it's right—"

Luca catches his lips on mine, and I kiss him the way Princess Ann would have kissed Joe Bradley if they could have been together.

Thirty-Six

When we get back to the apartment, my mom hugs Luca.

"Mrs. Herriot," he says, "I owe you the biggest apology. I should never have asked Story to lie to you. I don't know how you can stand me." He says it with genuine contrition, but without fear because he already knows he's forgiven.

"Well, I can't approve of the behavior of either of you," she says. "But . . . I think maybe you've both learned something important. And you got my daughter out of her shell, which I was beginning to think might never happen."

Luca and I smile at each other.

My mom goes to get us celebratory limonatas while Luca and I sit down. "How did you know where to find me this afternoon?"

"Jack texted me. He was worried about you."

"So you came back because of Jack?"

Luca takes my hand. "After you left Scotland, I didn't know

if I had any chance with you. I came to Rome to at least try. Then Jack told me you were probably losing Princeton, and I couldn't let you go in there on your own. When I saw you today and you left without even giving me a chance, I was afraid I should give up. But then you posted, and I had hope again."

"I wanted you—I wanted everyone—to know the truth. Even though I didn't think we could be together."

"I could hardly believe what I read. Then when Rowdy posted—"

"Wait, what did Jeremy say?"

My mom sets our limonatas on the coffee table and sits down.

"You didn't see it?"

"No, I turned my phone off after I posted. Plus, I don't follow him anyway."

"He backed you up. He said part of him will always love Jasmine, but the stuff her team was putting out there just wasn't true. It was pretty smart, actually, because he blamed her people so he doesn't have to get into a fan tug-of-war with her. He let everyone know she was lying without ever calling her a liar."

"Why would he do that for me?"

"Well, back when all this started, we had to fill him in. I was on the call, and we told him that you were going to do this, and he didn't trust you'd keep it a secret. He couldn't believe you weren't a fan and would still do it, until I explained what you wanted in return, and why. I told him you asked if helping us would help him. He was actually really touched."

"You never told me that."

"I didn't think it was important. Anyway, once Jeremy came out for you, then Dani felt like she could, too. I'm not going to tell you the Jasminers aren't going to make our lives miserable to the extent they can. But it's already cooling down with her running around with the superhero guy from the comics franchise. People who love her blindly will move on with her. The rest will see who she really is."

"Eventually," I say.

"Okay, I deserve that." He squints a little. "I have one more thing to tell you that might make you mad at me."

"Now what?" my mom and I say in unison.

He takes a deep breath. "Well, when you walked out on your school today, I asked my dad to talk to someone at Oxford. I just wanted to make sure you had somewhere to go. Anyway, they said they'd open your offer back up if you're still interested."

"Really?" I turn to my mom. "Is that ethical?"

She shrugs. "You got in before on your own merit. All Luca's dad did was ask them to give you a second chance to accept the offer."

"And you'd be okay with me going to school in England?"

"You'd be closer than if you were in the States. But it's your decision." She puts her hands up to let me know I'm my own adult now.

Luca weaves his fingers into mine. "So?"

I let it sink in. "I guess I'm going to Oxford?"

Luca hugs me. "You're going to love it, I know it."

322

We talk about Oxford for a while, and then my mom says she has work tomorrow, so she wishes us good night. Luca and I share a gelato as he tells me more about my new school, and then he wraps me up in his arms.

"There are so many places I want to go with you, so many things I want us to do together."

"Gray seal pups this fall?"

"Definitely. And Amsterdam next summer, and Maine." He strokes my hair, his heartbeat against my cheek. "Although, I don't know if anywhere could be as magical as Rome. I came here chasing false gold, just like Pietraforte. And, somehow, I met a girl who gave me the formula for the real thing. Maybe that could only have happened in a place known as the Eternal City."

"Well, you know what they say." I pull away just enough to see his beautiful eyes.

"All roads lead to Rome," we say together. And, when he kisses me, I know it's true.

Acknowledgments

Writing the acknowledgments is the beautiful part of the book process because it means that you've reached the finish line and it gives you the chance to thank all the people who helped you get there.

I'd like to thank my wonderful agent, Michelle Hauck of Storm Literary Agency, for her unstinting support, not just of my work but also of me as a person. It has truly been a gift to work with her. And thanks to everyone at Storm for the many ways they support my work. Thank you to my editor, the great Wendy Loggia, and her team at Delacorte Press, for giving these characters a place in the world and for their guidance, support, and skill in shaping the story. When Michelle told me she was planning on submitting this story to Wendy, all I could say was "Wow, Wendy Loggia is going to see *my* story?" I didn't really expect to get to work with Wendy, but I'm so glad I did!

Thank you to my darling critique group, particularly Sally Alexander, Cristina Rouvalis, Jane Ackerman, Heidi Brayer,

Alan Irvine, Linda Casey Kustra, and Dave Crawley, for your constant love, impeccable writing advice, and endless encouragement. Special thanks to Cristina for always being my cheerleader and for pushing me to keep on submitting (and for the lemon tarts) and to Jane for reading the whole thing again.

Thank you to the people who have loved me and sustained me in all of this—my family, my friends, and my mentors along the way. Special shout-out to Cynthia Platt for being the call I get when I send the big news text before I can share that news with the rest of the world. Thank you to Amanda Hooper and Lisa Slage Robinson for always being there for me. Special, forever thanks to my chief shenaniganator, my daughter, who put up with me making her get off her bed and hold hands and jump up and down like idiots so I could tell her the news of the offer. And thank you to every one of you who buys a copy of this book, or checks it out at your library, or writes a review (fingers crossed it will be positive), or tells someone about it, or posts about it on social media. I hope you will love Story and Luca as much as I do. Thank you to Wyatt, who fills every day with love and laughter. Thanks to my cats for letting me be part of their pride and for being excellent office mates. And, finally, most humbly, thank you to Rita Fedel for giving me so much love in her lifetime that I will never go without.

About the Author

Sabrina Fedel has worked as a litigator and a civilian environmental compliance attorney. She earned her MFA in creative writing from Lesley University and has taught in the English department at Robert Morris University as an adjunct professor. Her fiction and poetry have appeared in various journals. Sabrina loves Italy and the Cape Hatteras National Seashore, animals, chocolate in any form, Oxford commas, and, most of all, her kids.

sabrinafedel.com